JONNA
AND THE UNPOSSIBLE MONSTERS

AN ONI PRESS PUBLICATION

JONNA
AND THE UNPOSSIBLE MONSTERS

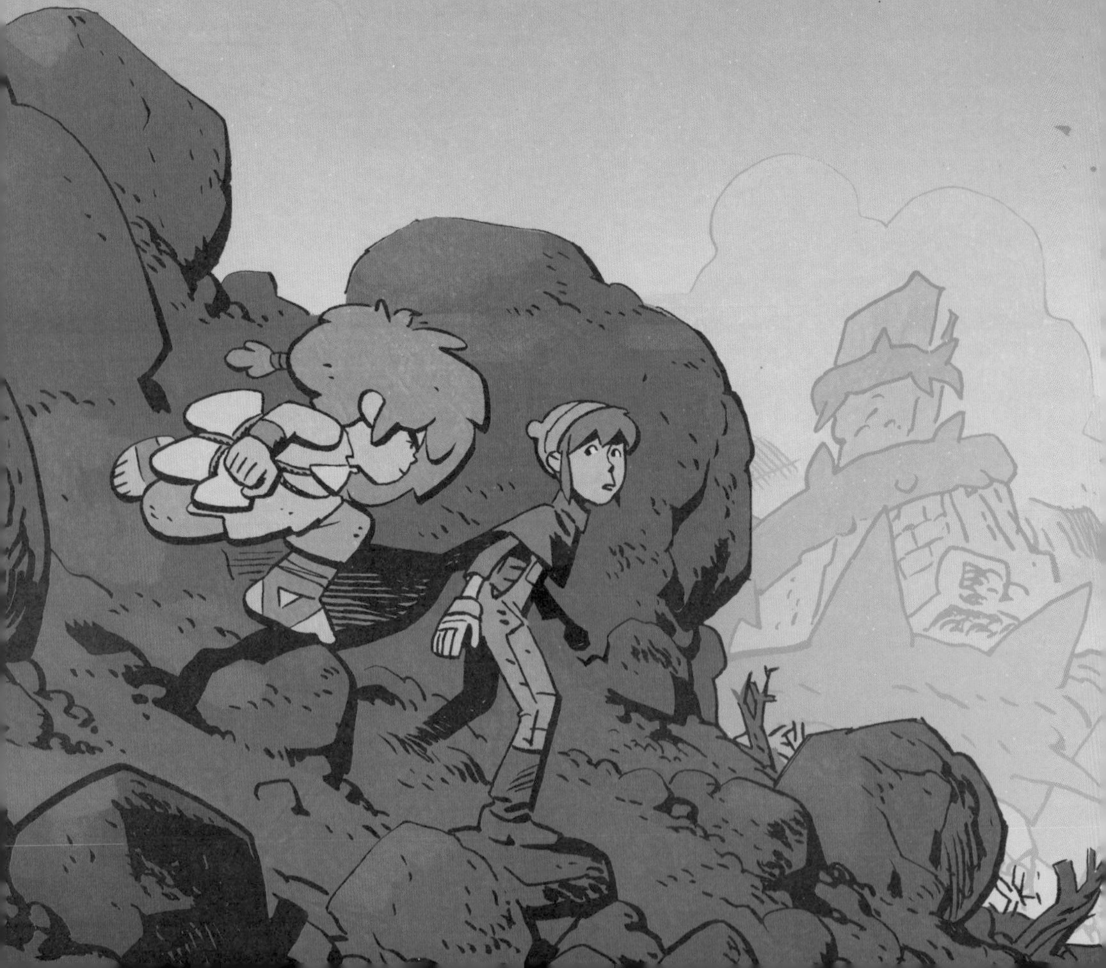

Written by
CHRIS SAMNEE & LAURA SAMNEE

Art by	Colors by	Letters by
CHRIS SAMNEE	MATTHEW WILSON	CRANK!

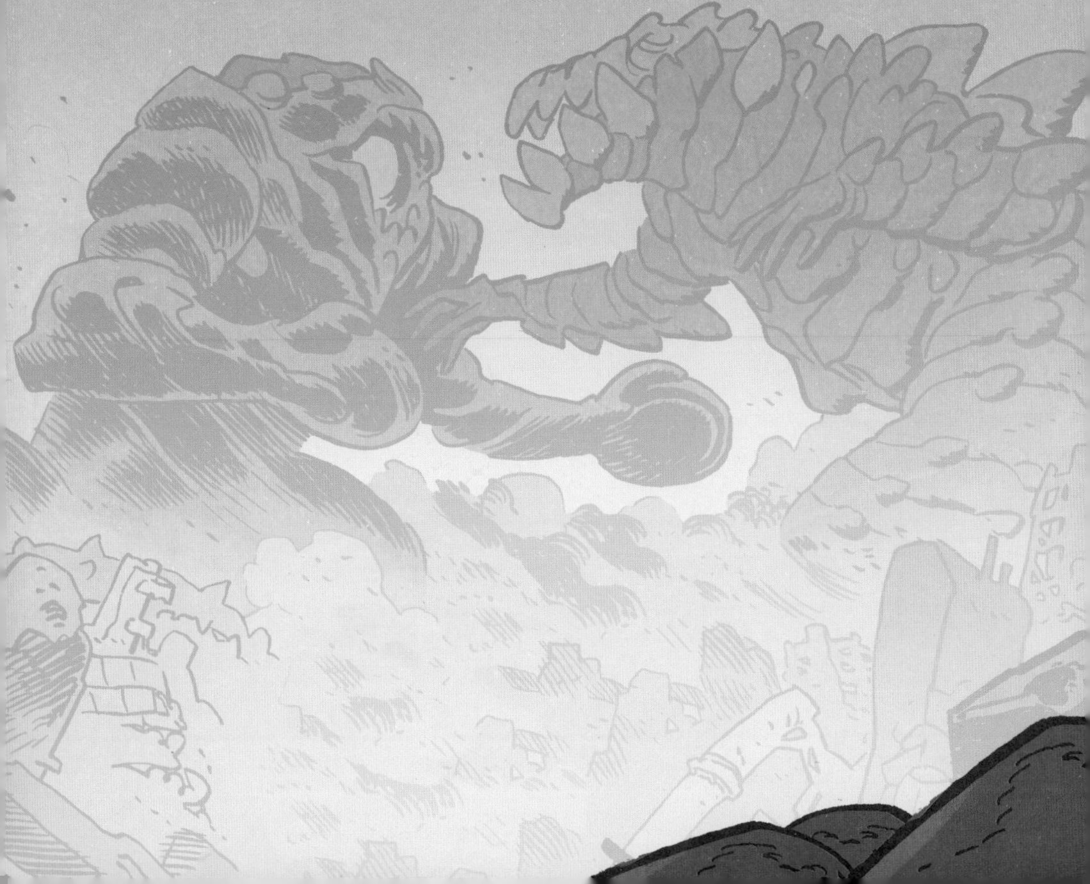

Logo Design by RICKY DELUCCO
Book Design by ANGIE KNOWLES with SONJA SYNAK
Edited by ZACK SOTO

Published by Oni-Lion Forge Publishing Group, LLC.

James Lucas Jones, president & publisher • Charlie Chu, e.v.p. of creative & business development • Steve Ellis, s.v.p. of games & operations • Alex Segura, s.v.p of marketing & sales • Michelle Nguyen, associate publisher • Brad Rooks, director of operations Amber O'Neill, special projects manager • Margot Wood, director of marketing & sales Katie Sainz, marketing manager • Henry Barajas, sales manager • Tara Lehmann, publicist Holly Aitchison, consumer marketing manager • Troy Look, director of design & production Angie Knowles, production manager • Kate Z. Stone, senior graphic designer • Carey Hall, graphic designer • Sarah Rockwell, graphic designer • Hilary Thompson, graphic designer Vincent Kukua, digital prepress technician • Chris Cerasi, managing editor Jasmine Amiri, senior editor • Shawna Gore, senior editor • Amanda Meadows, senior editor • Robert Meyers, senior editor, licensing • Desiree Rodriguez, editor Grace Scheipeter, editor • Zack Soto, editor • Ben Eisner, game developer Jung Lee, logistics coordinator • Kuian Kellum, warehouse assistant

Joe Nozemack, publisher emeritus

onipress.com
[f] [v] [o]

[v] @ChrisSamnee | [v] @COLORnMATT | [v] @ccrank

[o] @chrissamnee | [o] @colornmatt | [o] @ccrank

First Edition: April 2022

ISBN 978-1-63715-021-4
eISBN 978-1-63715-030-6

Printed in China

Library of Congress Control Number: 2020947317

1 2 3 4 5 6 7 8 9 10

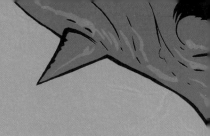

For Patti

CHAPTER 5

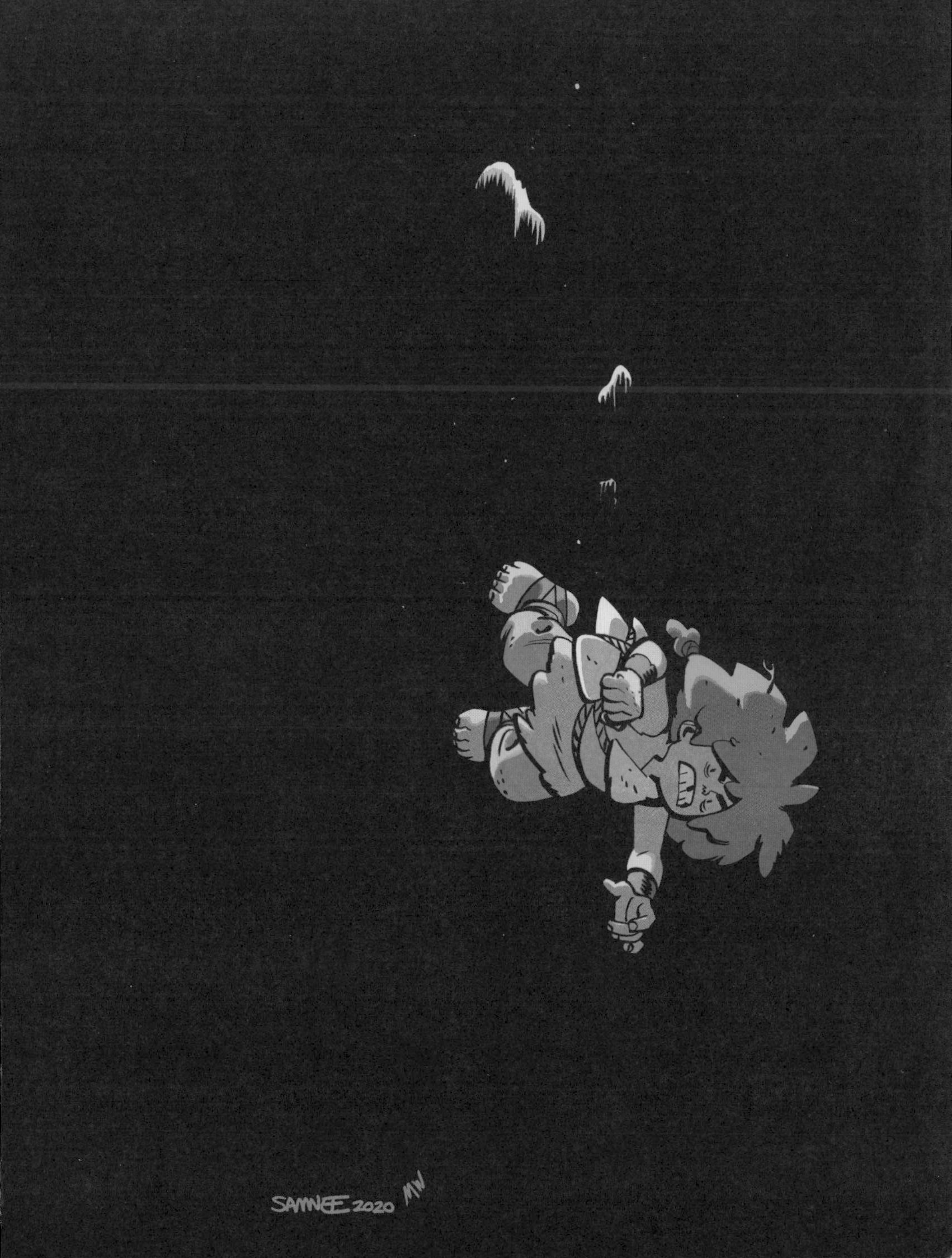
SAMNEE 2020 MW

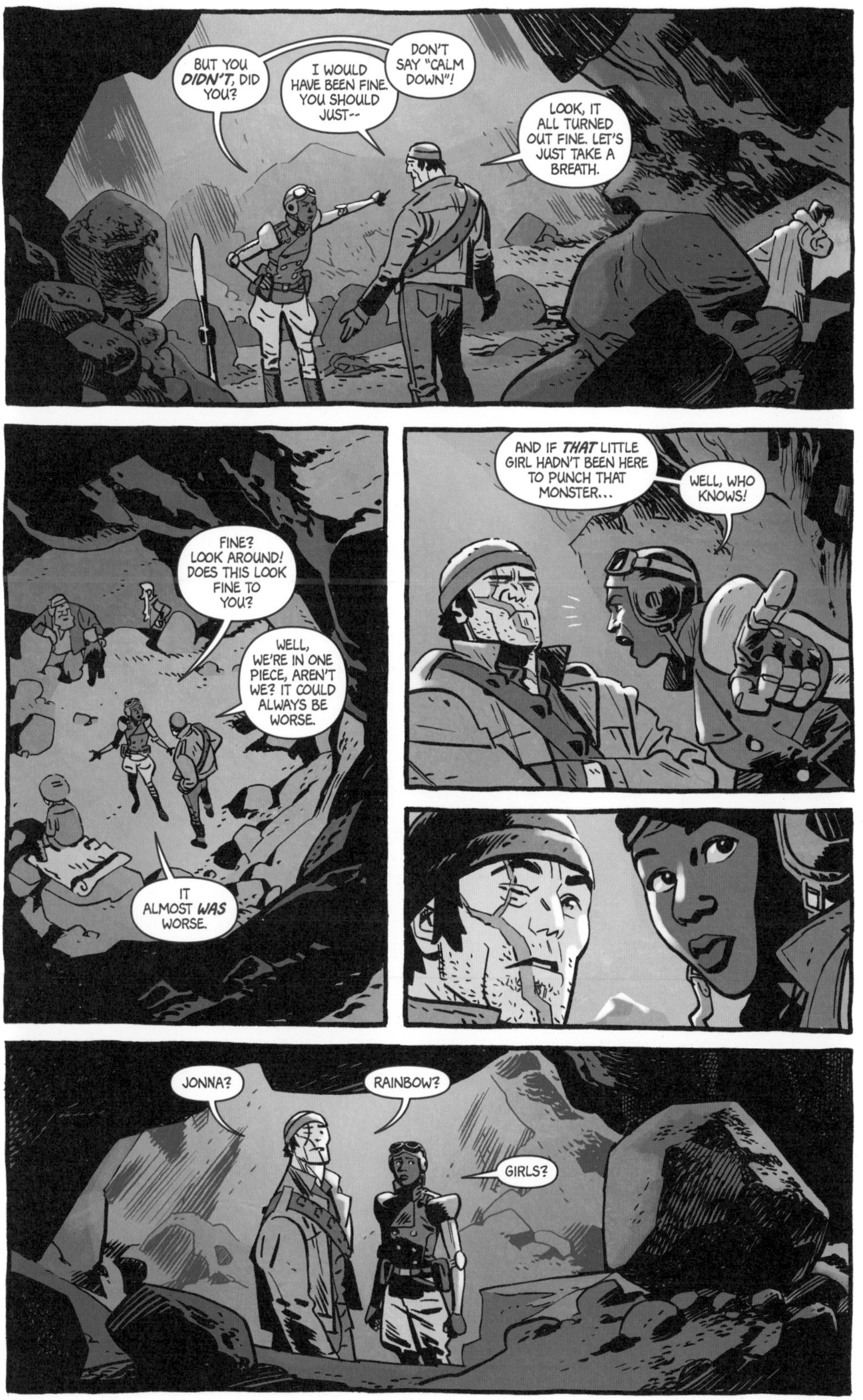
BUT YOU DIDN'T, DID YOU?
I WOULD HAVE BEEN FINE. YOU SHOULD JUST--
DON'T SAY "CALM DOWN"!
LOOK, IT ALL TURNED OUT FINE. LET'S JUST TAKE A BREATH.
FINE? LOOK AROUND! DOES THIS LOOK FINE TO YOU?
WELL, WE'RE IN ONE PIECE, AREN'T WE? IT COULD ALWAYS BE WORSE.
IT ALMOST WAS WORSE.
AND IF THAT LITTLE GIRL HADN'T BEEN HERE TO PUNCH THAT MONSTER...
WELL, WHO KNOWS!
JONNA?
RAINBOW?
GIRLS?

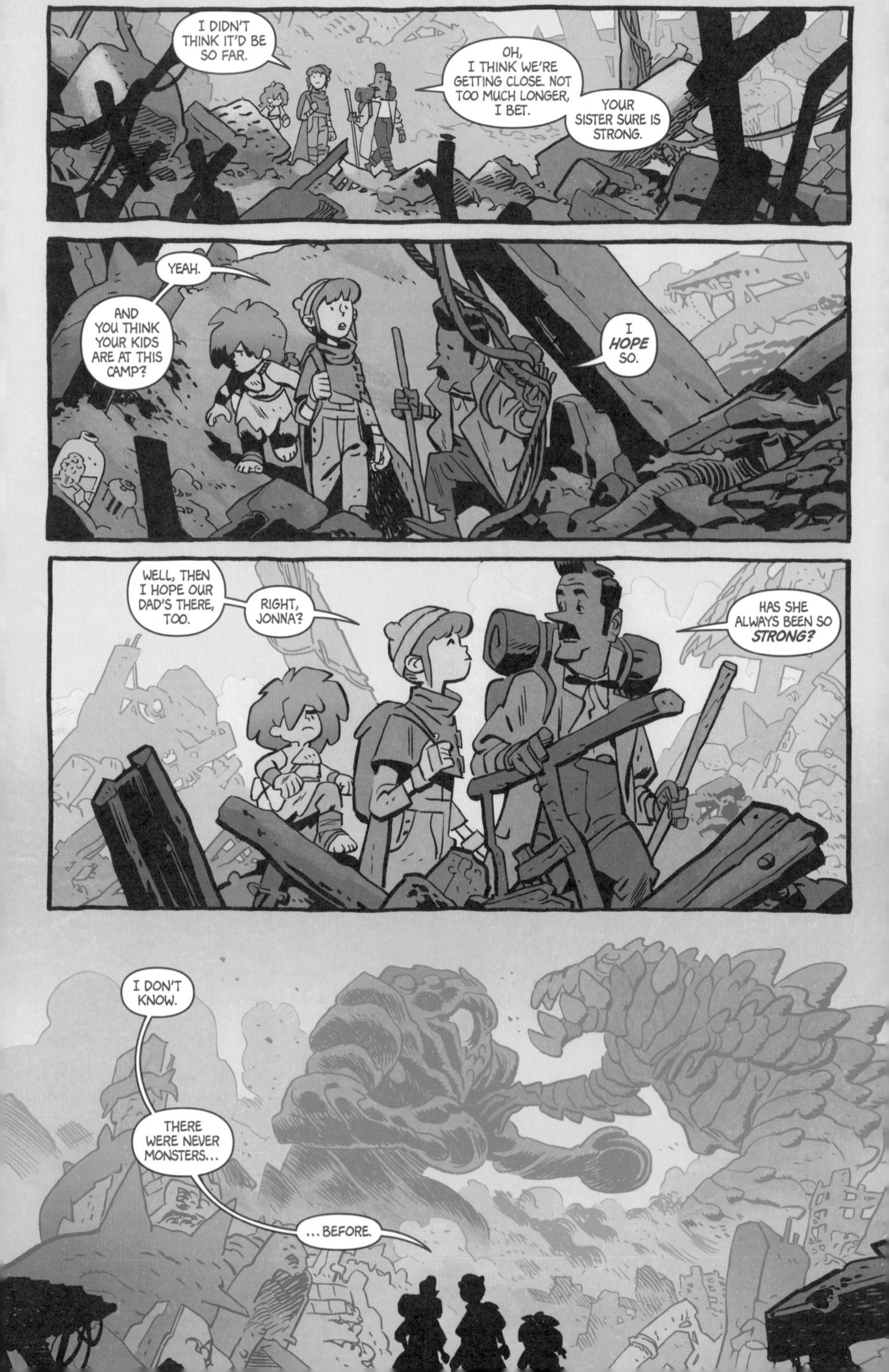
I DIDN'T THINK IT'D BE SO FAR.
OH, I THINK WE'RE GETTING CLOSE. NOT TOO MUCH LONGER, I BET.
YOUR SISTER SURE IS STRONG.
YEAH.
AND YOU THINK YOUR KIDS ARE AT THIS CAMP?
I *HOPE* SO.
WELL, THEN I HOPE OUR DAD'S THERE, TOO.
RIGHT, JONNA?
HAS SHE ALWAYS BEEN SO *STRONG?*
I DON'T KNOW.
THERE WERE NEVER MONSTERS...
...BEFORE.

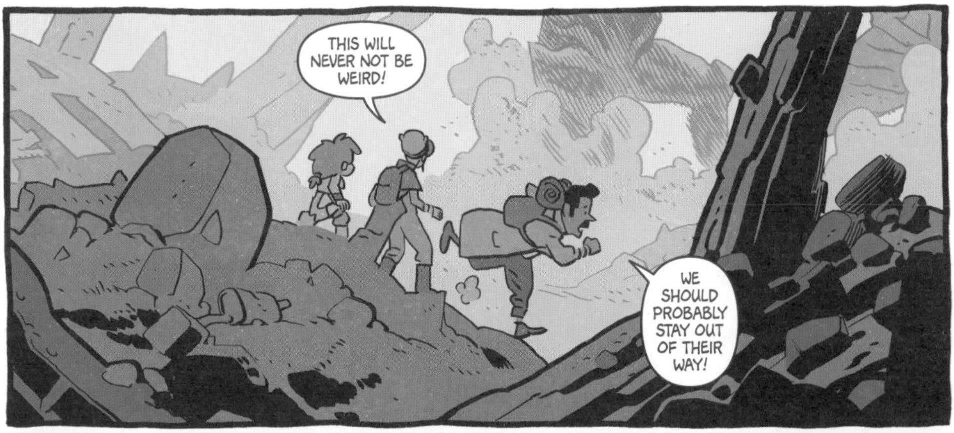
THIS WILL NEVER NOT BE WEIRD!
WE SHOULD PROBABLY STAY OUT OF THEIR WAY!

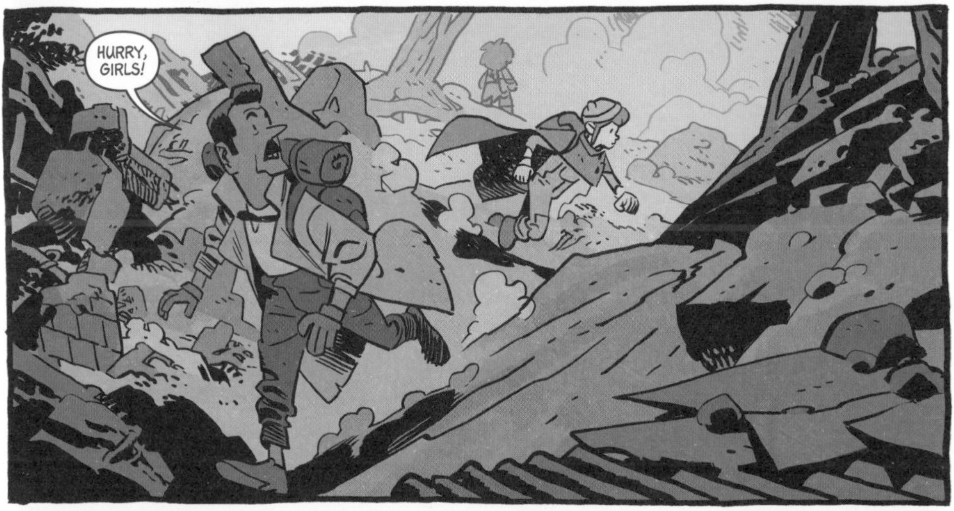
HURRY, GIRLS!

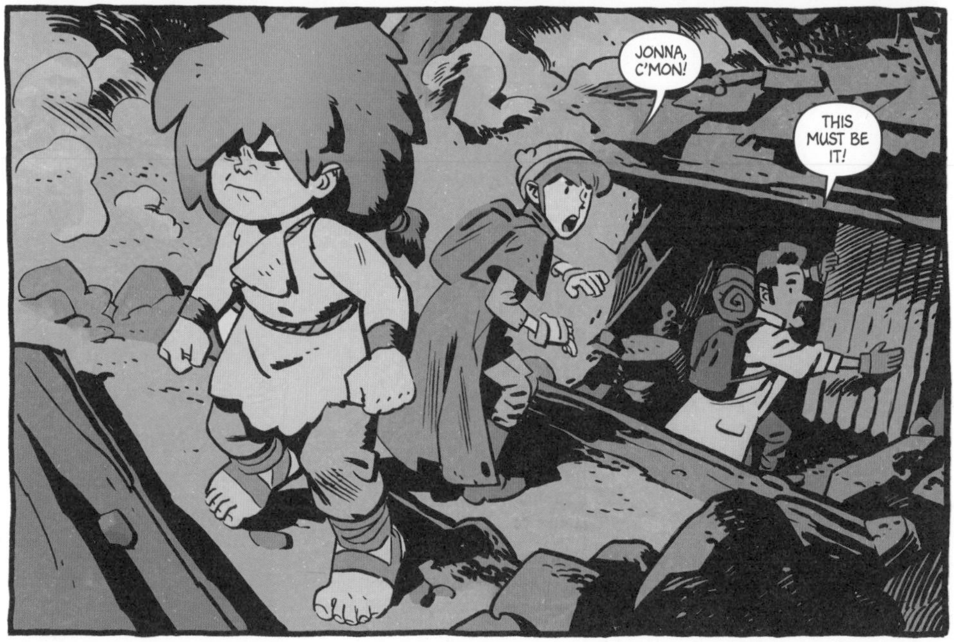
JONNA, C'MON!
THIS MUST BE IT!

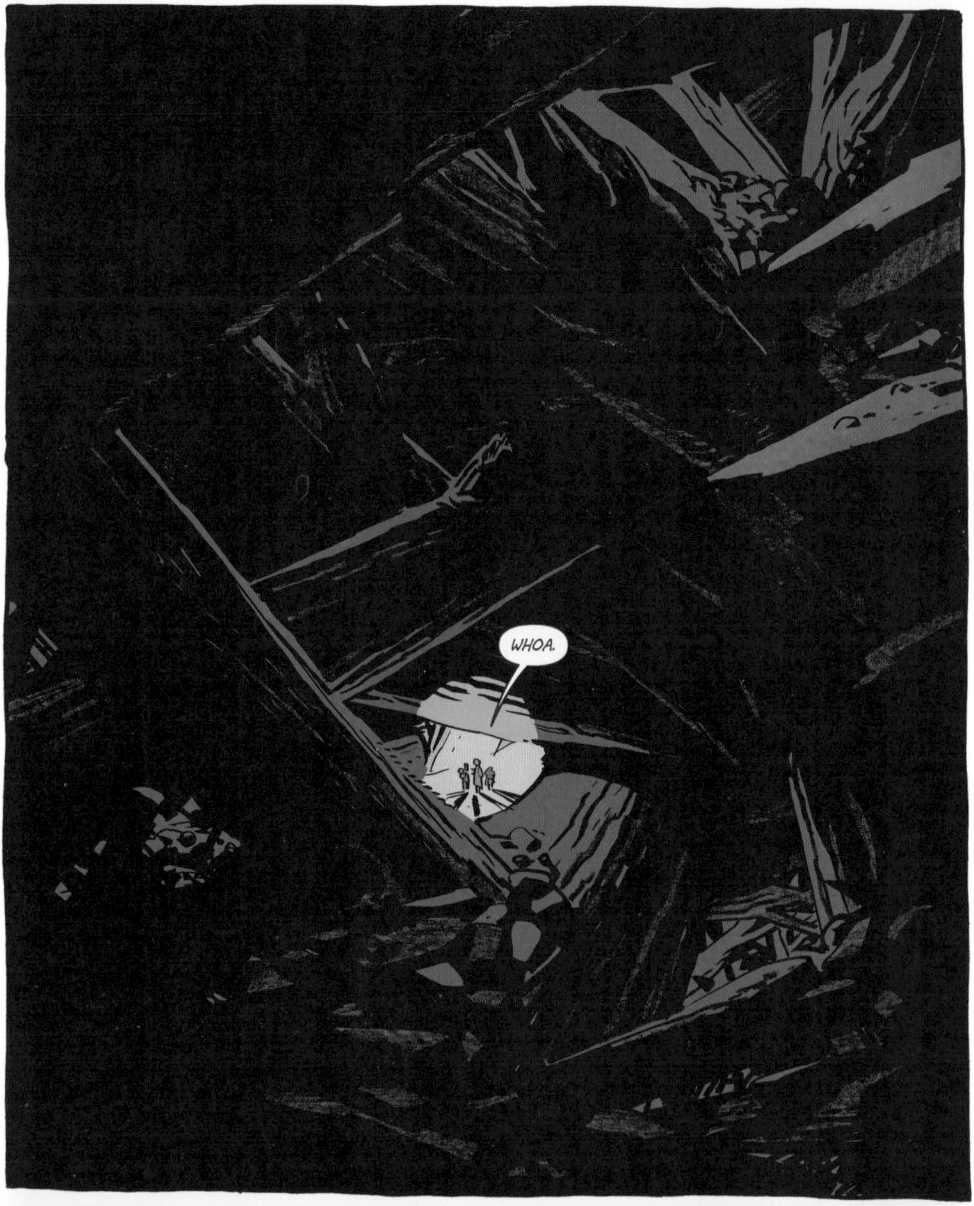
WHOA.

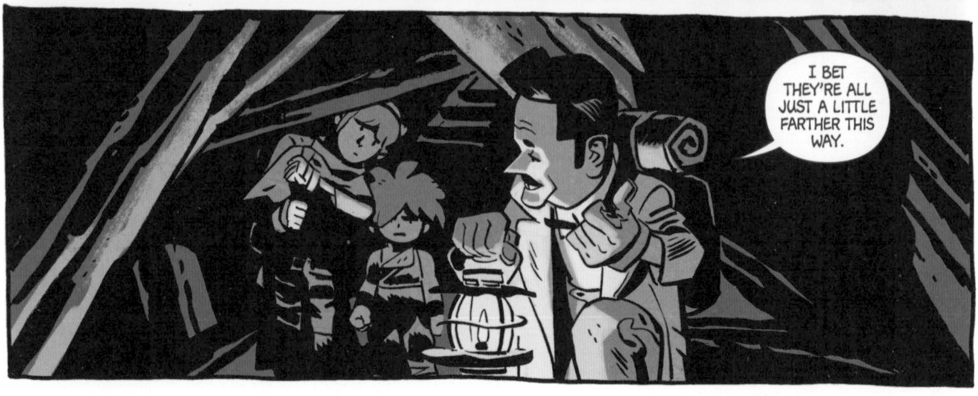
I BET THEY'RE ALL JUST A LITTLE FARTHER THIS WAY.

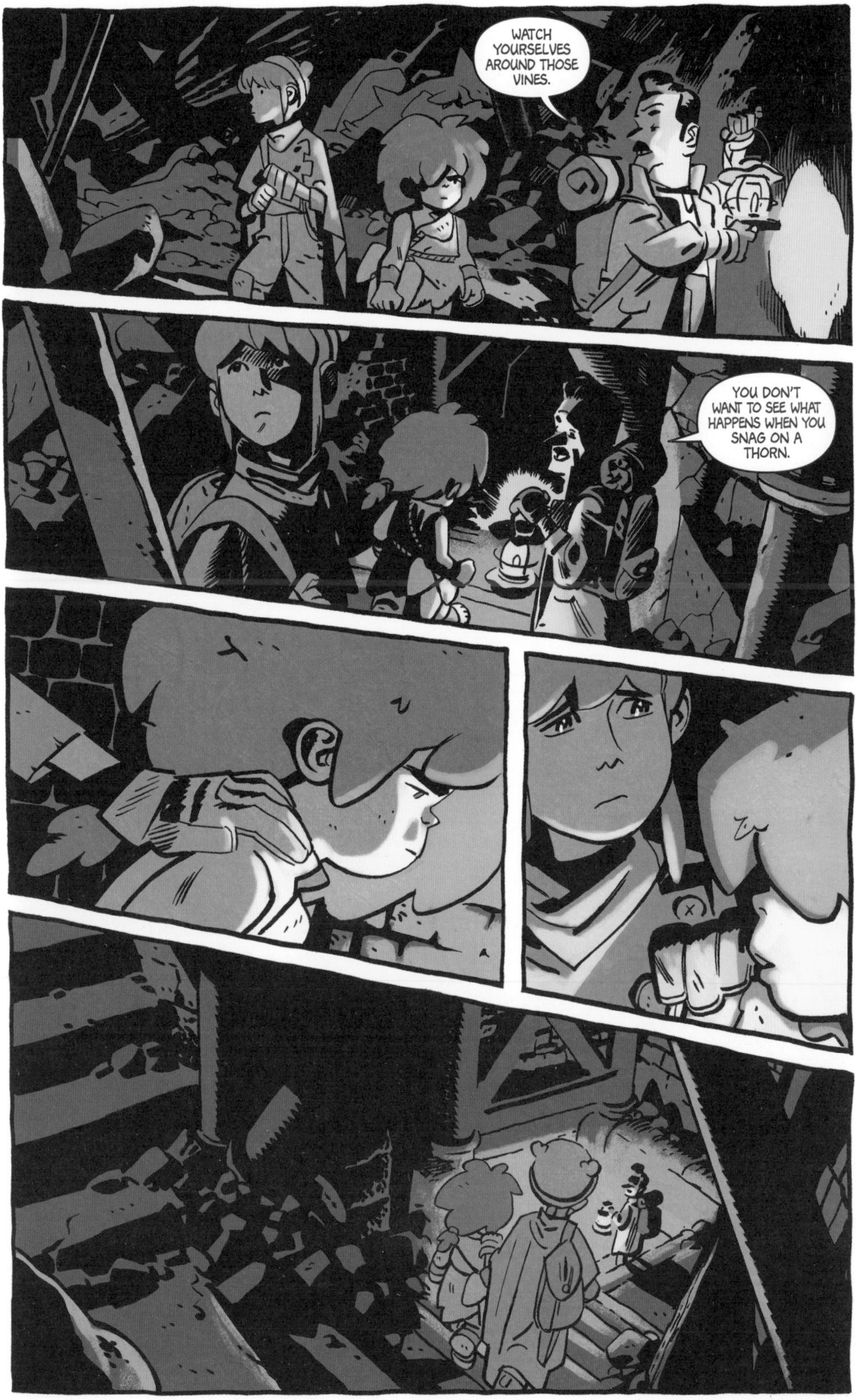
WATCH YOURSELVES AROUND THOSE VINES.
YOU DON'T WANT TO SEE WHAT HAPPENS WHEN YOU SNAG ON A THORN.

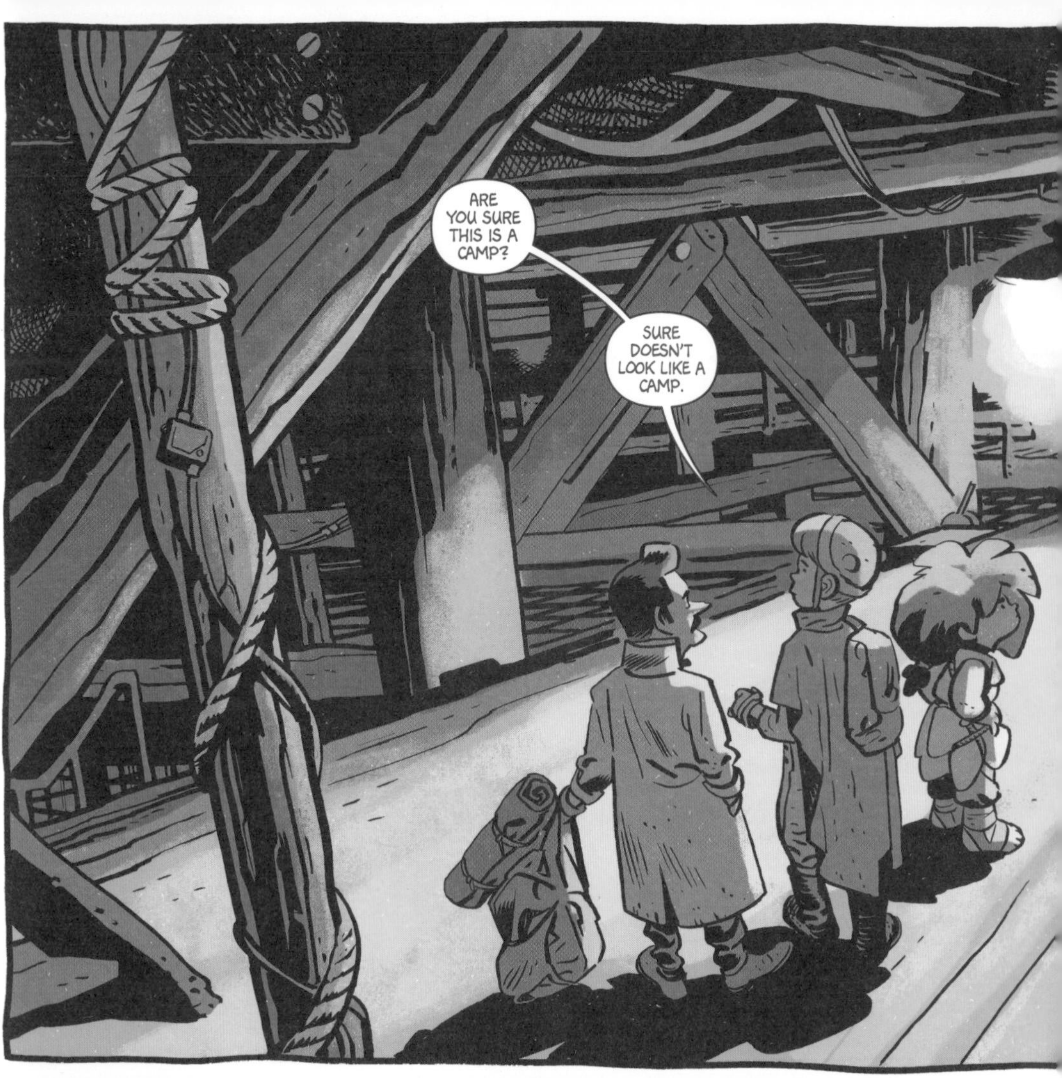
ARE YOU SURE THIS IS A CAMP?
SURE DOESN'T LOOK LIKE A CAMP.

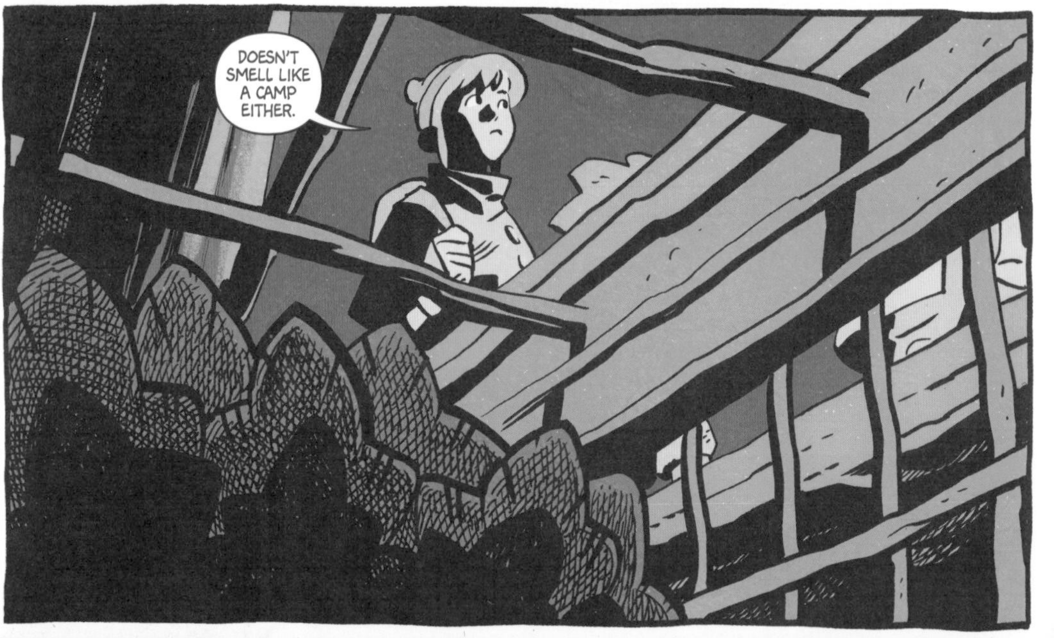
DOESN'T SMELL LIKE A CAMP EITHER.

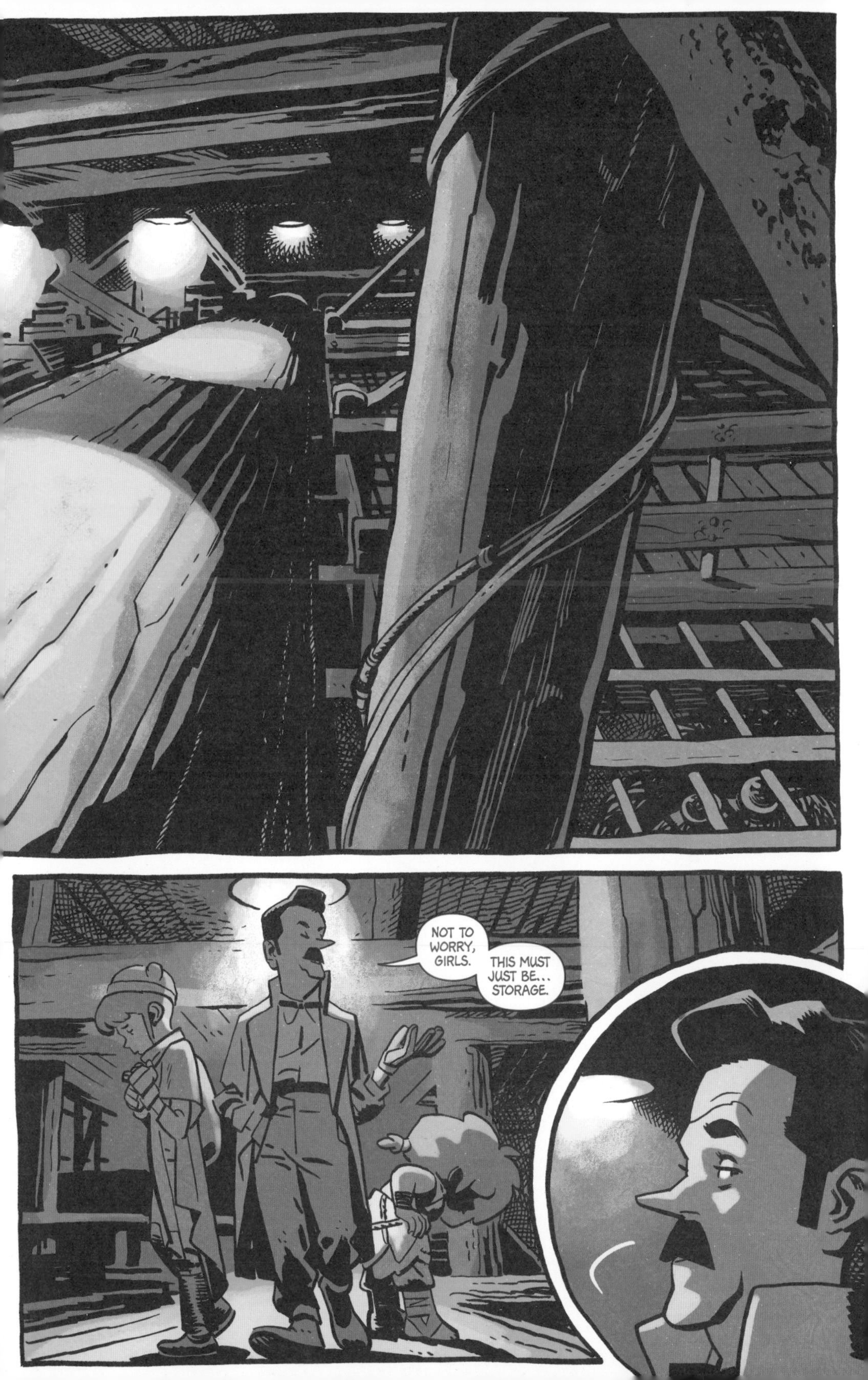
NOT TO WORRY, GIRLS.
THIS MUST JUST BE... STORAGE.

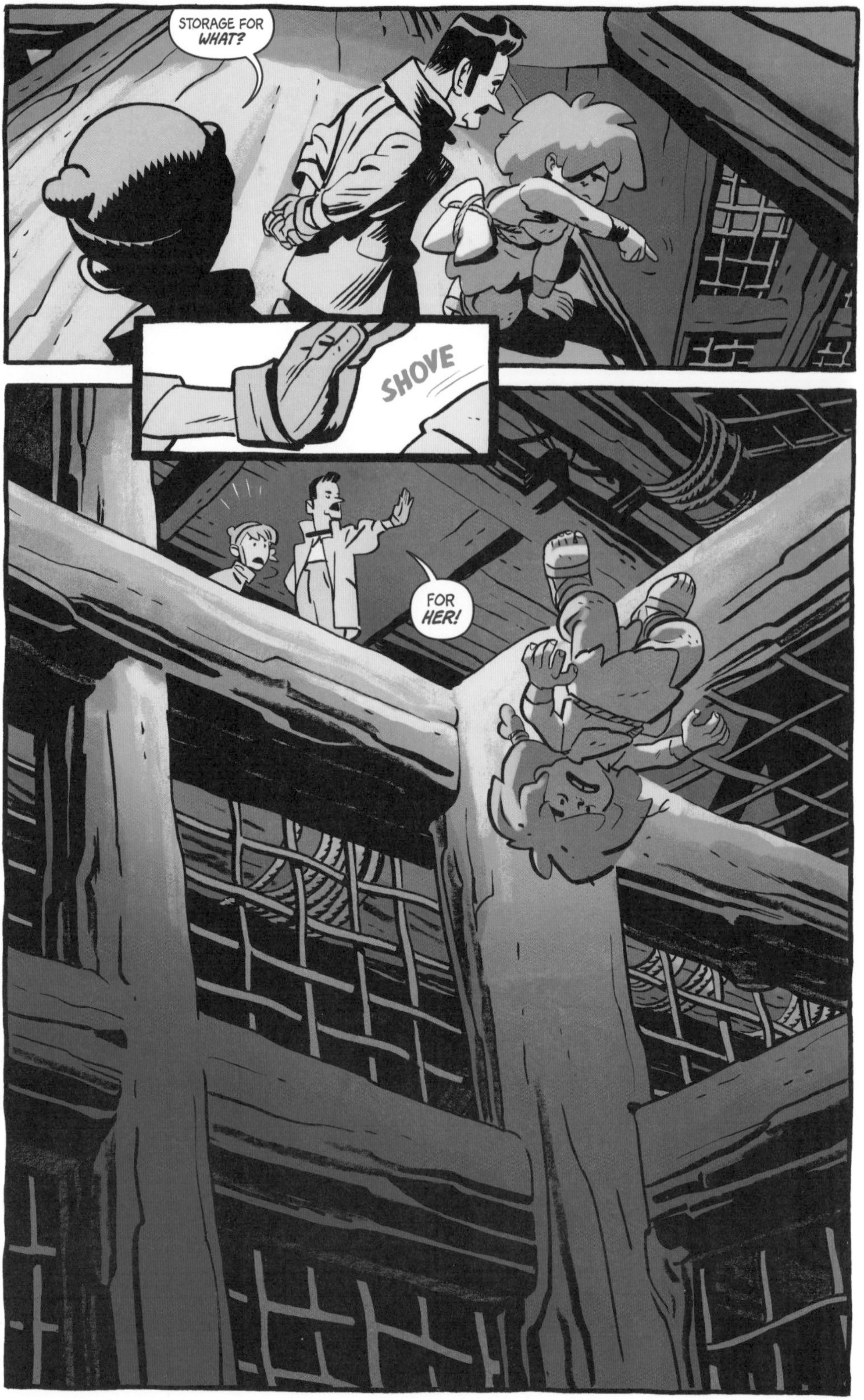
STORAGE FOR *WHAT?*
SHOVE
FOR *HER!*

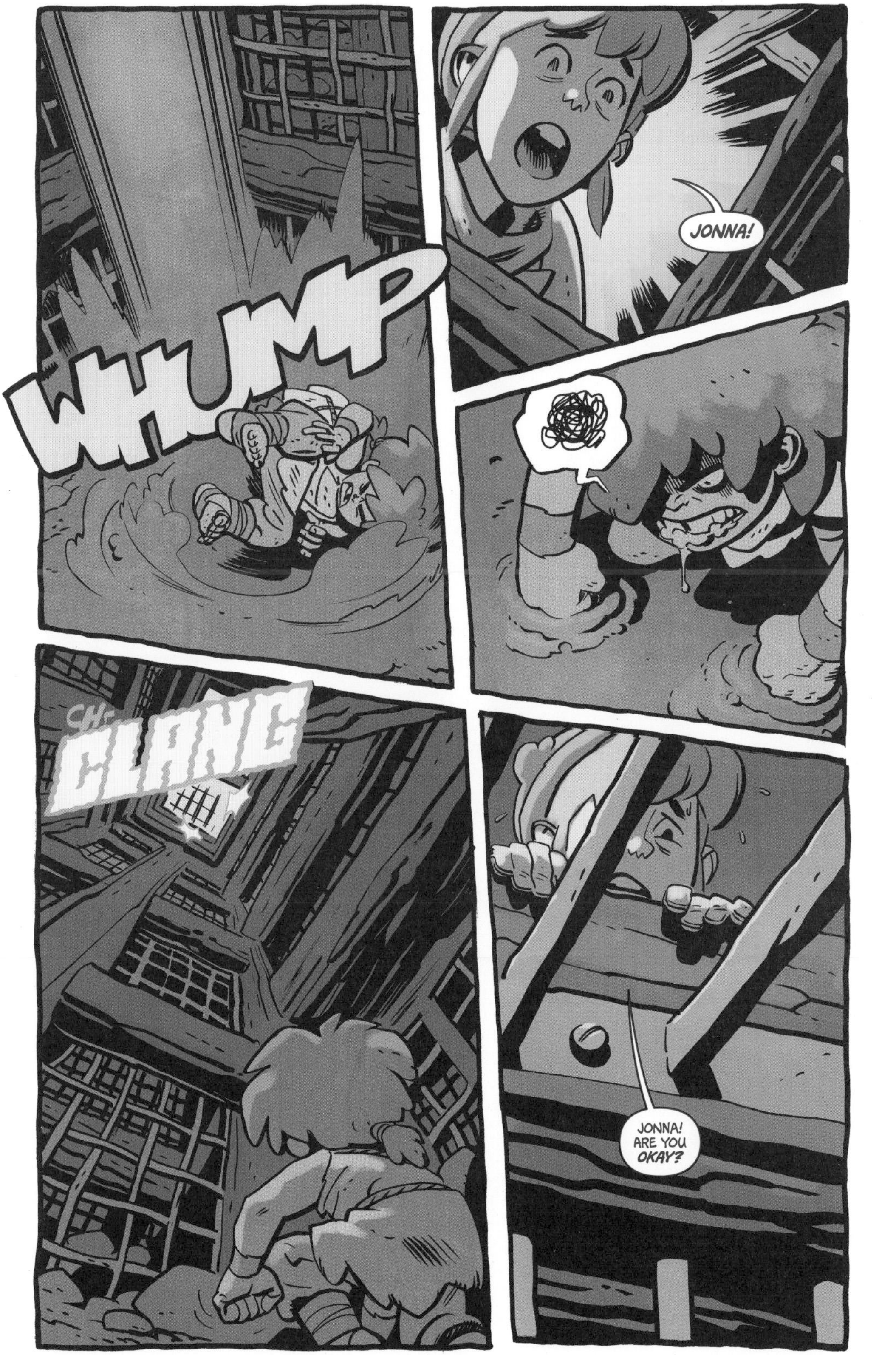
WHUMP
JONNA!
CH-CLANG
JONNA! ARE YOU OKAY?

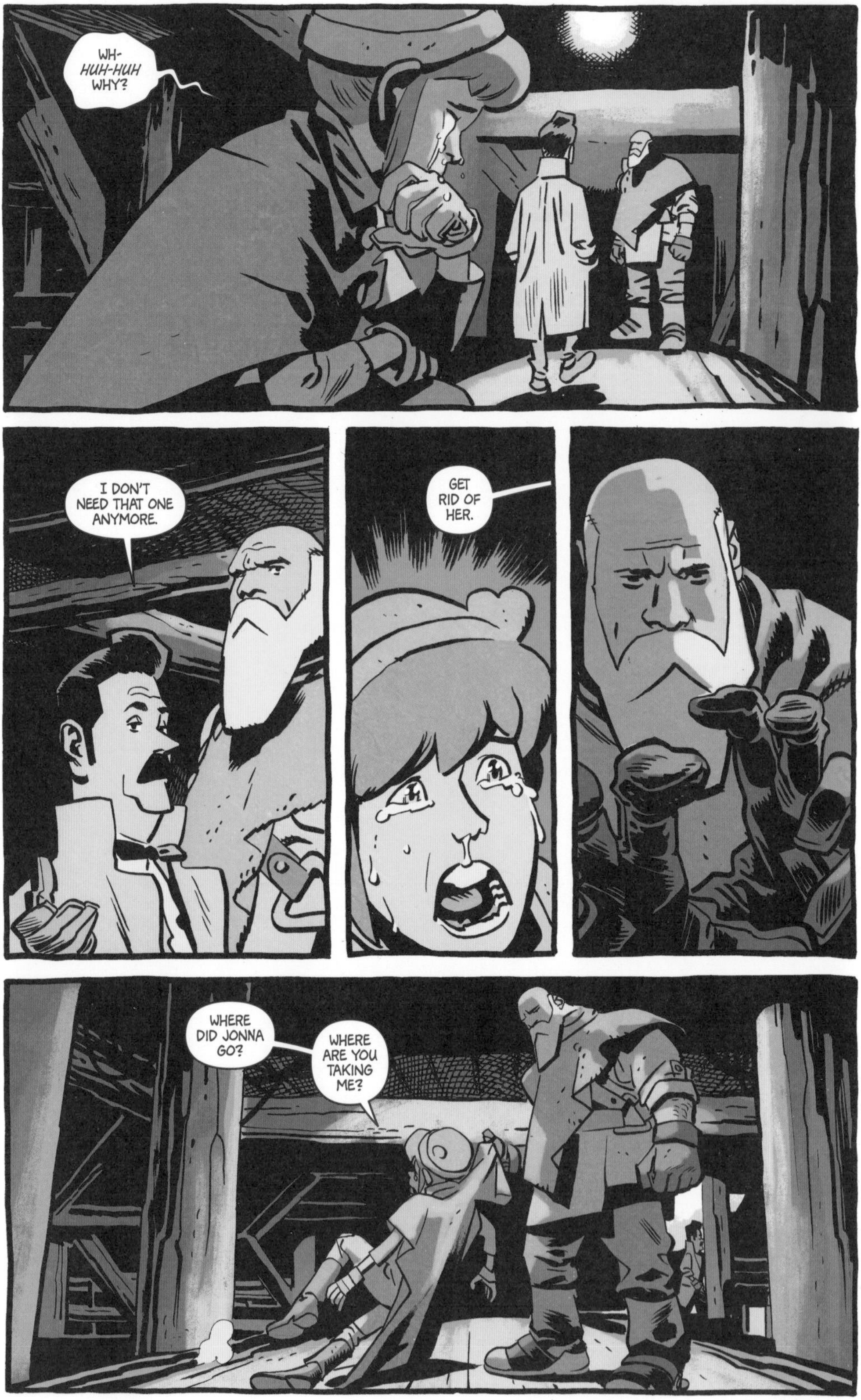
WH-
HUH-HUH
WHY?
I DON'T NEED THAT ONE ANYMORE.
GET RID OF HER.
WHERE DID JONNA GO?
WHERE ARE YOU TAKING ME?

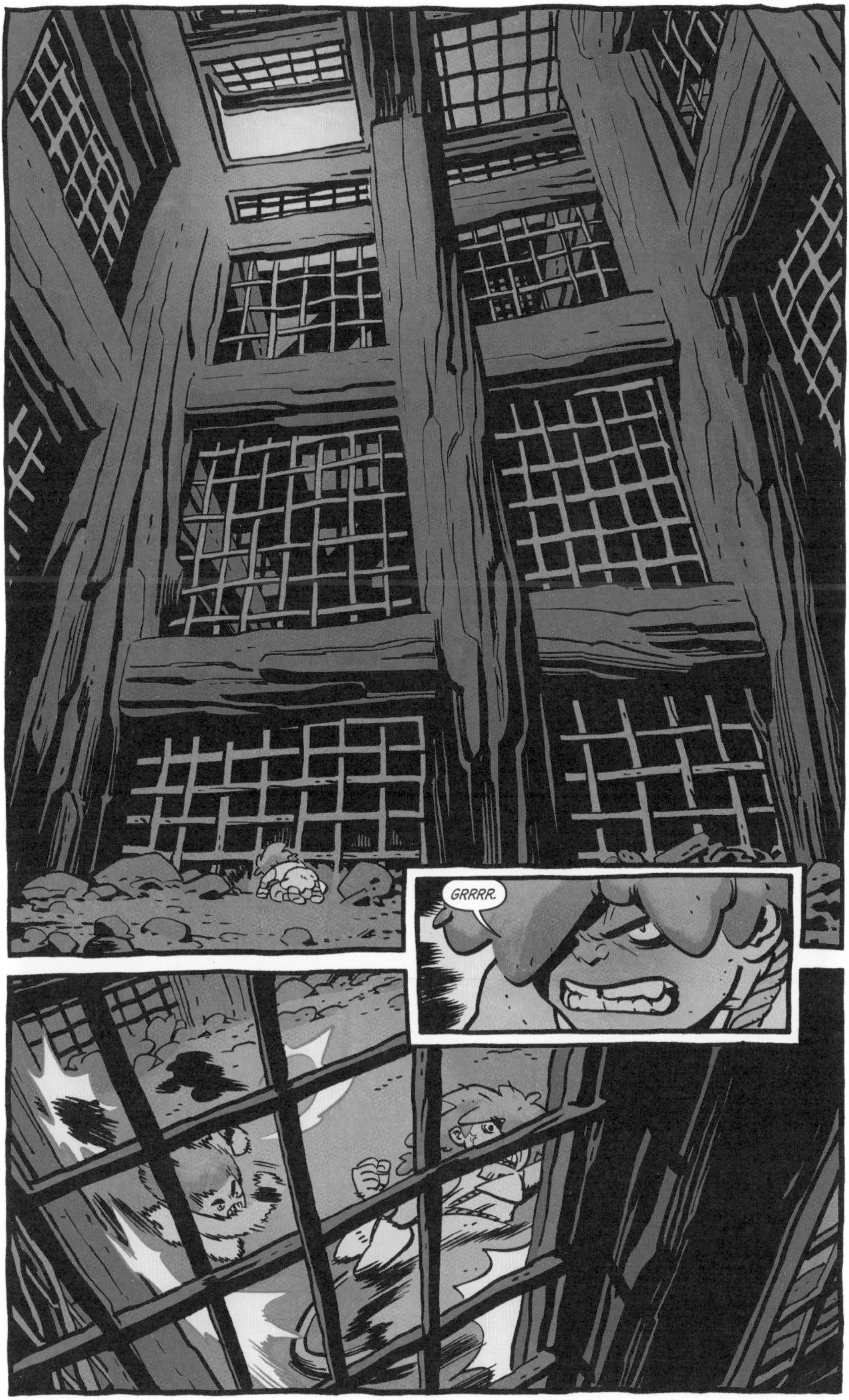
GRRRR.

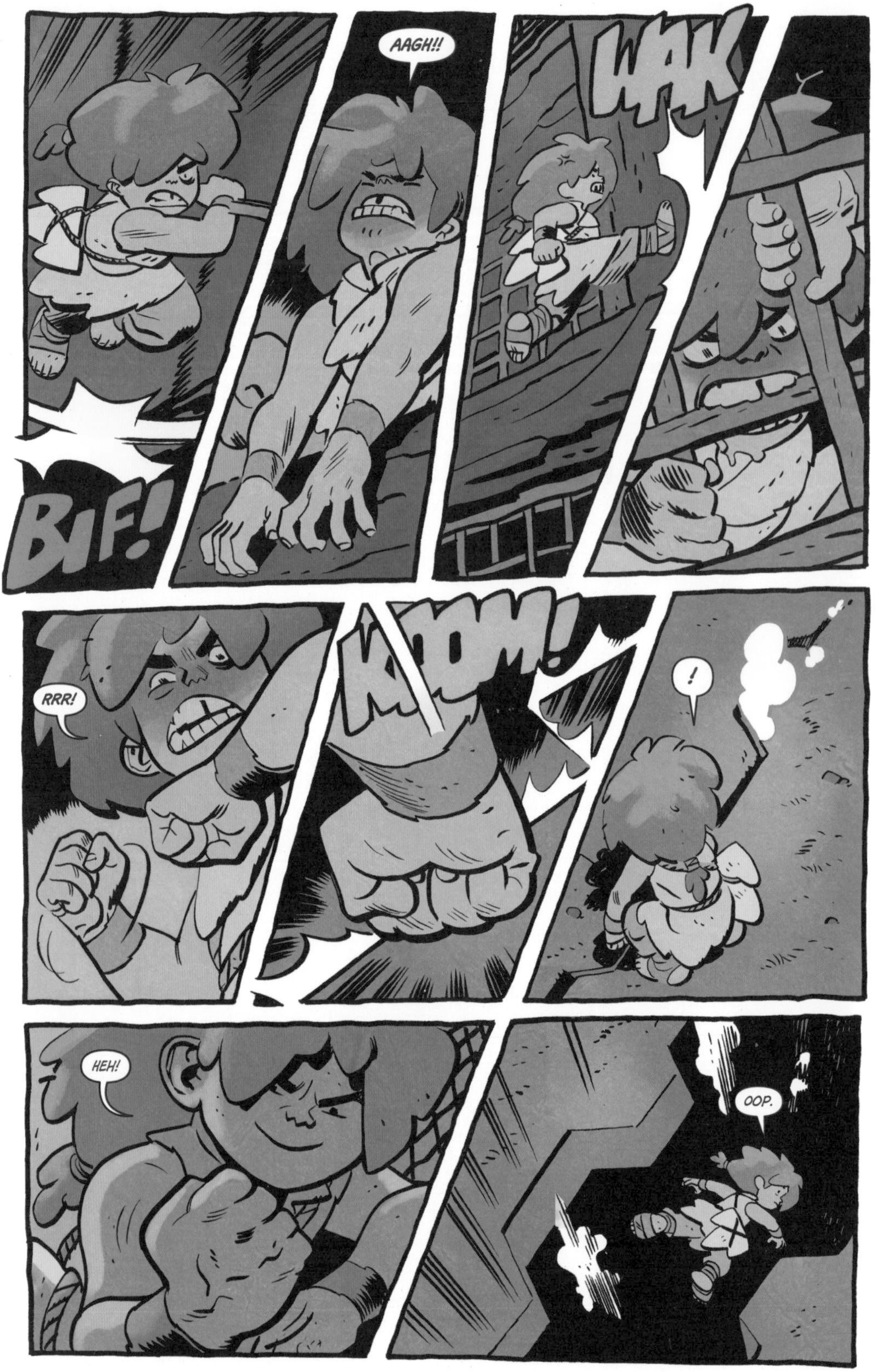

BIF!
AAGH!!
WAK
RRR!
KADOOM!
!
HEH!
OOP.

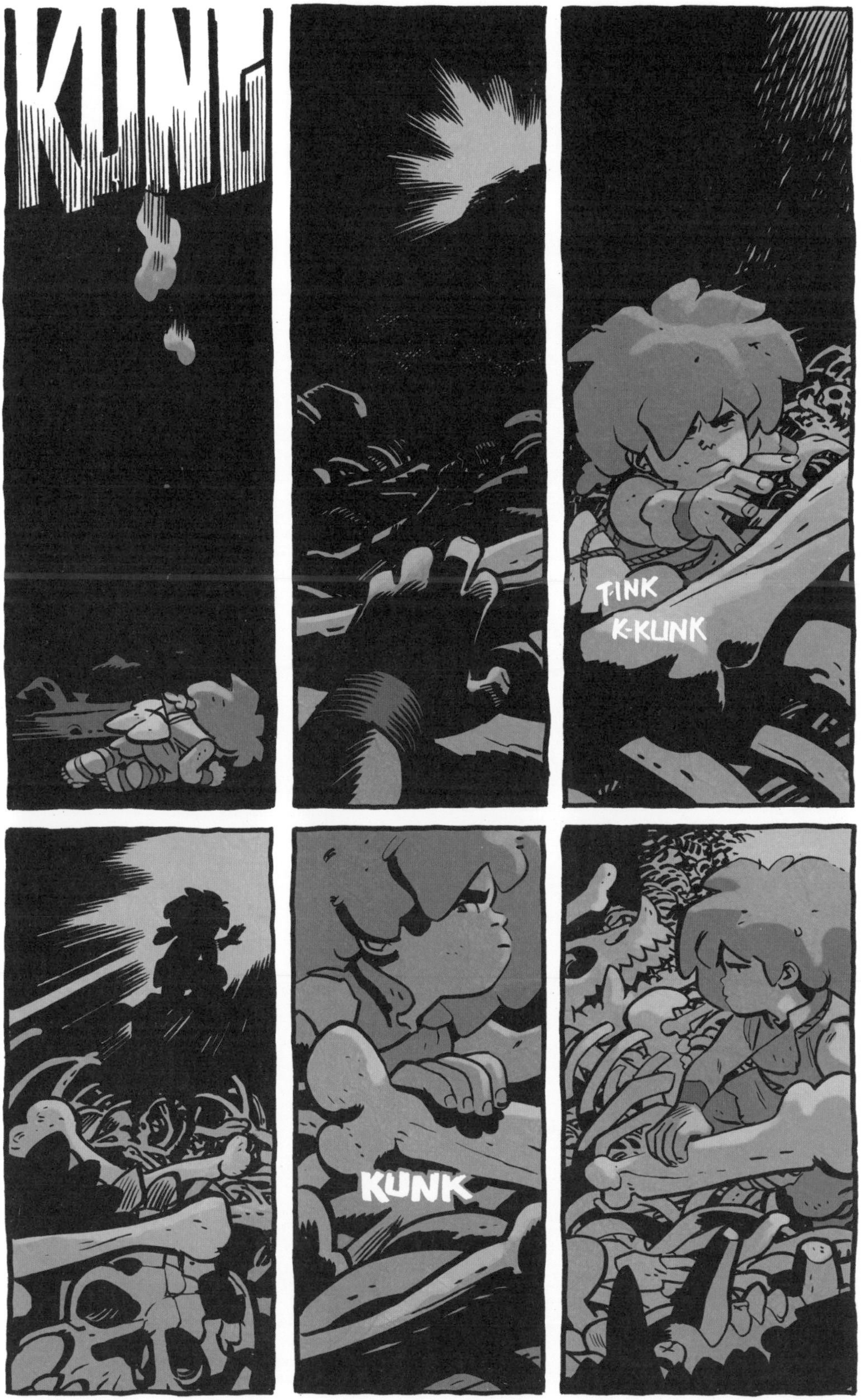
KUNK
T-INK
K-KUNK
KUNK

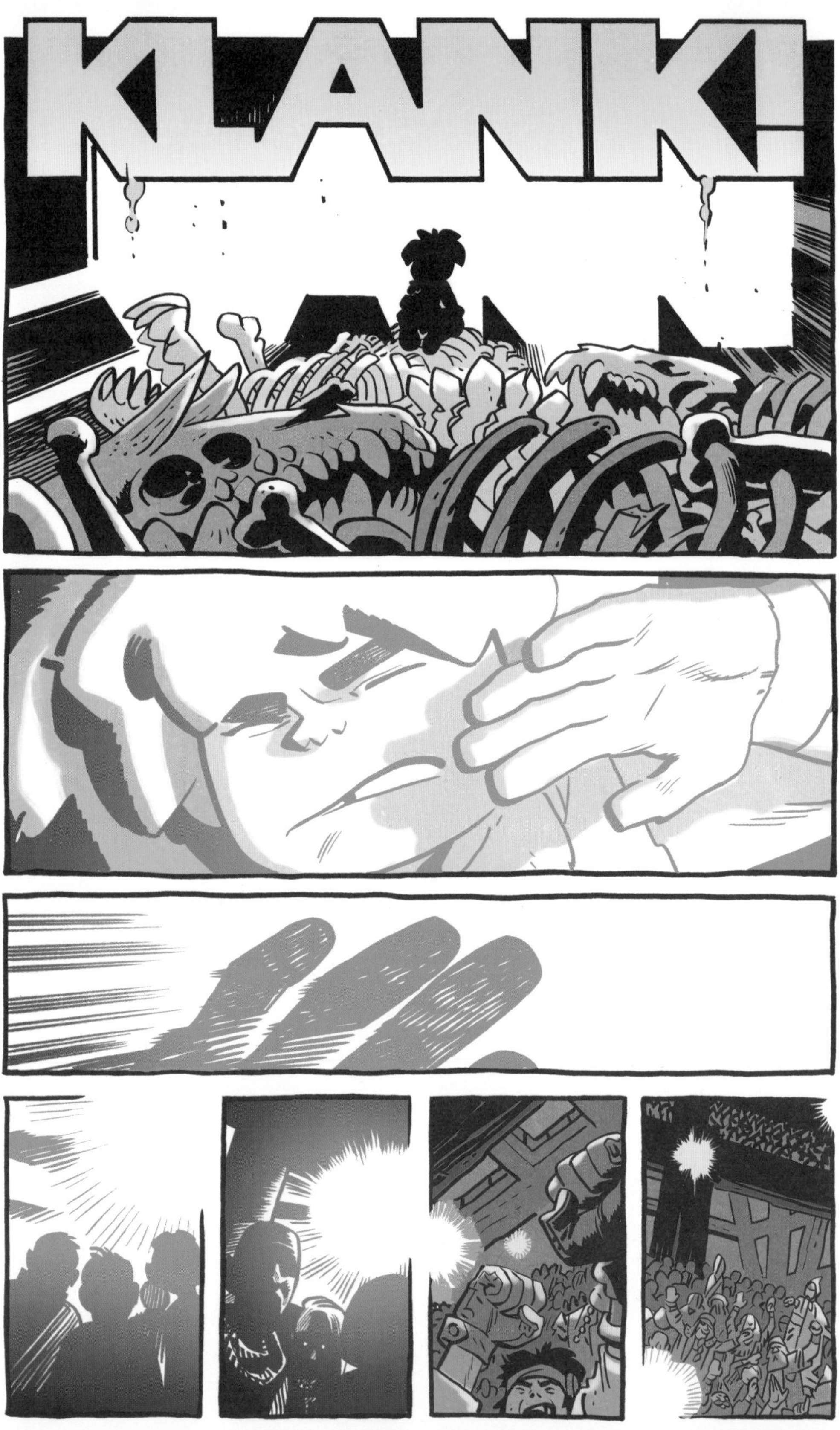
KLANK!

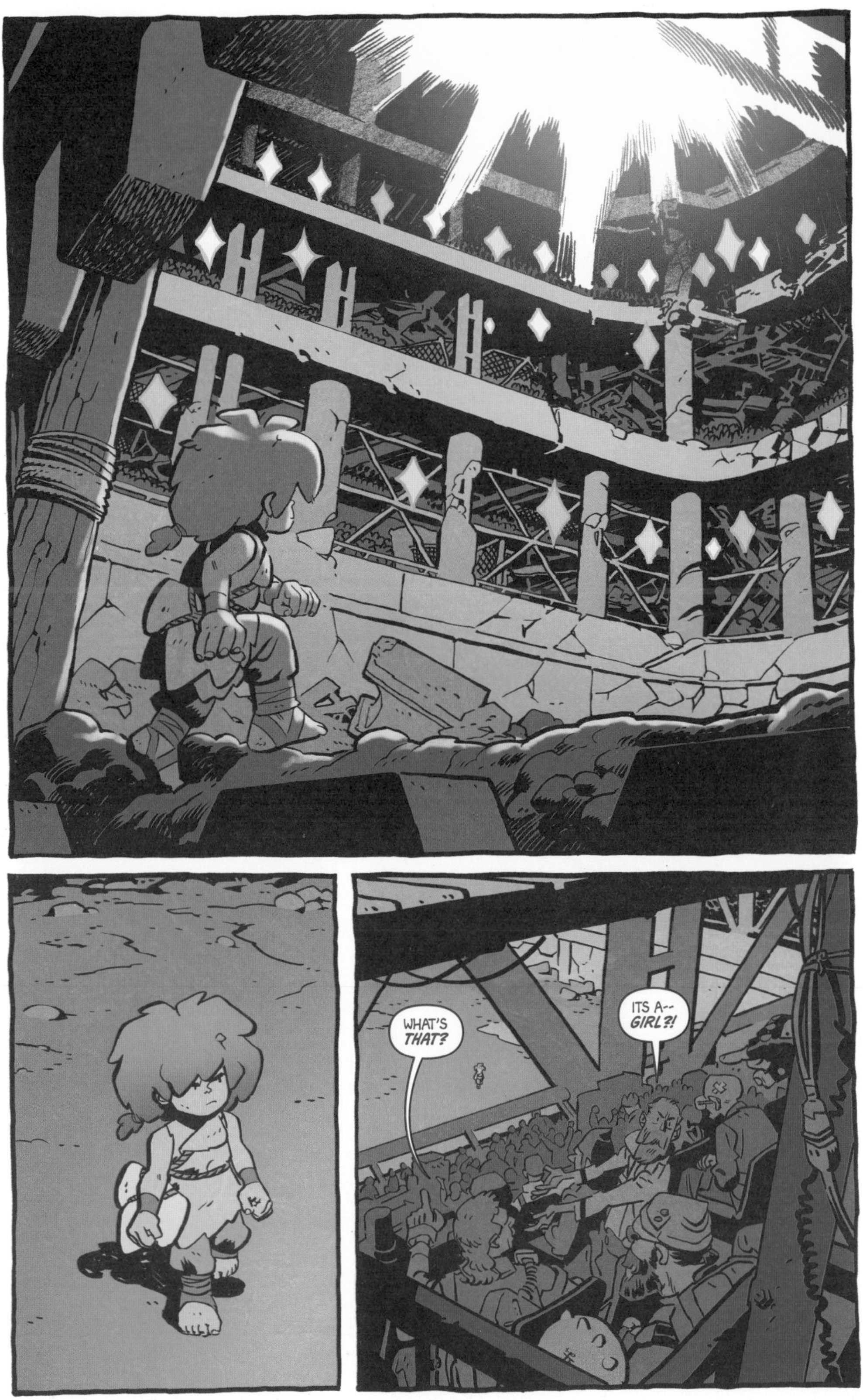
WHAT'S
THAT?
ITS A--
GIRL?!

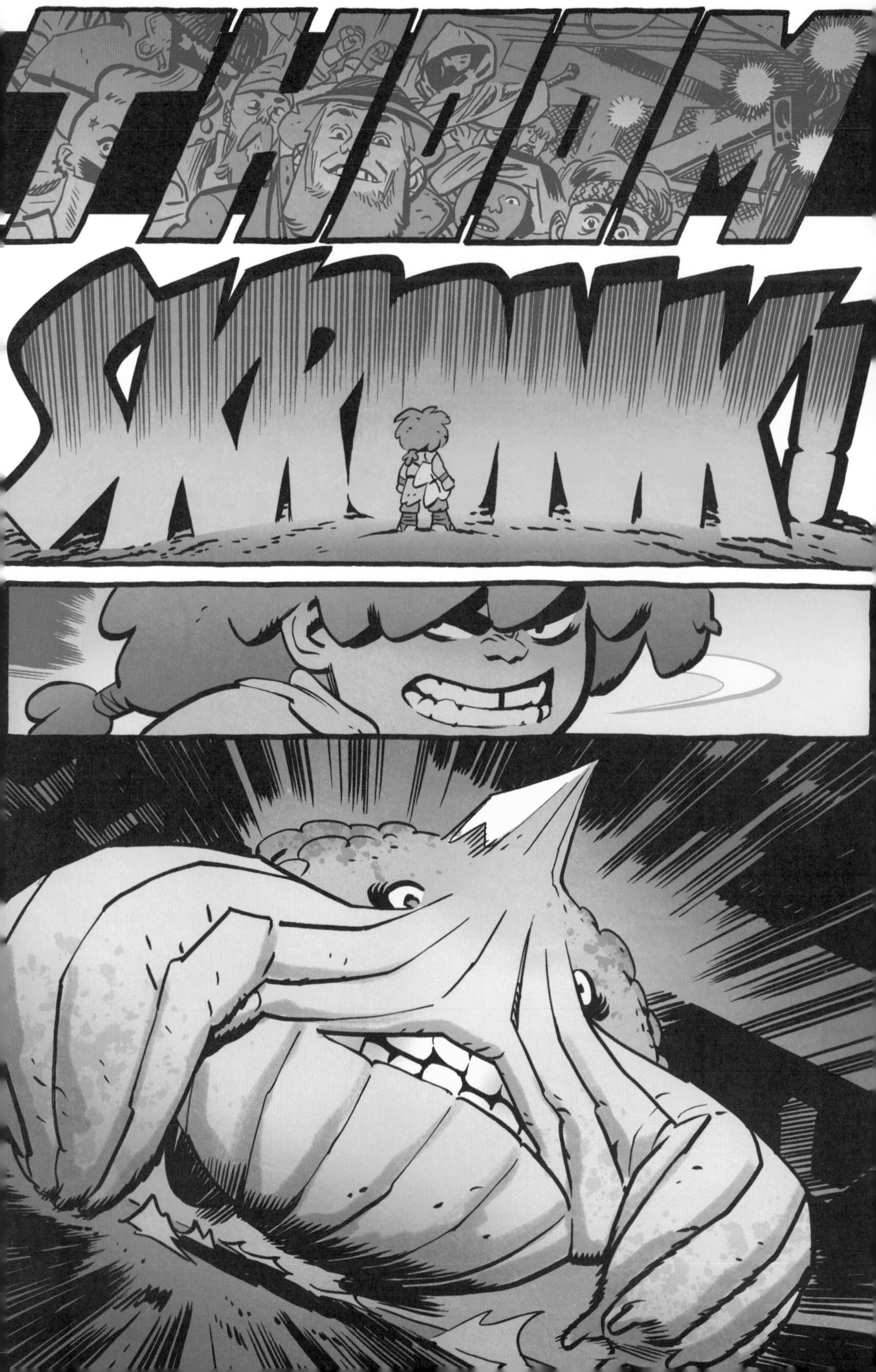
THOOM
SKRUNK!

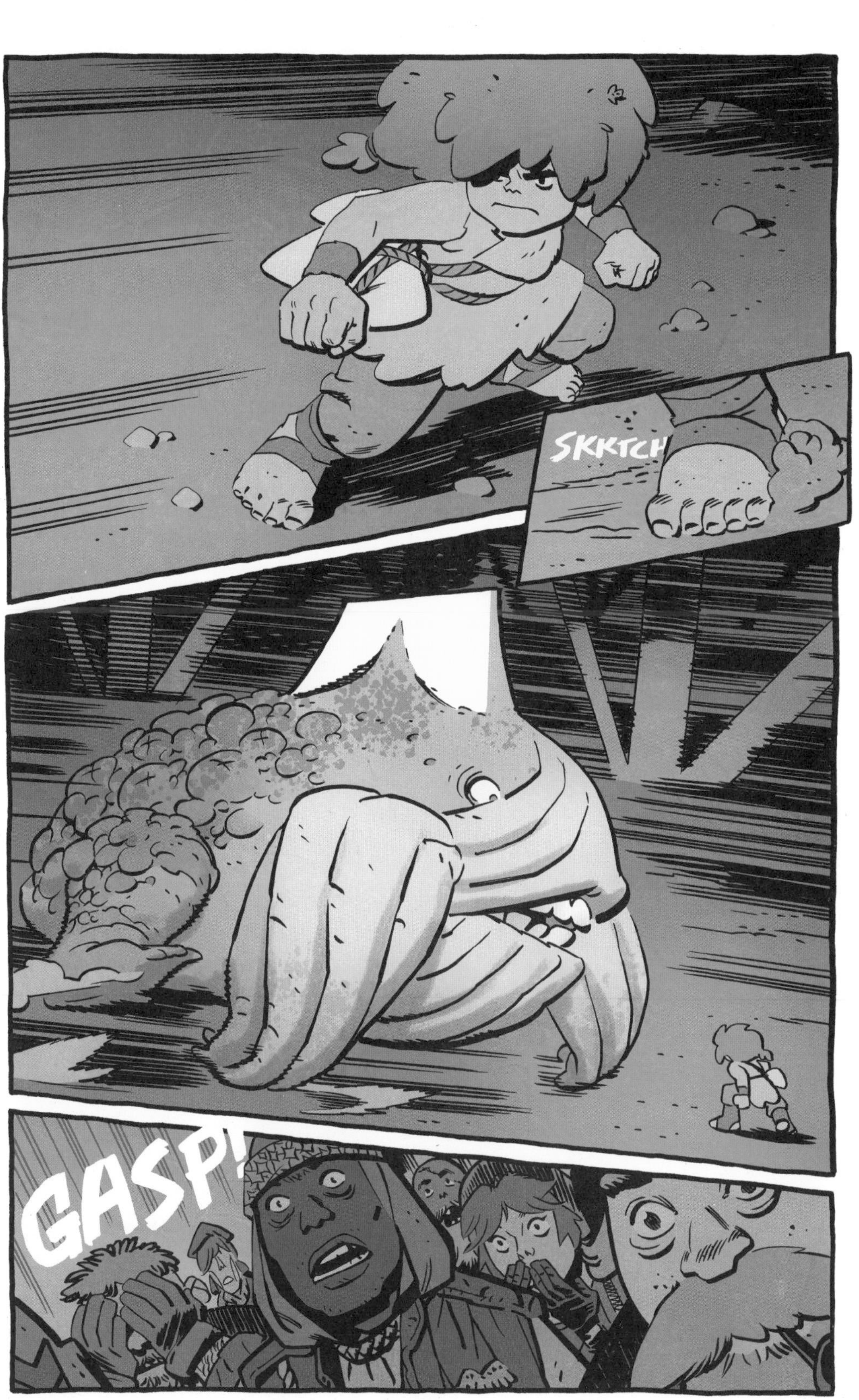
SKKTCH
GASP!

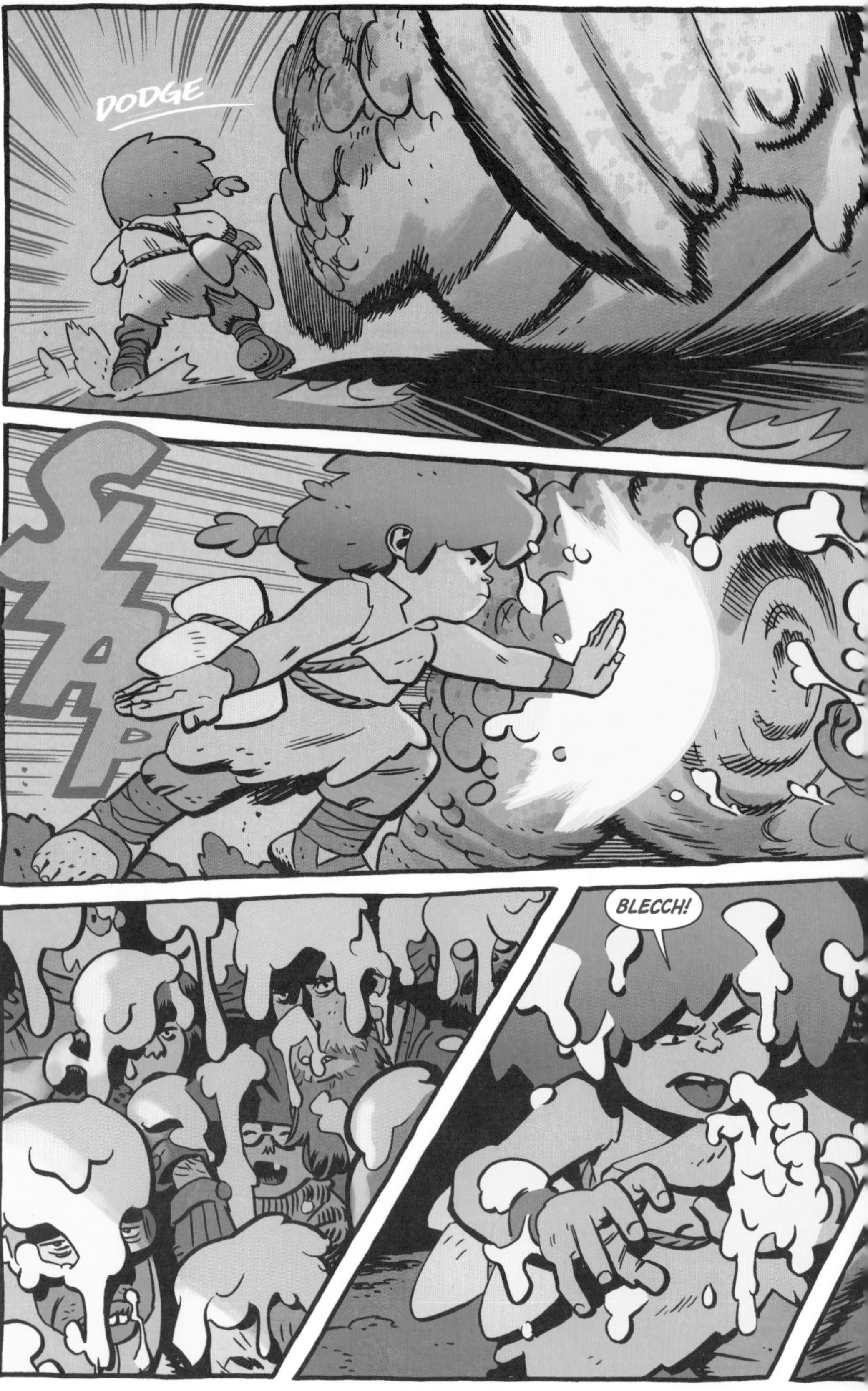
DODGE
BLECCH!

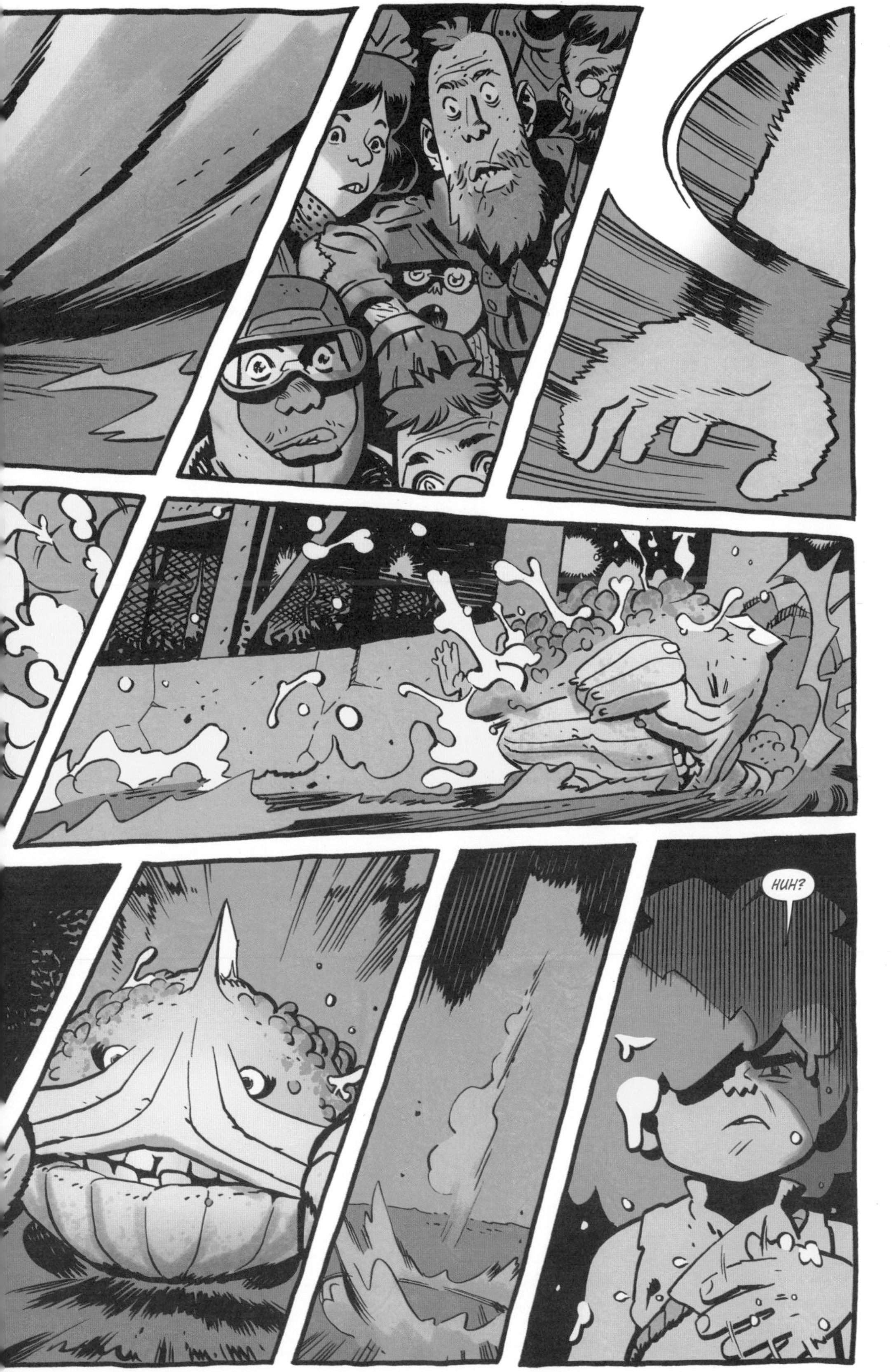
HUH?

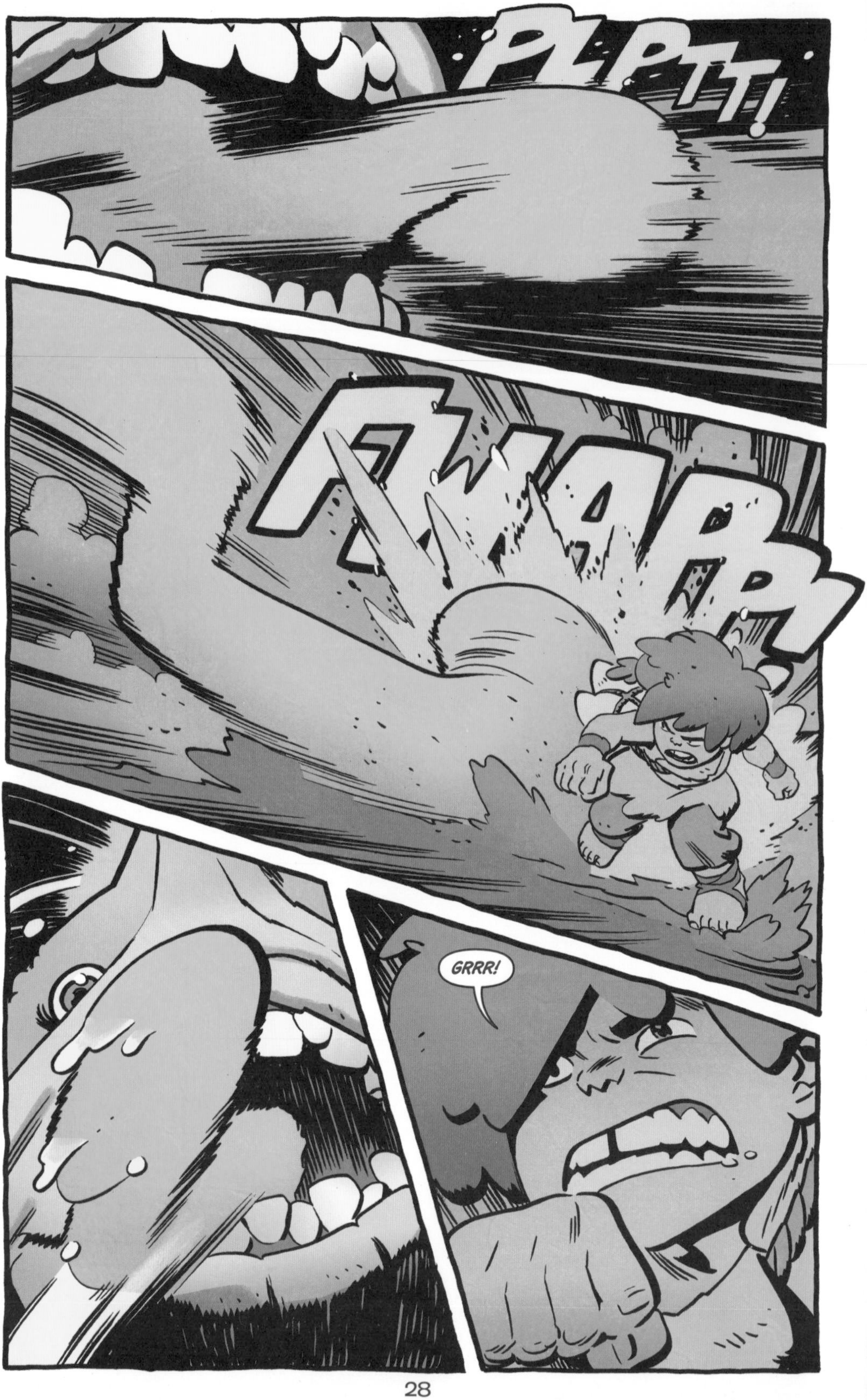
PLPTTT!
FWAP!
GRRR!

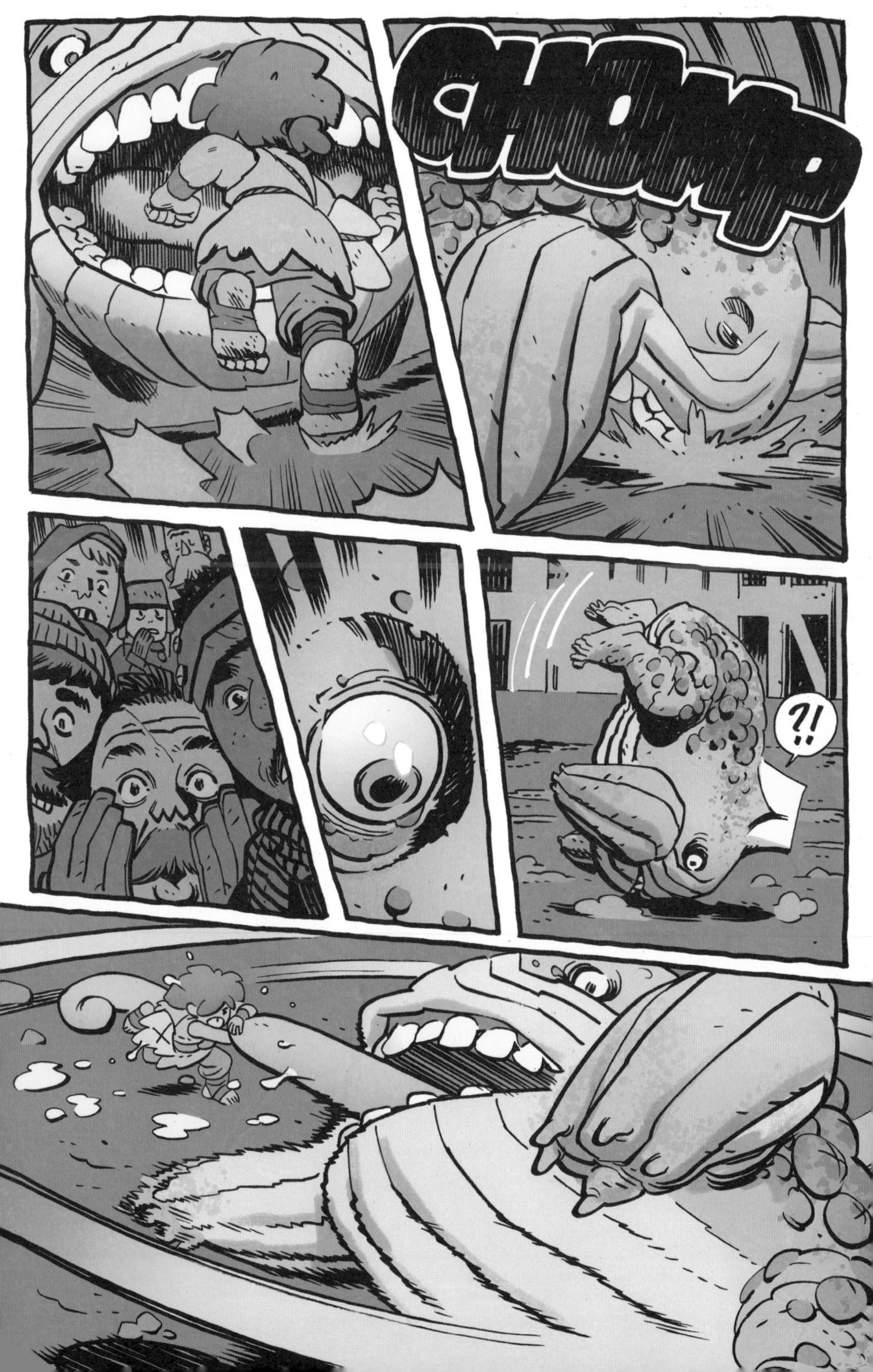
CHOMP
?!

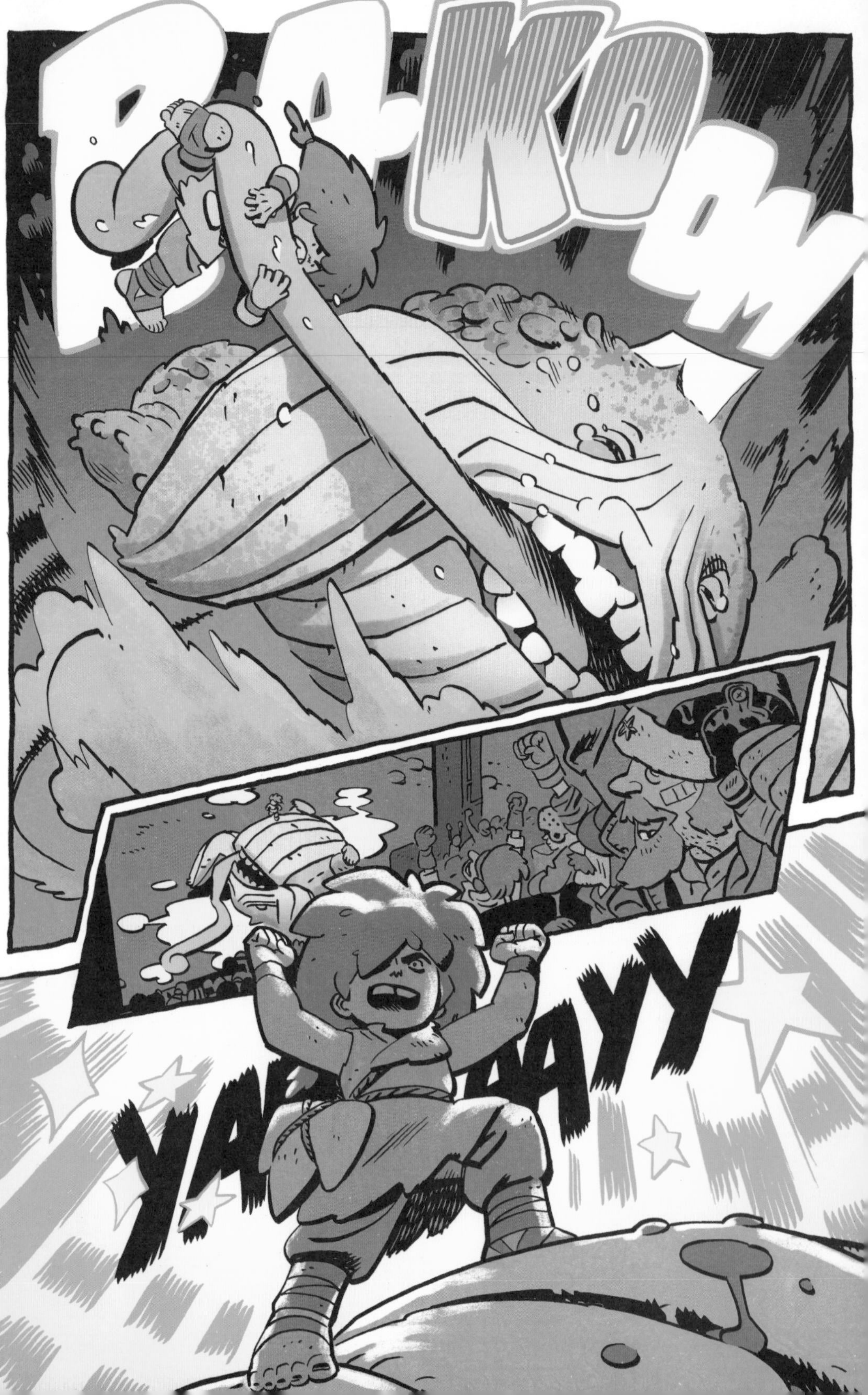
BA-KOOM
YA AYY

CHAPTER 6

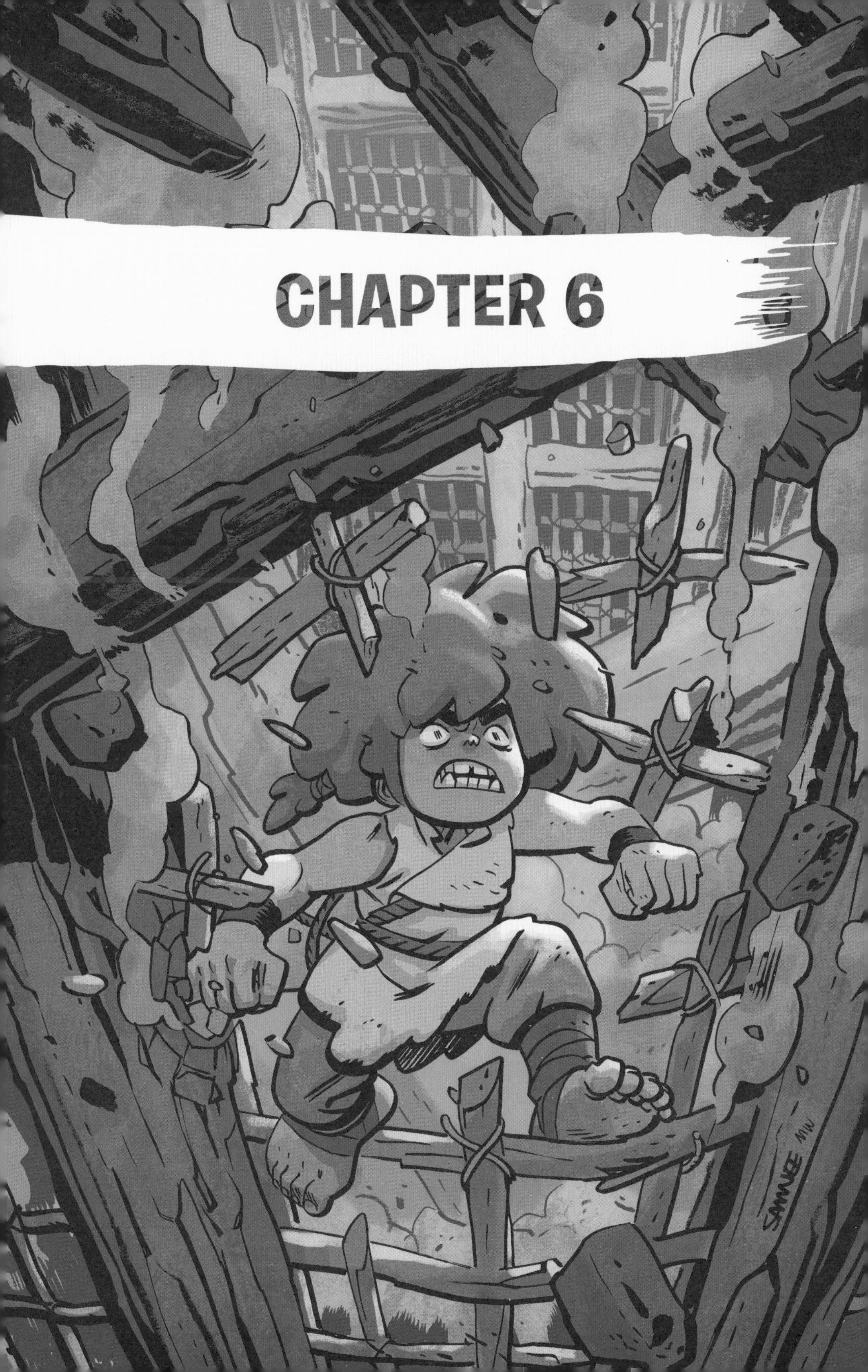
SAMNEE MW

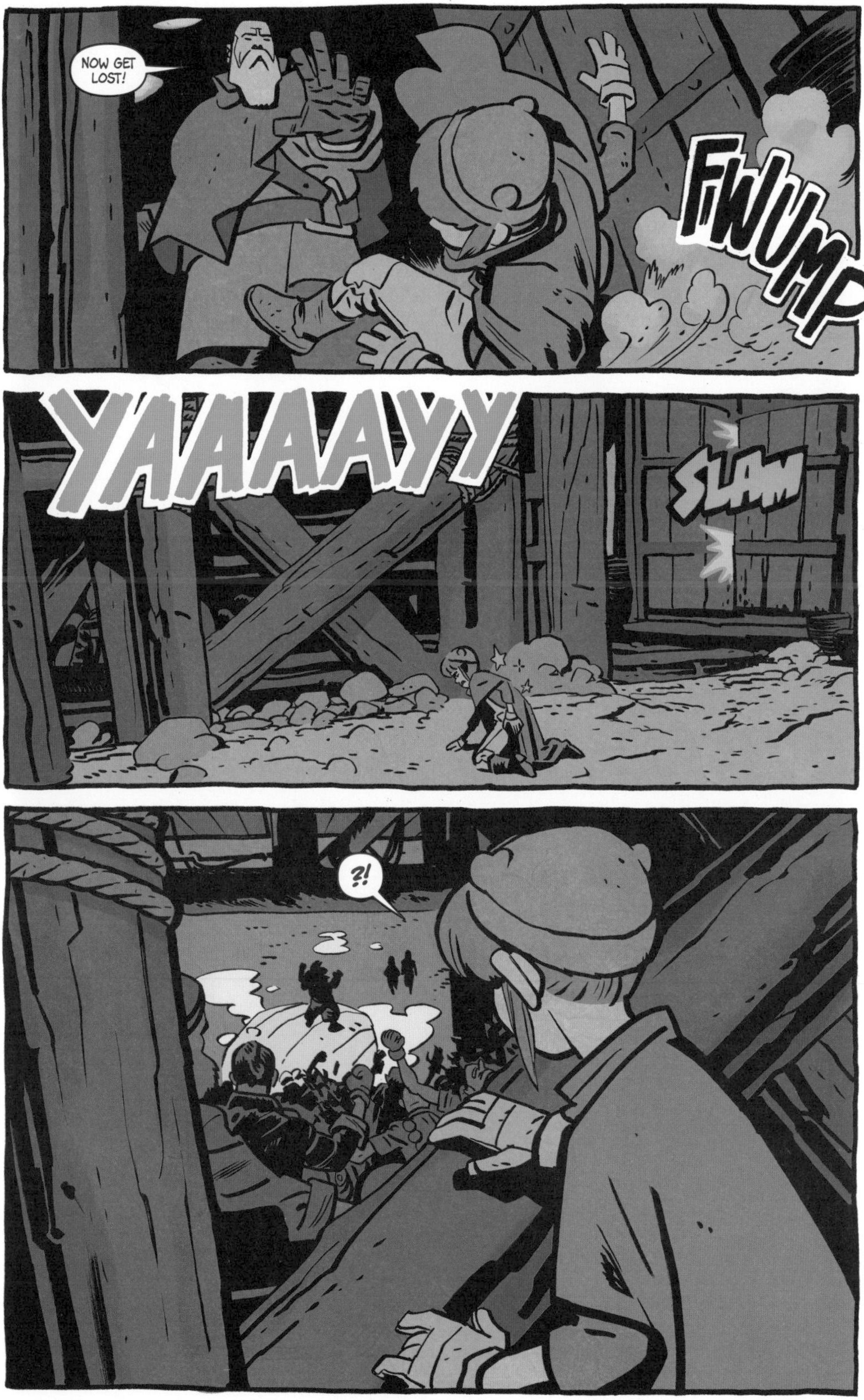
NOW GET LOST!
FWUMP
YAAAAYY
SLAM
?!

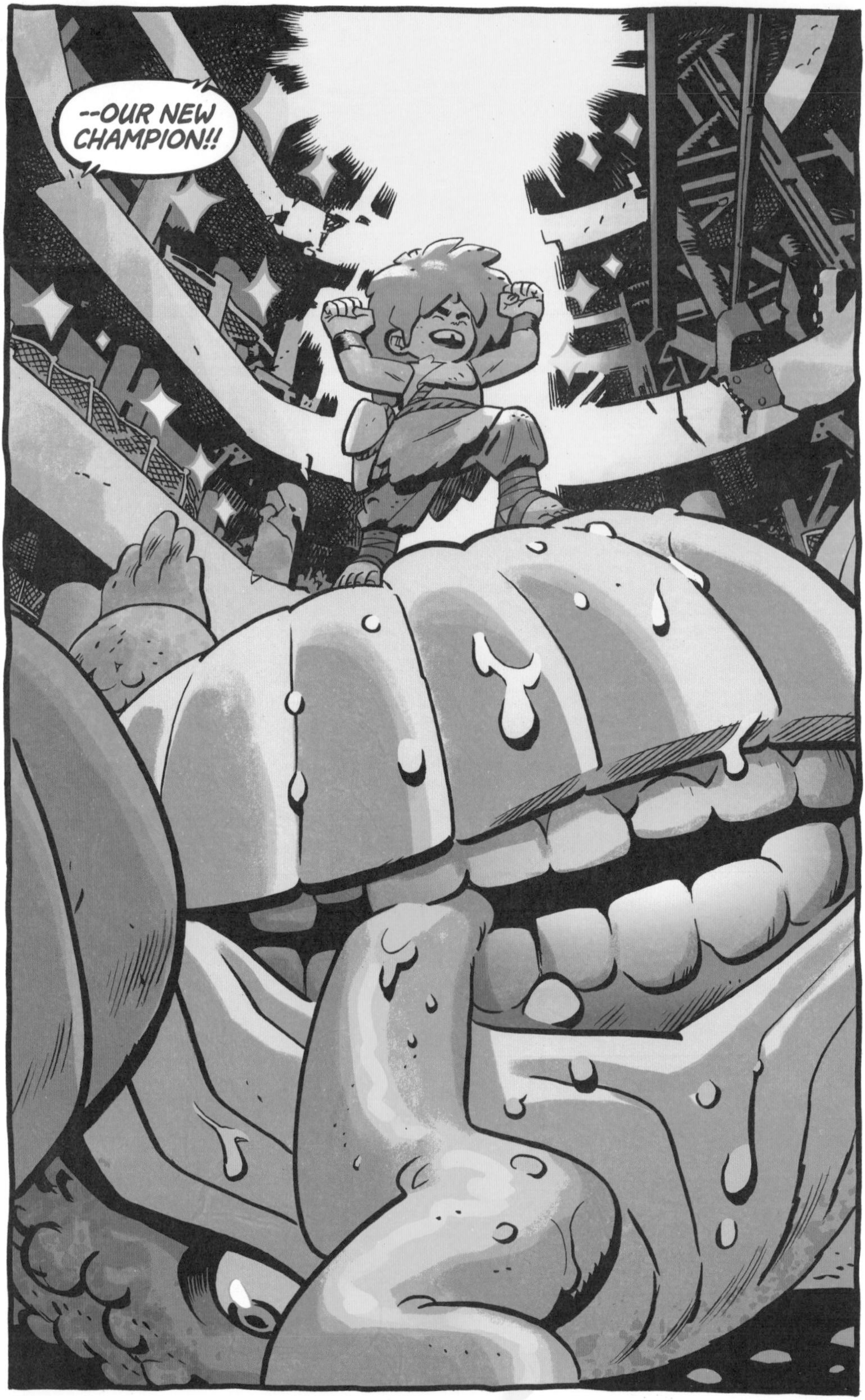
--OUR NEW CHAMPION!!

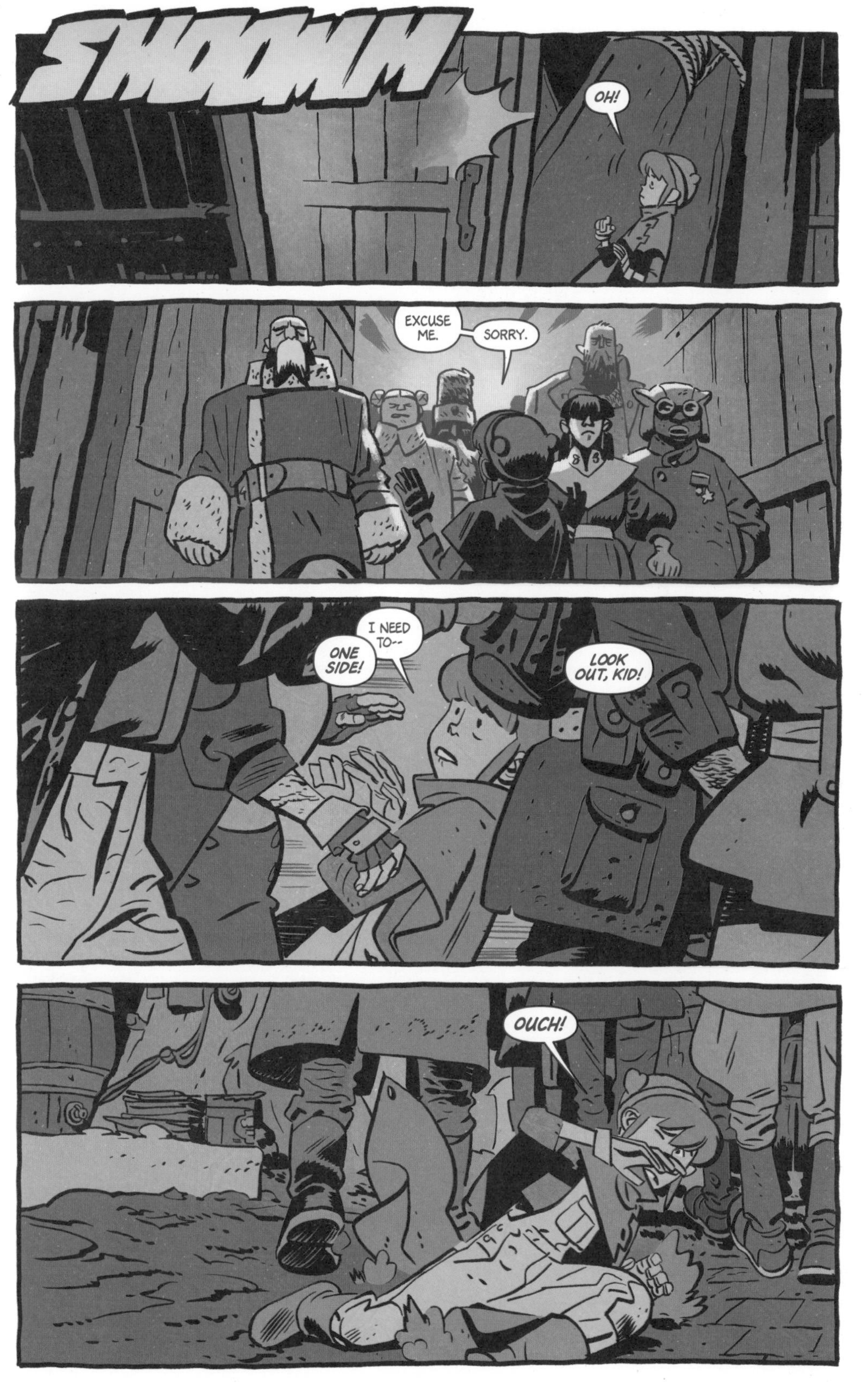
SHOOM
OH!
EXCUSE ME.
SORRY.
ONE SIDE!
I NEED TO--
LOOK OUT, KID!
OUCH!

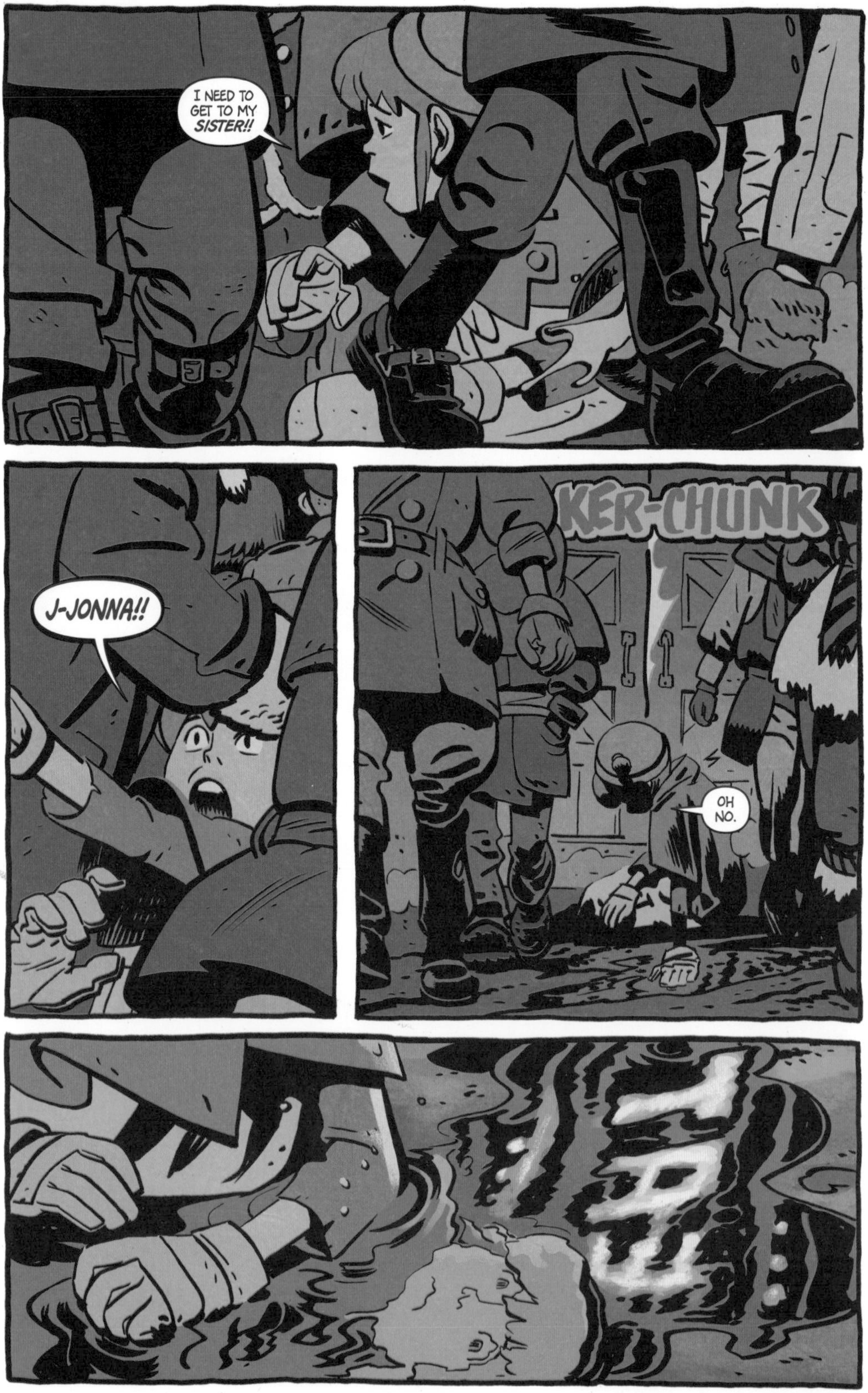

I NEED TO GET TO MY SISTER!!
J-JONNA!!
KER-CHUNK
OH NO.

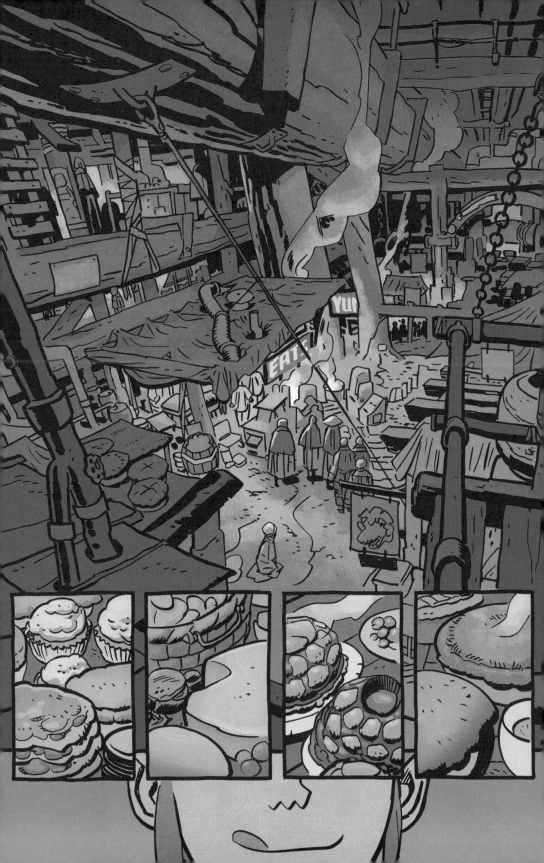

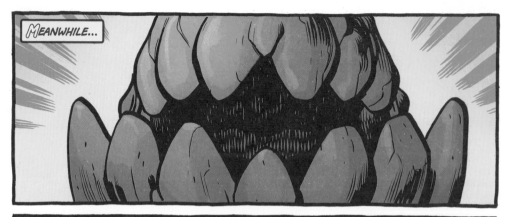

MEANWHILE...

KA-CHOOM

YOU AND YOUR BIG *MOUTH!*

IF YOU HADN'T PICKED A FIGHT WITH *ME,* THOSE GIRLS WOULDN'T HAVE WANDERED *OFF!*

MY BIG MOUTH?! I DIDN'T START THAT FIGHT!

AND HOW AM I SUPPOSED TO HAVE KEPT AN EYE ON THEM? I'VE ONLY GOT ONE GOOD ONE!

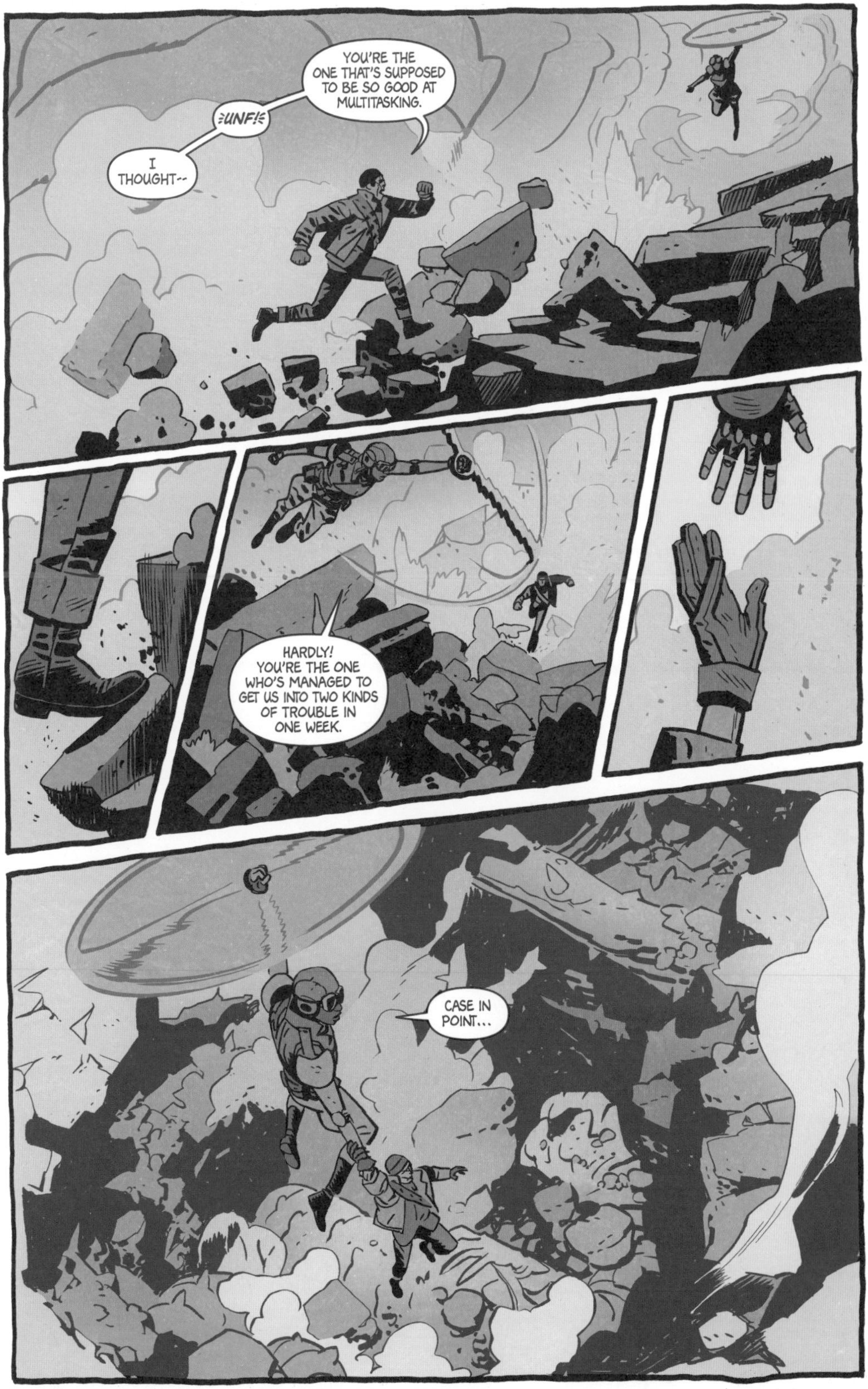
I THOUGHT--
UNF!
YOU'RE THE ONE THAT'S SUPPOSED TO BE SO GOOD AT MULTITASKING.
HARDLY! YOU'RE THE ONE WHO'S MANAGED TO GET US INTO TWO KINDS OF TROUBLE IN ONE WEEK.
CASE IN POINT...

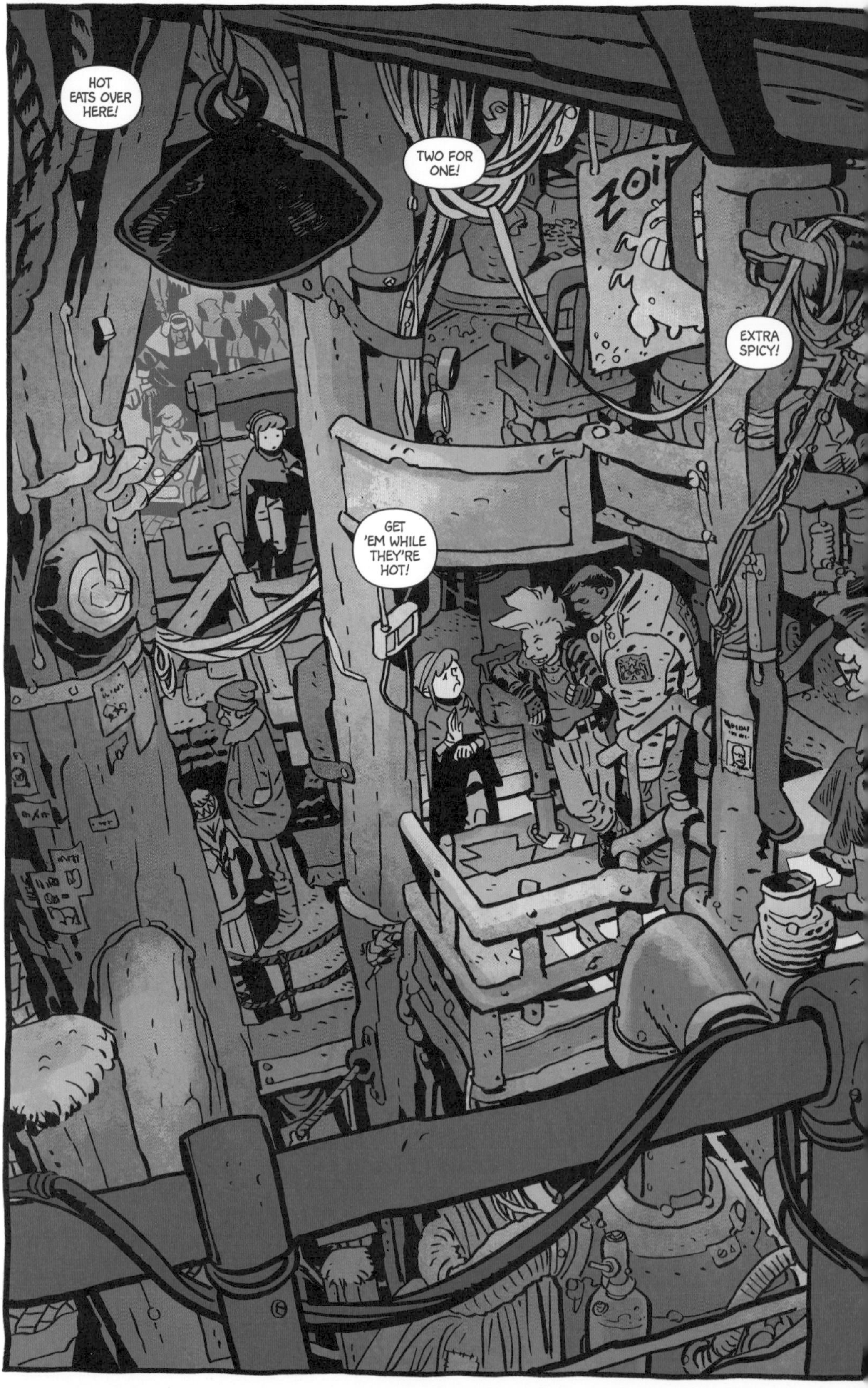
HOT EATS OVER HERE!
TWO FOR ONE!
EXTRA SPICY!
GET 'EM WHILE THEY'RE HOT!

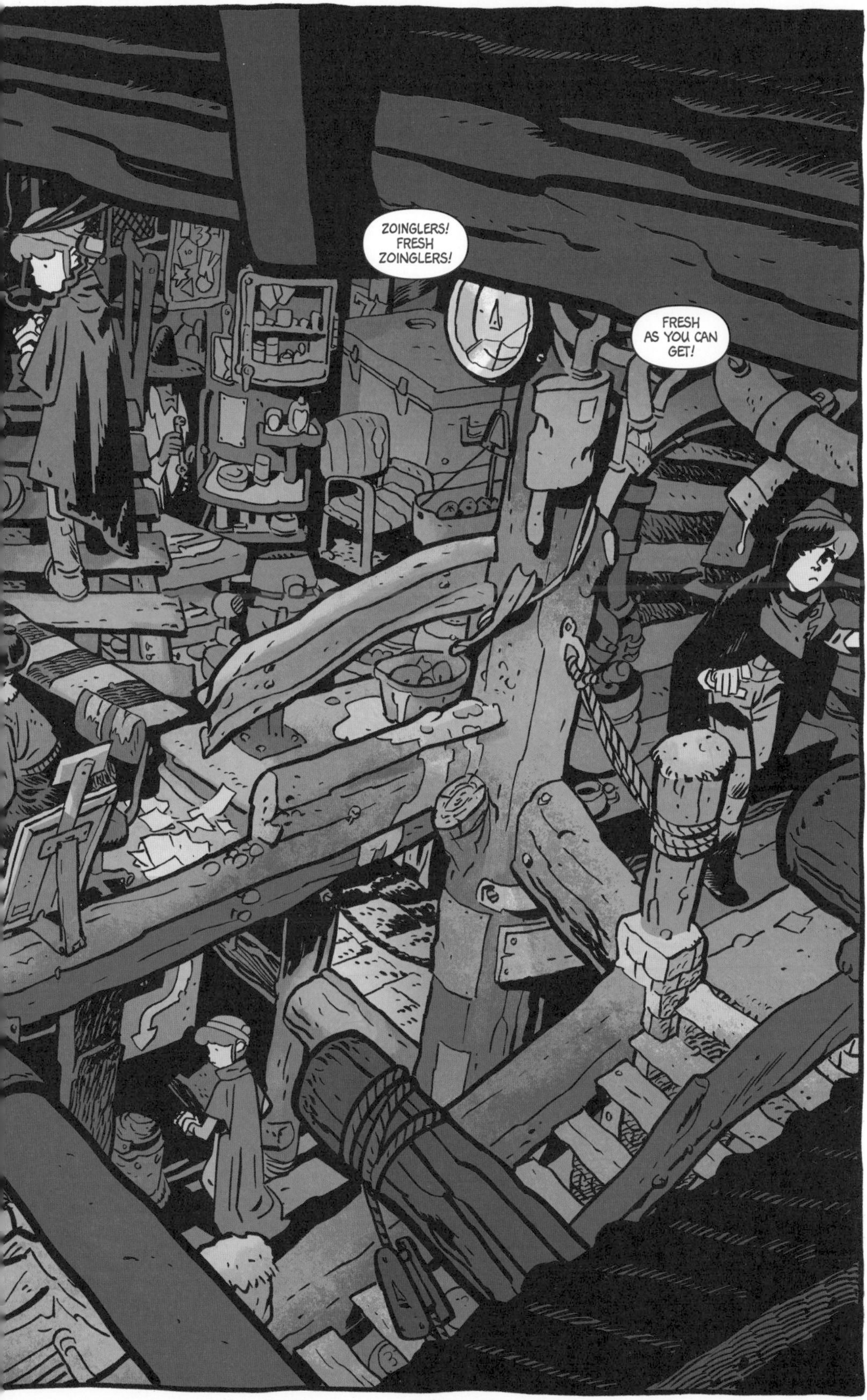
ZOINGLERS! FRESH ZOINGLERS!
FRESH AS YOU CAN GET!

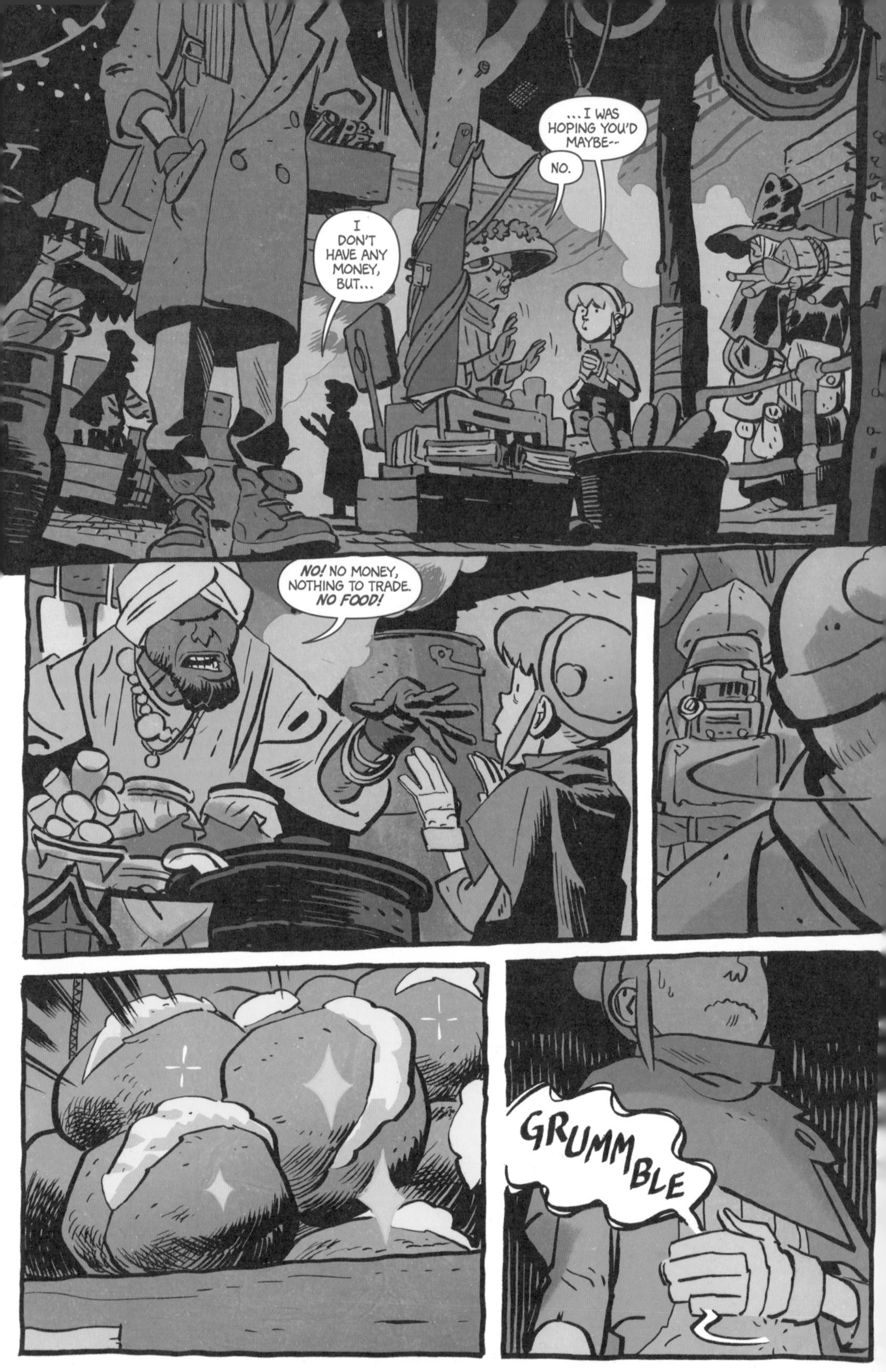
I DON'T HAVE ANY MONEY, BUT...
...I WAS HOPING YOU'D MAYBE--
NO.
NO! NO MONEY, NOTHING TO TRADE. NO FOOD!
GRUMMBLE

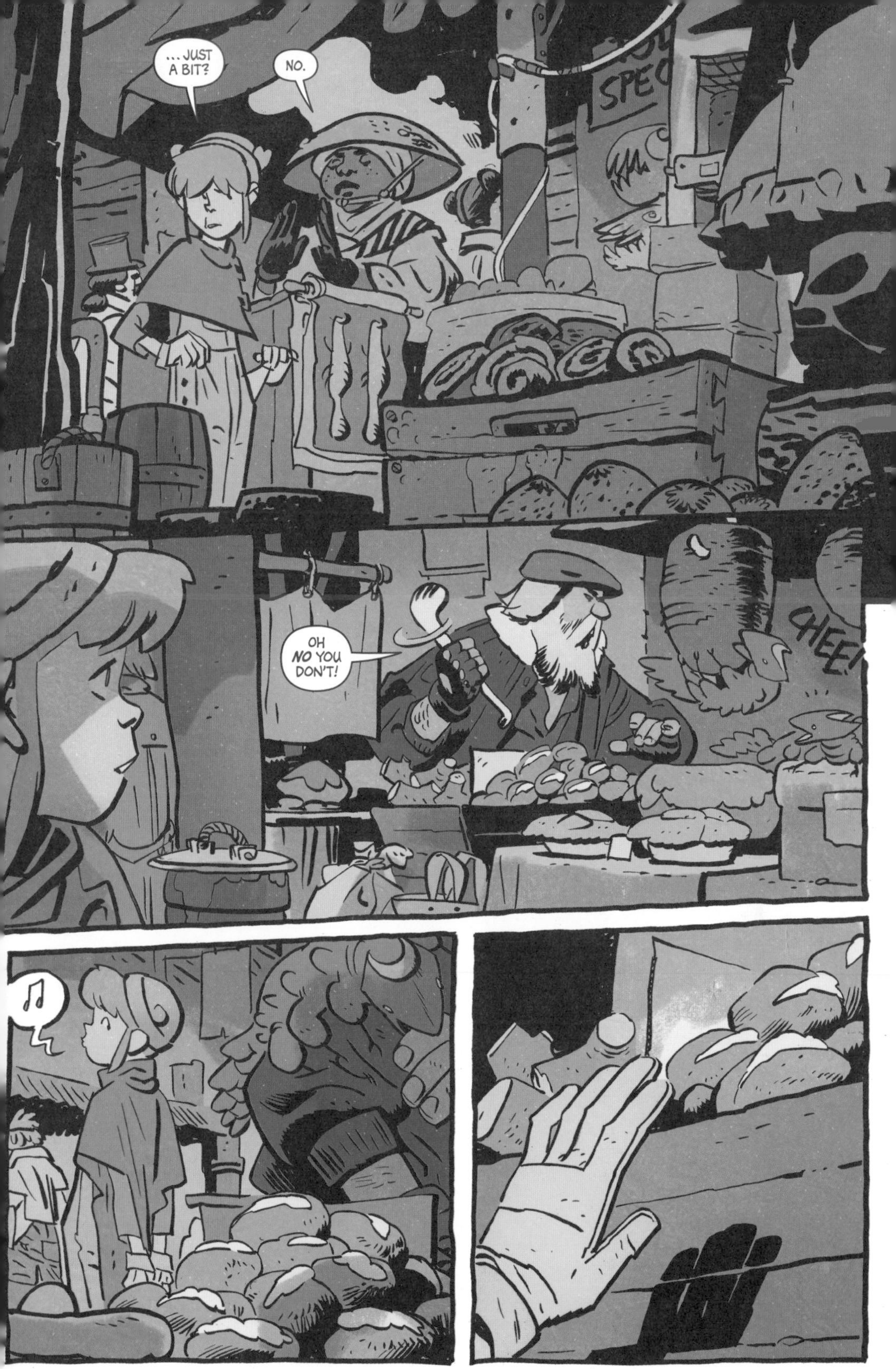
...JUST A BIT?
NO.
SPEC
OH NO YOU DON'T!
CHEE
♫

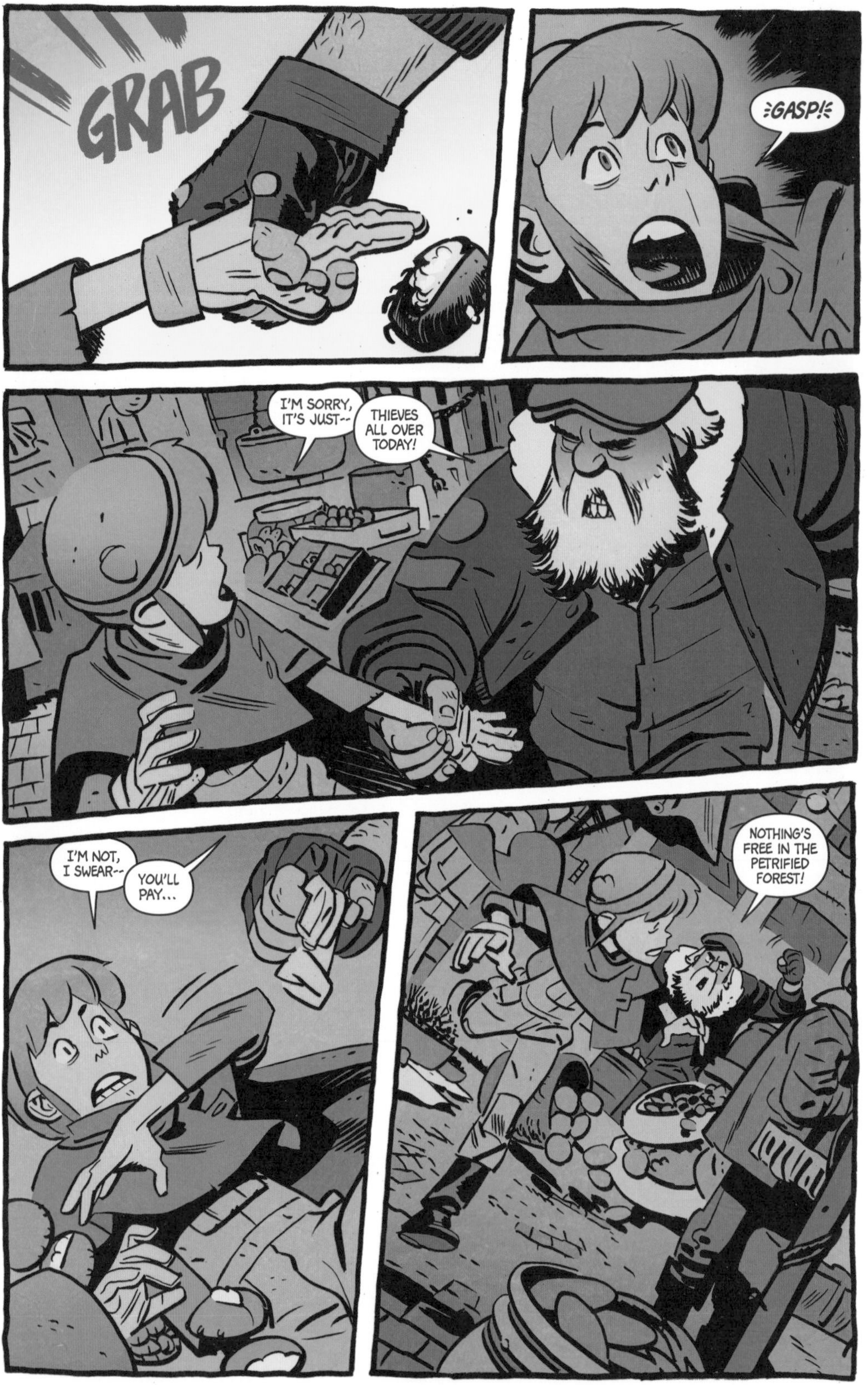
GRAB
GASP!
I'M SORRY, IT'S JUST--
THIEVES ALL OVER TODAY!
I'M NOT, I SWEAR--
YOU'LL PAY...
NOTHING'S FREE IN THE PETRIFIED FOREST!

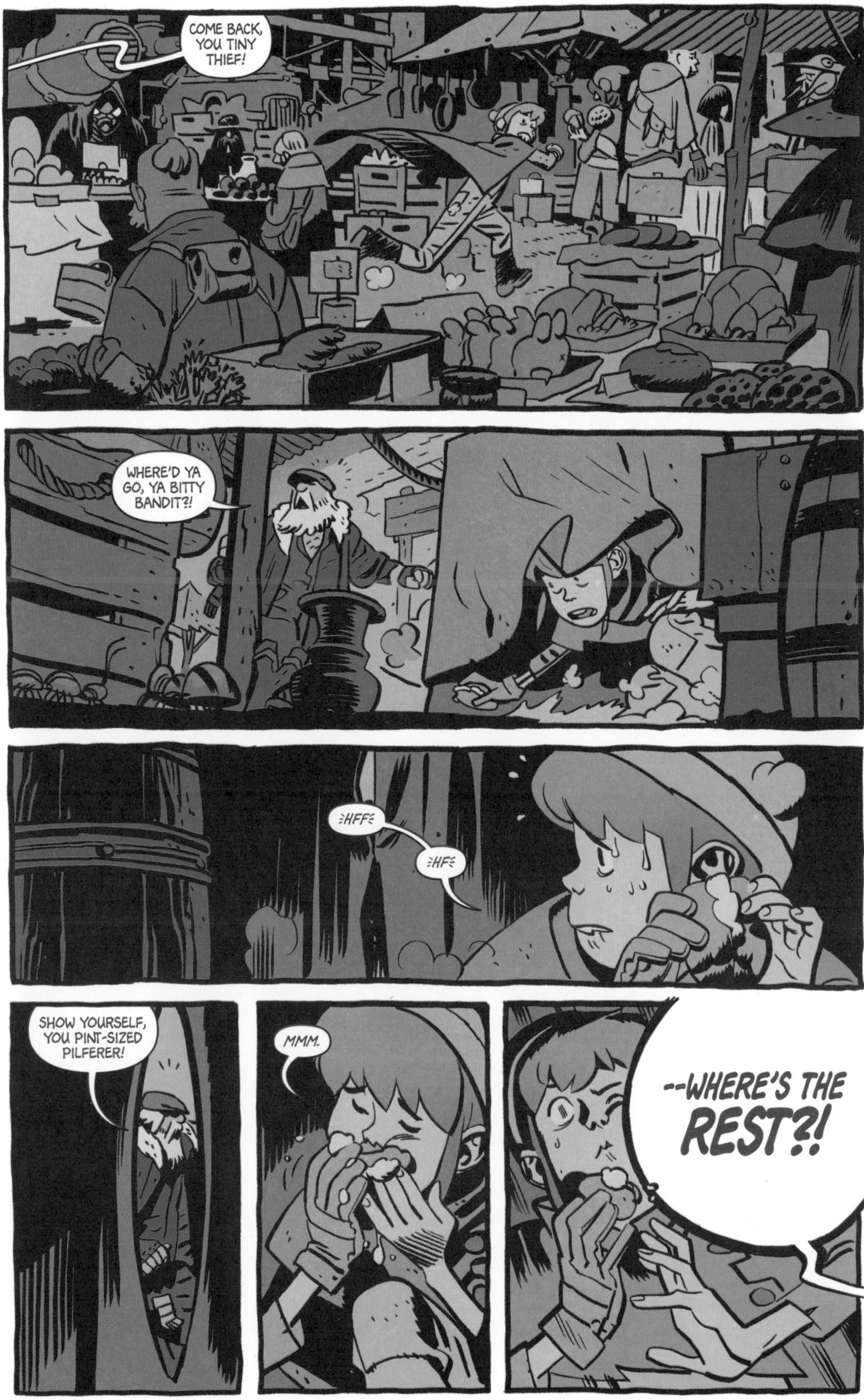
COME BACK, YOU TINY THIEF!
WHERE'D YA GO, YA BITTY BANDIT?!
HFF
HF
SHOW YOURSELF, YOU PINT-SIZED PILFERER!
MMM.
--WHERE'S THE REST?!

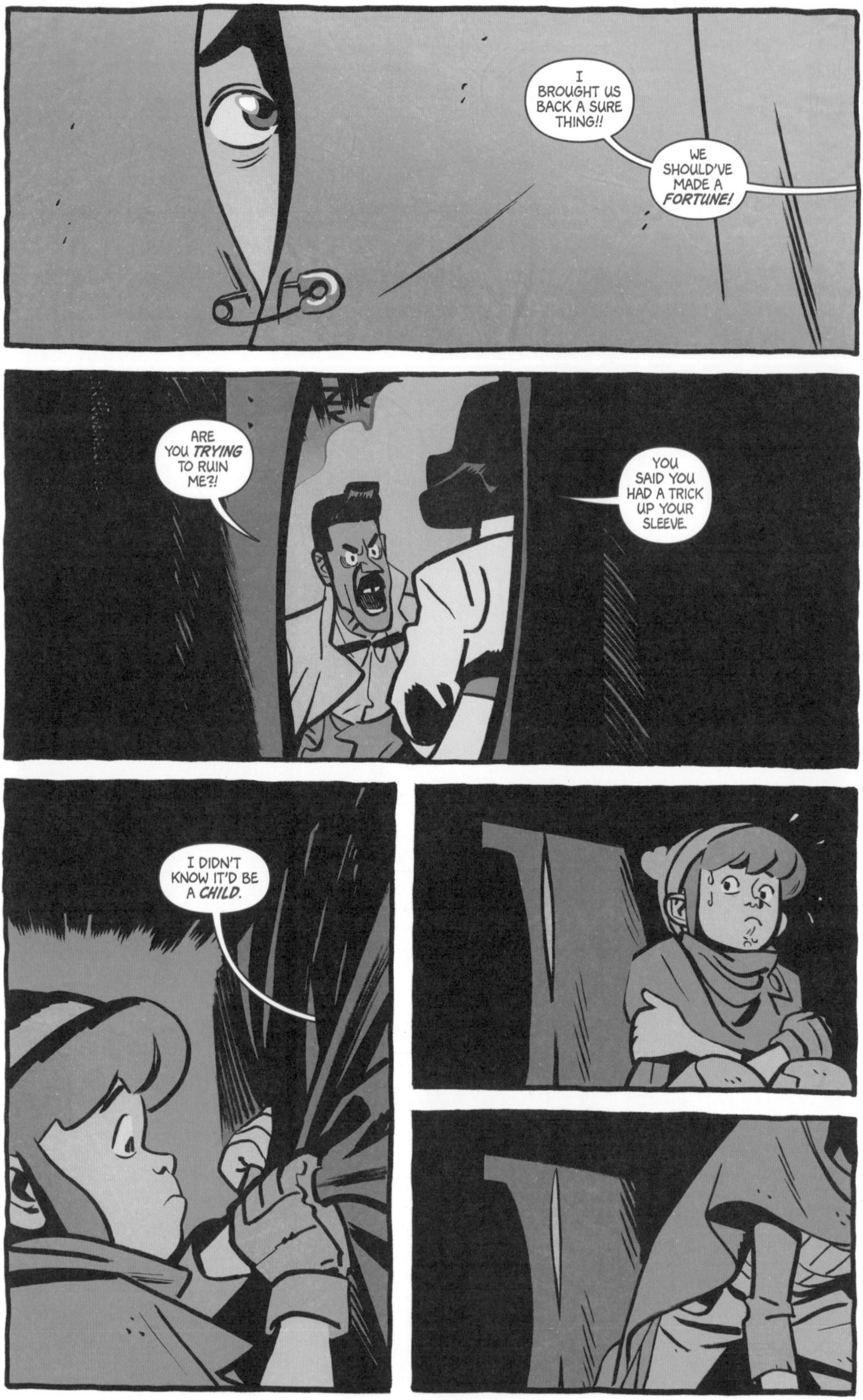
I BROUGHT US BACK A SURE THING!!
WE SHOULD'VE MADE A ***FORTUNE!***
ARE YOU ***TRYING*** TO RUIN ME?!
YOU SAID YOU HAD A TRICK UP YOUR SLEEVE.
I DIDN'T KNOW IT'D BE A ***CHILD***.

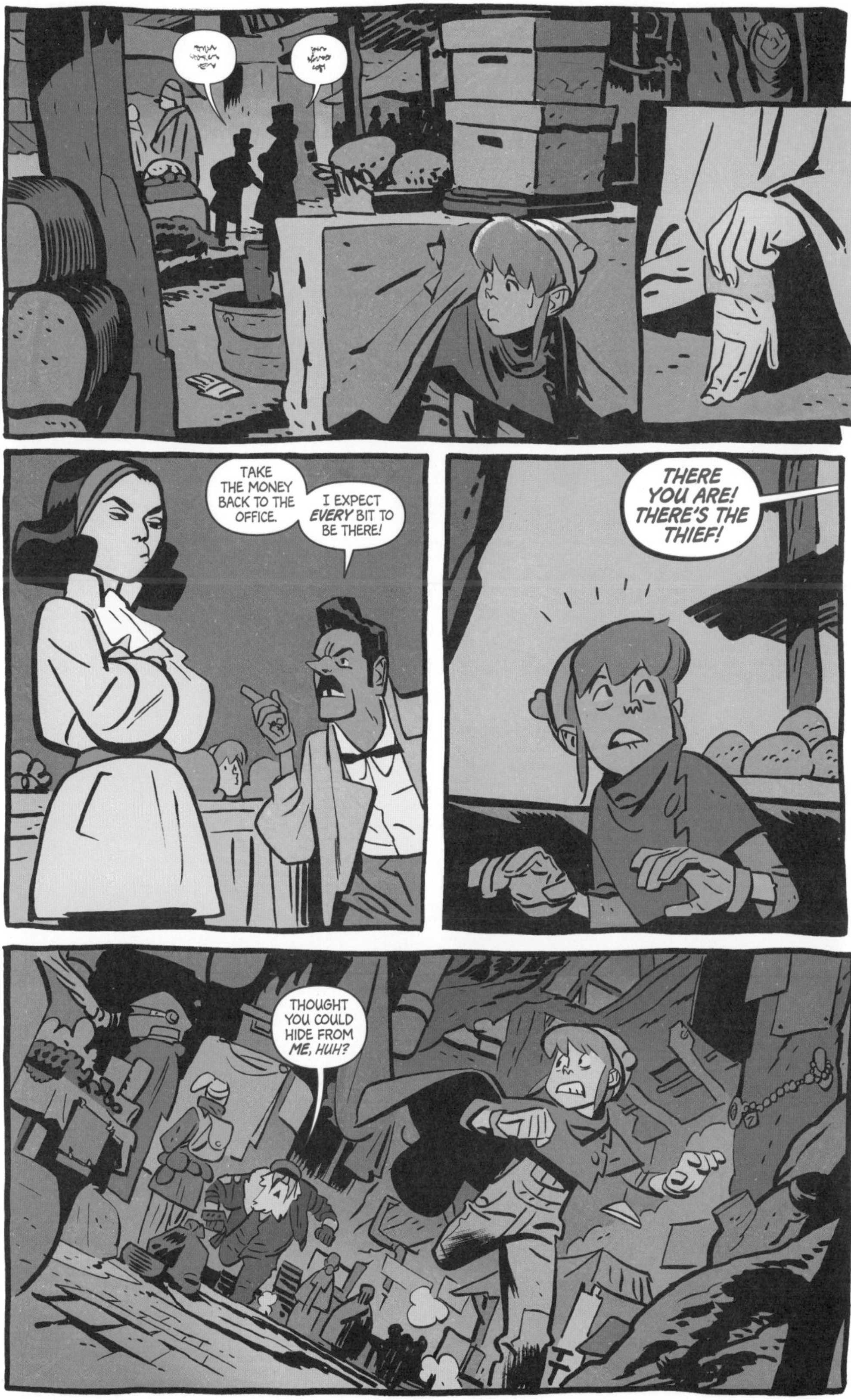

TAKE THE MONEY BACK TO THE OFFICE.
I EXPECT EVERY BIT TO BE THERE!
THERE YOU ARE! THERE'S THE THIEF!
THOUGHT YOU COULD HIDE FROM ME, HUH?

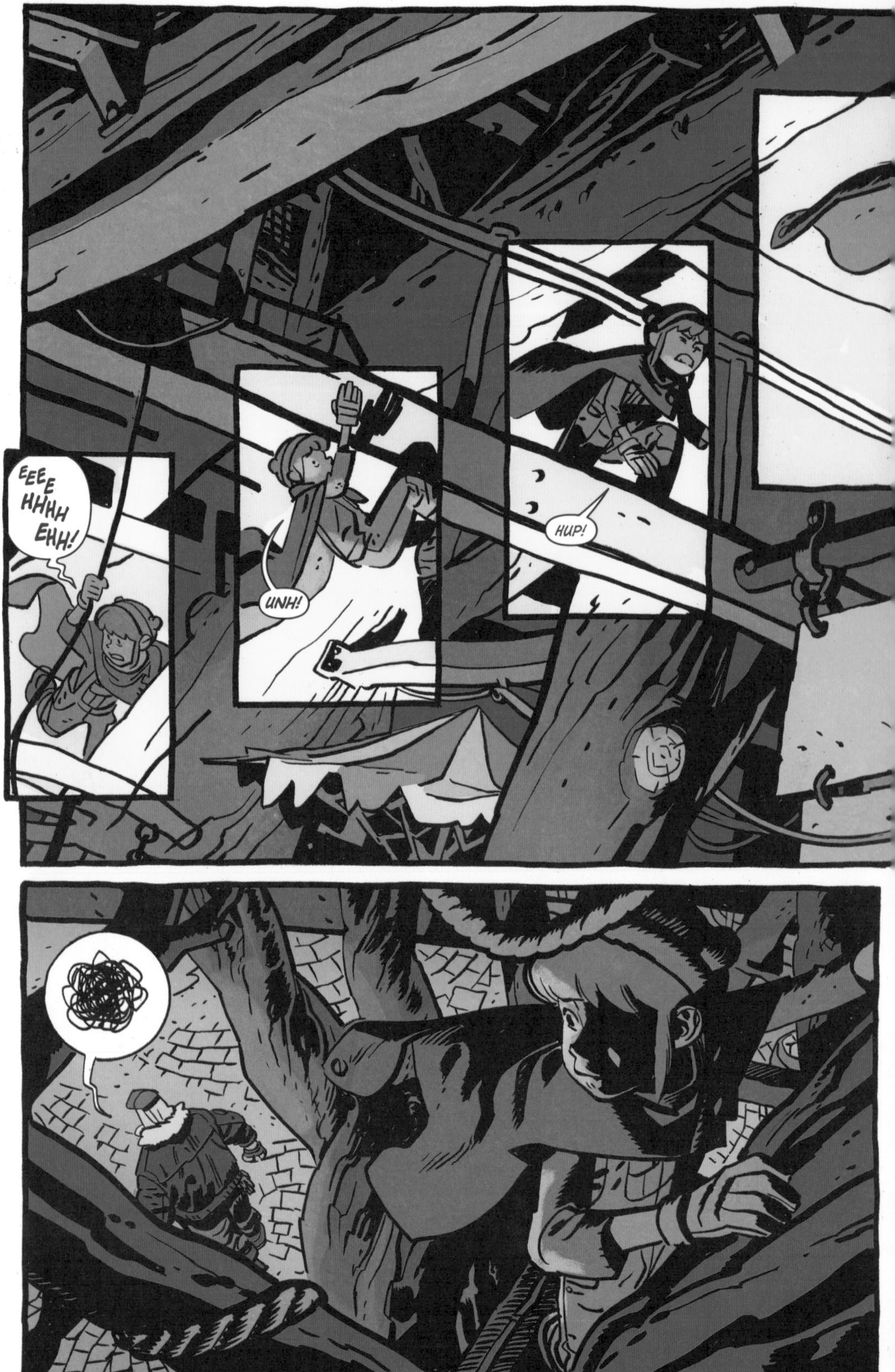
EEEE HHHH EHH!
UNH!
HUP!

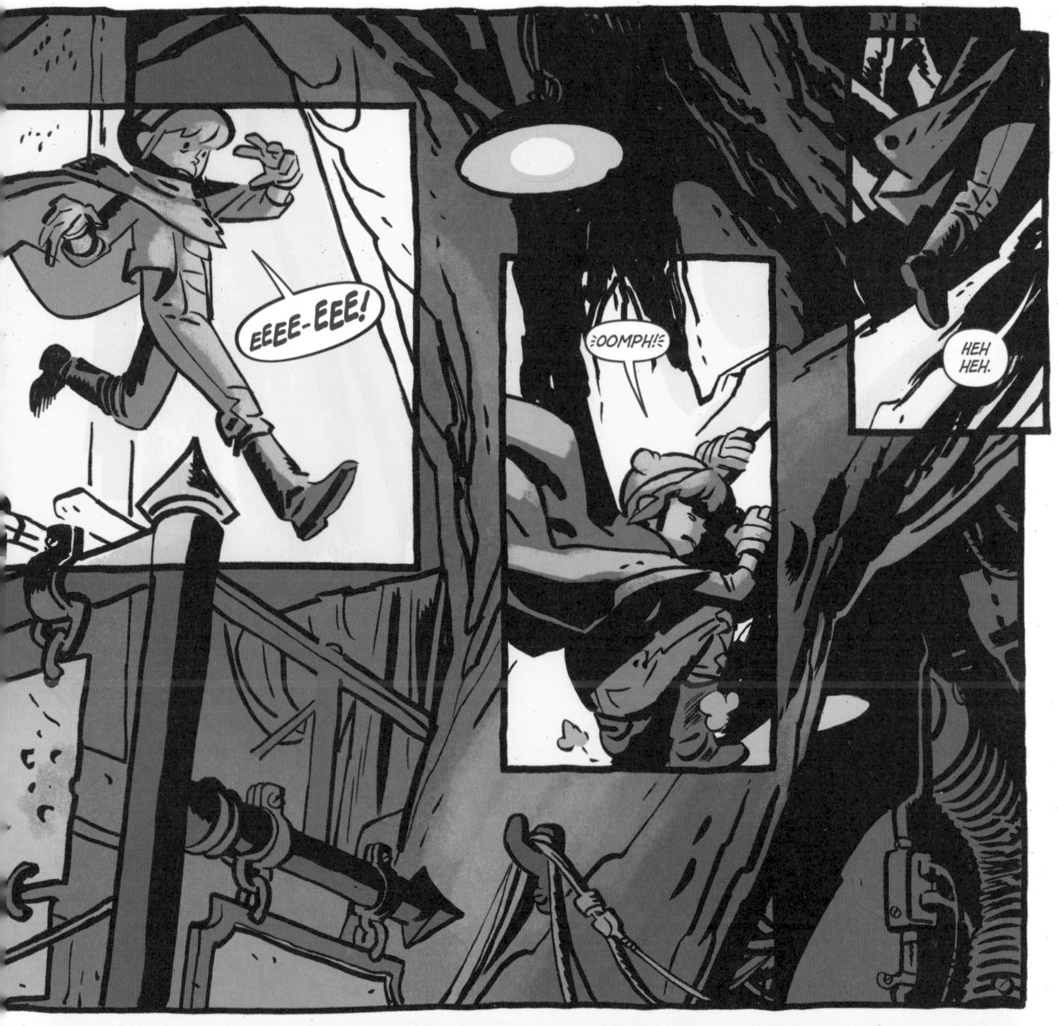
EEEE-EEE!
OOMPH!
HEH HEH.

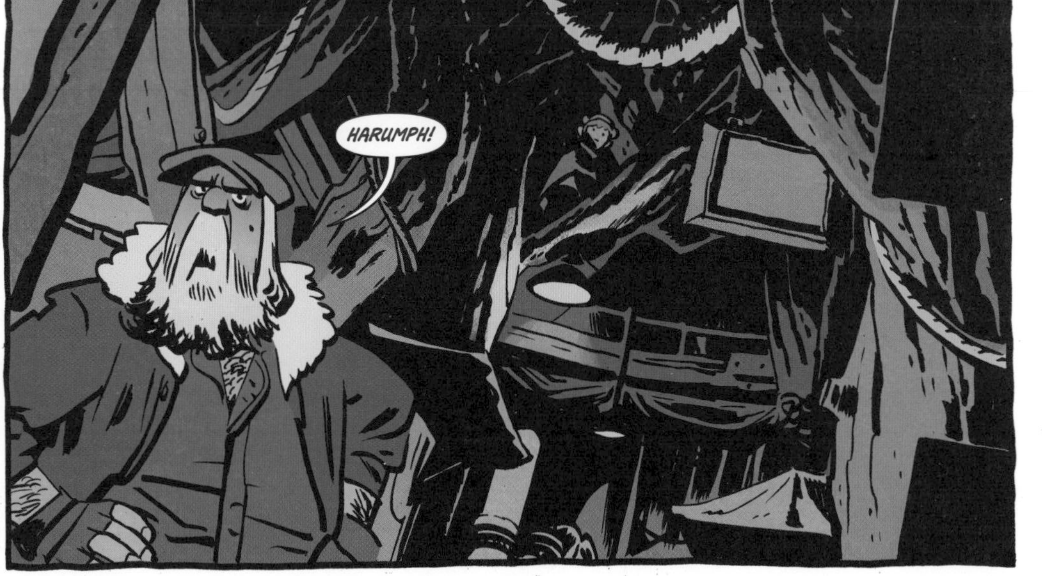
HARUMPH!

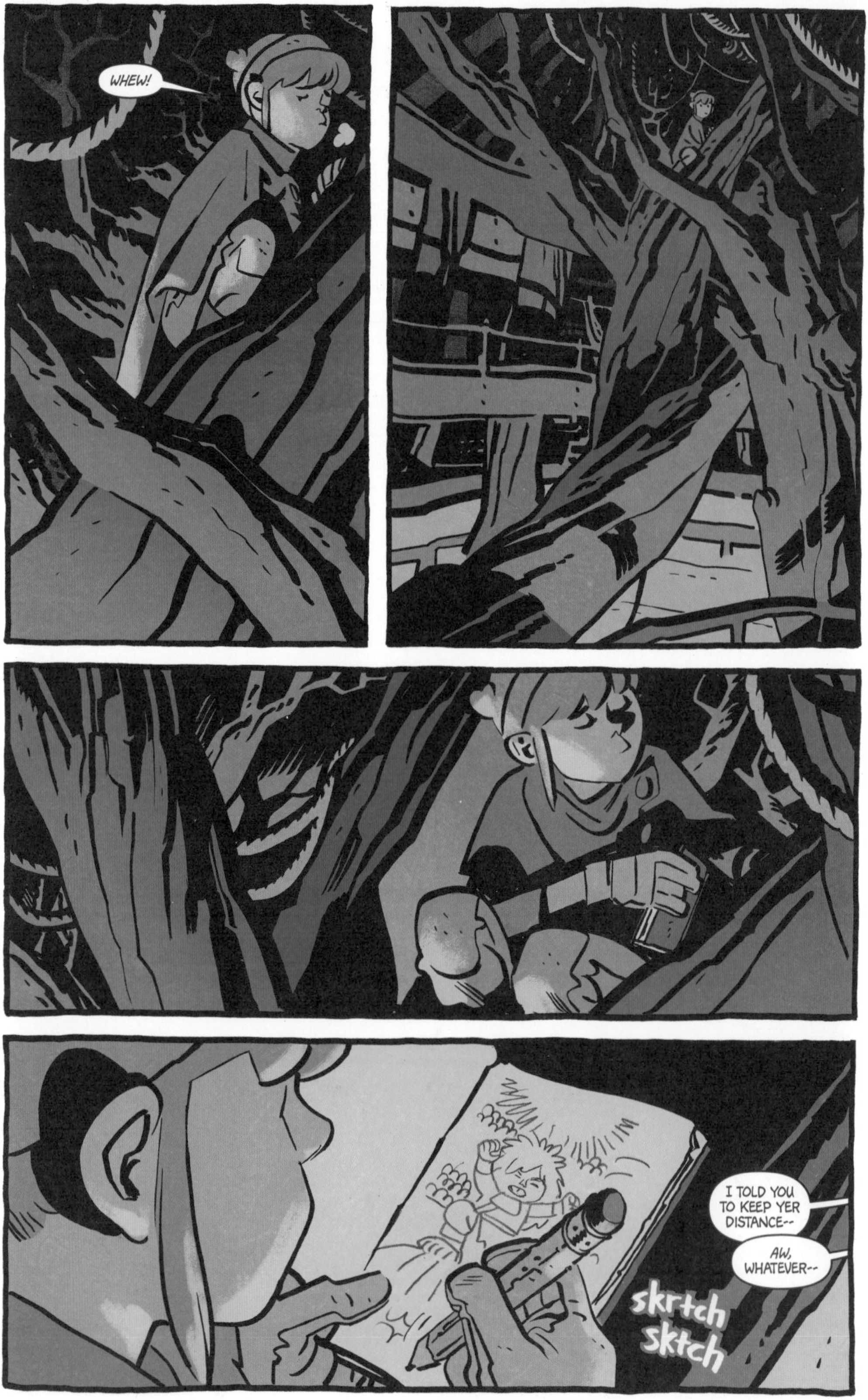
WHEW!
I TOLD YOU TO KEEP YER DISTANCE--
AW, WHATEVER--
skrtch
sktch

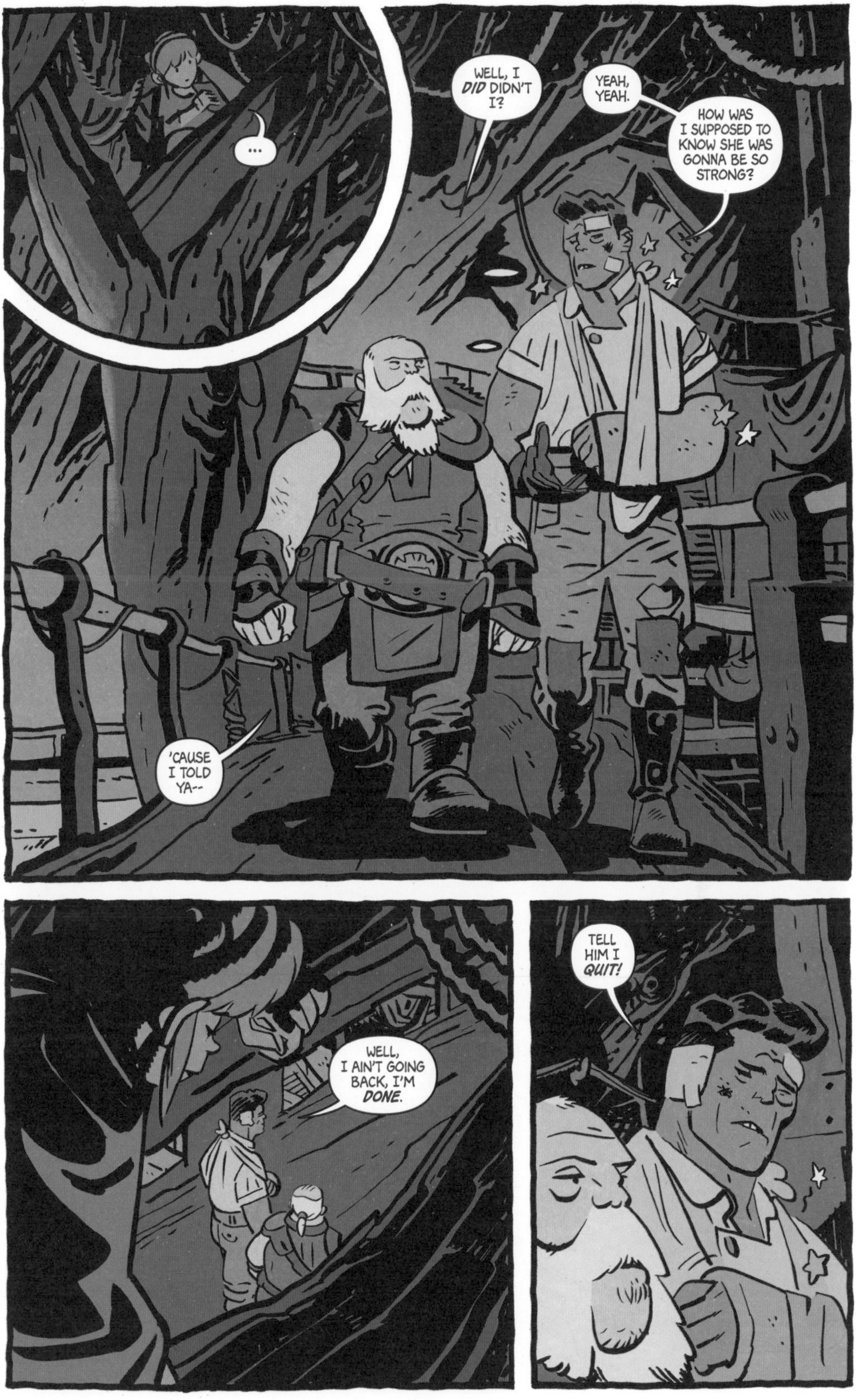
...
WELL, I DID DIDN'T I?
YEAH, YEAH.
HOW WAS I SUPPOSED TO KNOW SHE WAS GONNA BE SO STRONG?
'CAUSE I TOLD YA--
WELL, I AIN'T GOING BACK, I'M DONE.
TELL HIM I QUIT!

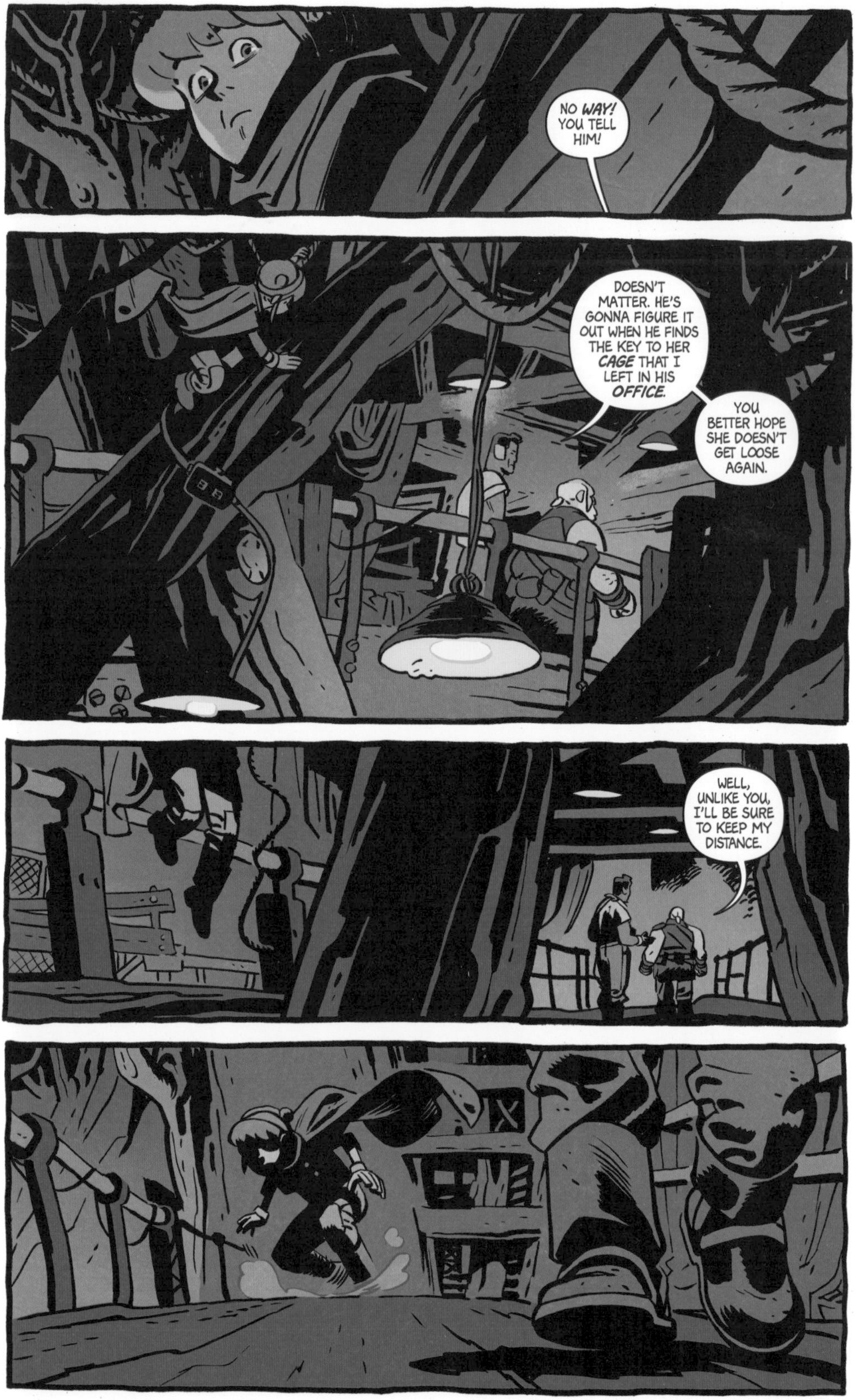
NO WAY! YOU TELL HIM!
DOESN'T MATTER. HE'S GONNA FIGURE IT OUT WHEN HE FINDS THE KEY TO HER CAGE THAT I LEFT IN HIS OFFICE.
YOU BETTER HOPE SHE DOESN'T GET LOOSE AGAIN.
WELL, UNLIKE YOU, I'LL BE SURE TO KEEP MY DISTANCE.

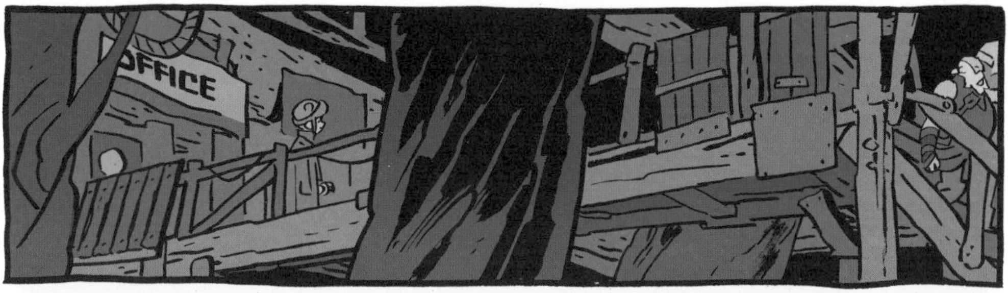
OFFICE

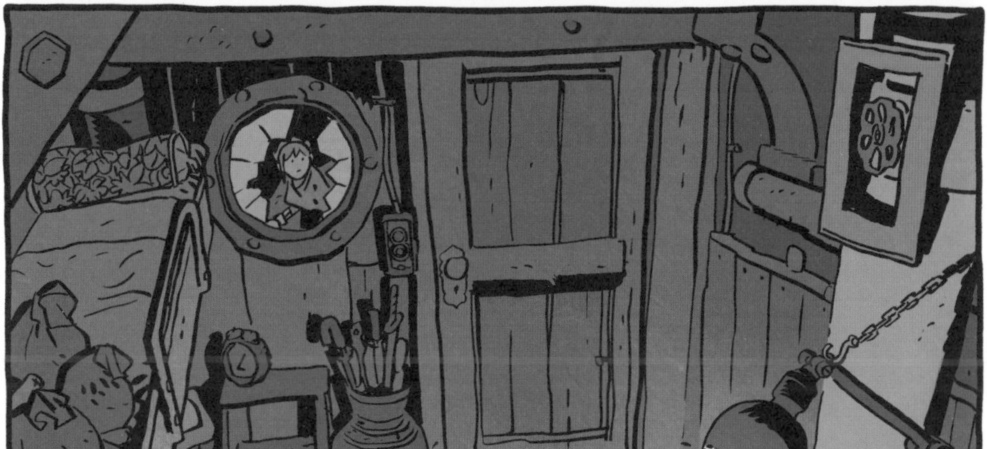

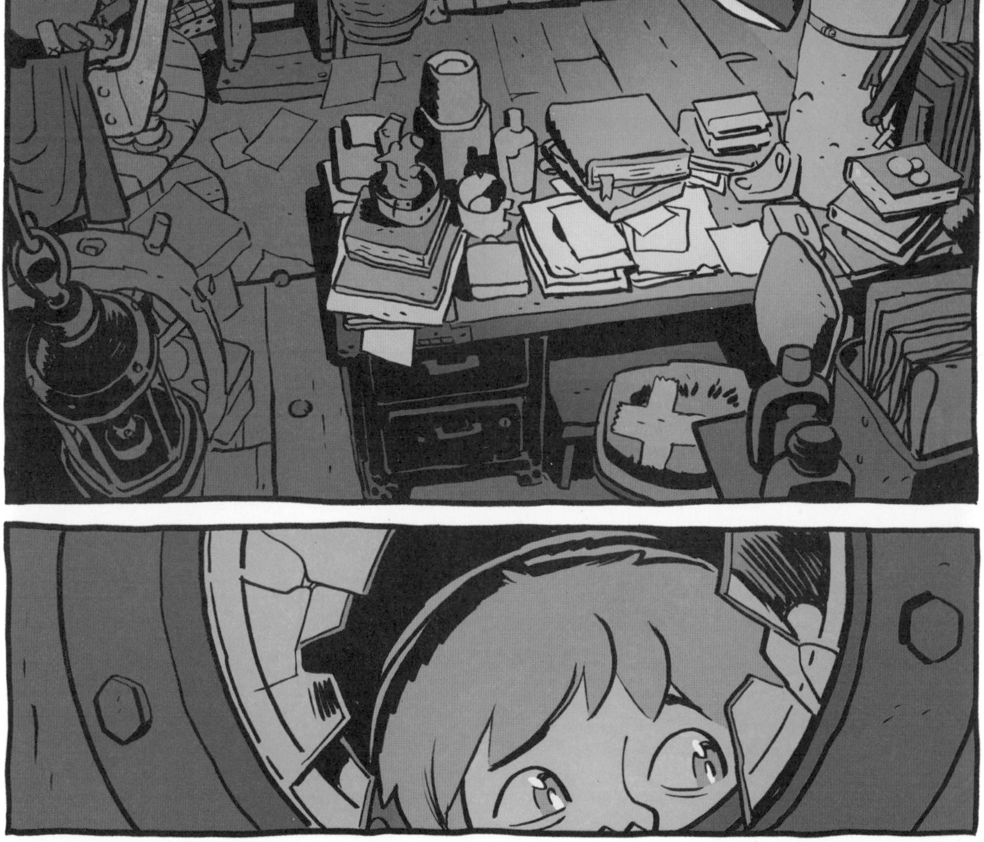

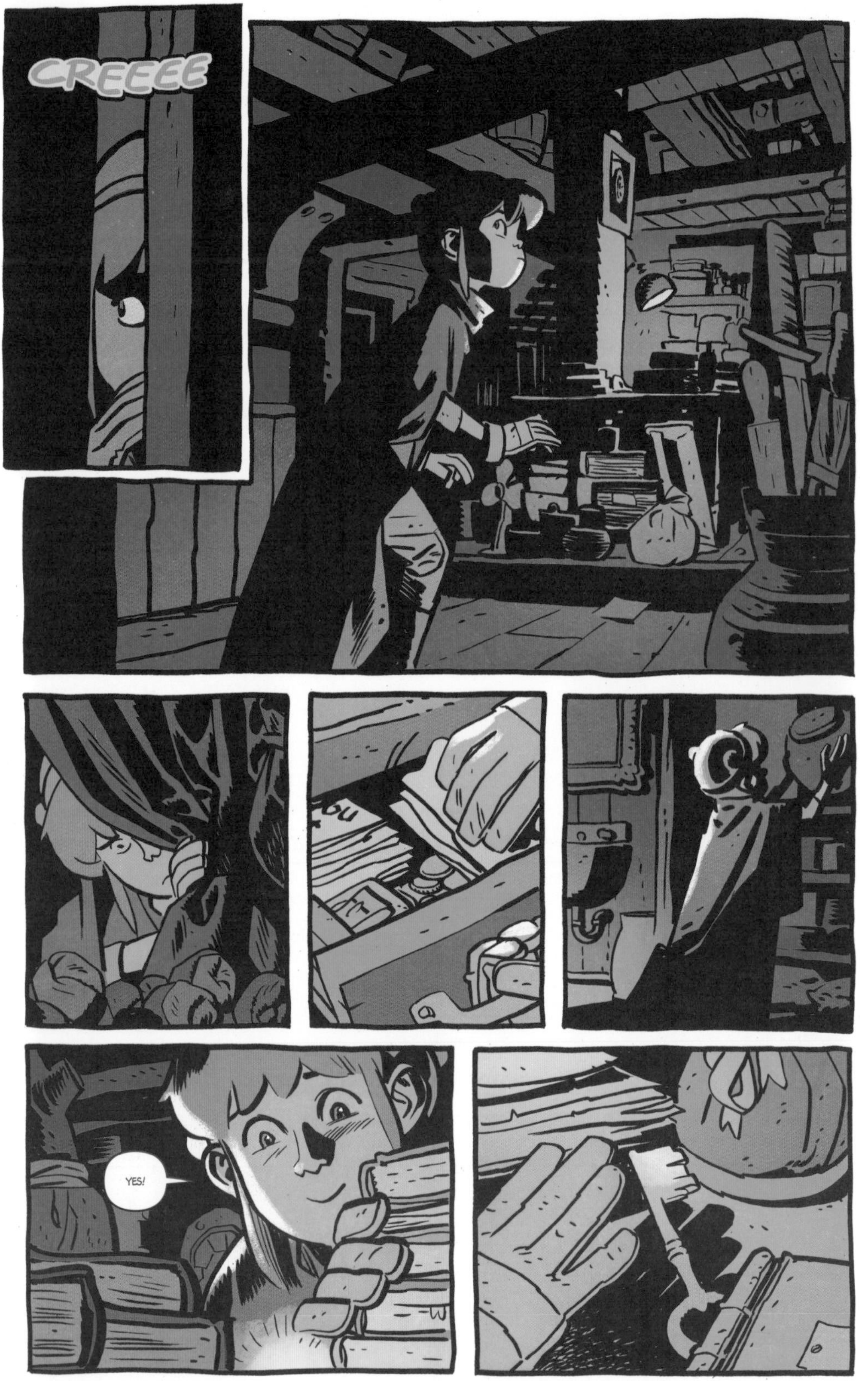
CREEEE
YES!

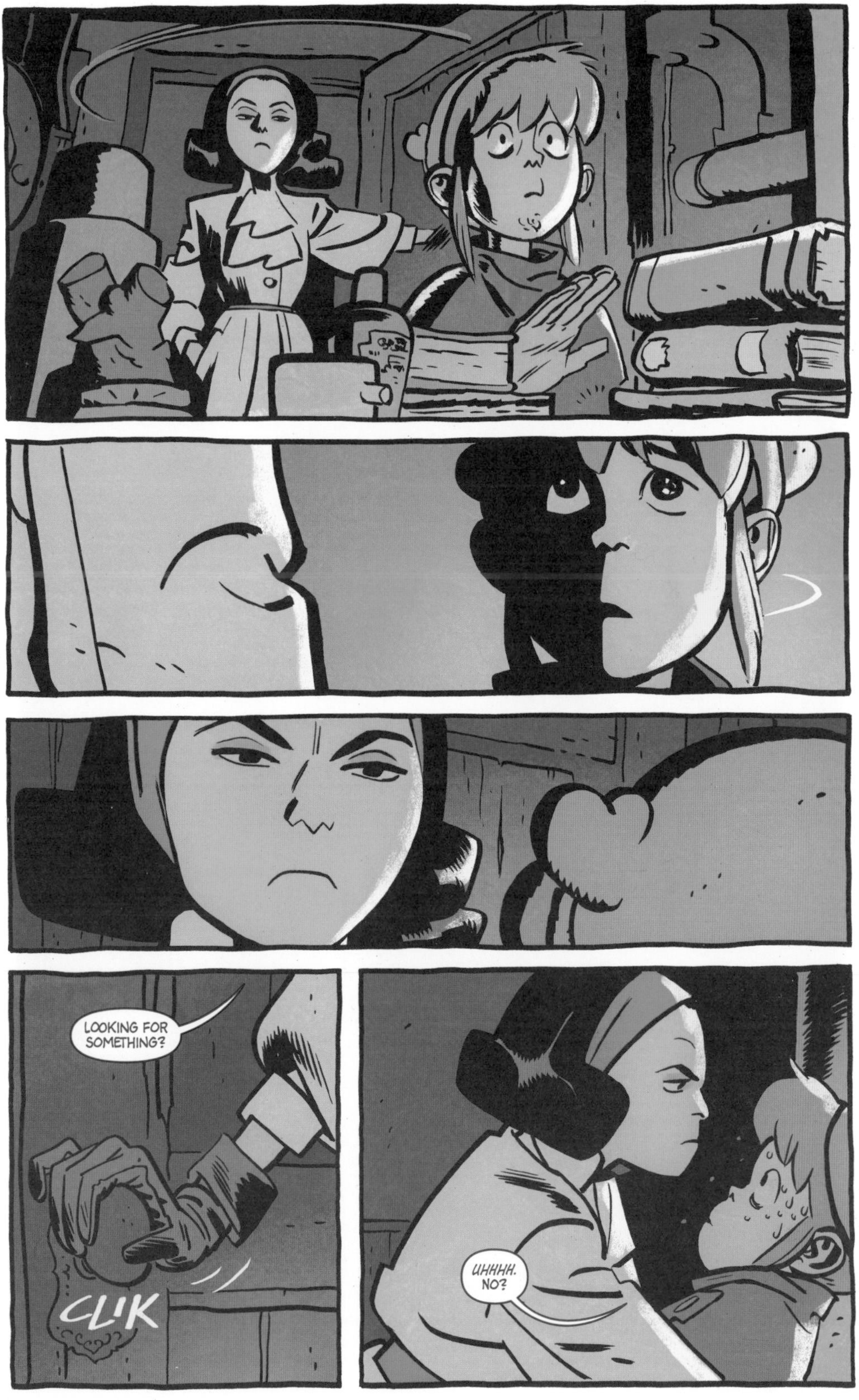
LOOKING FOR SOMETHING?
CLIK
UHHHH. NO?

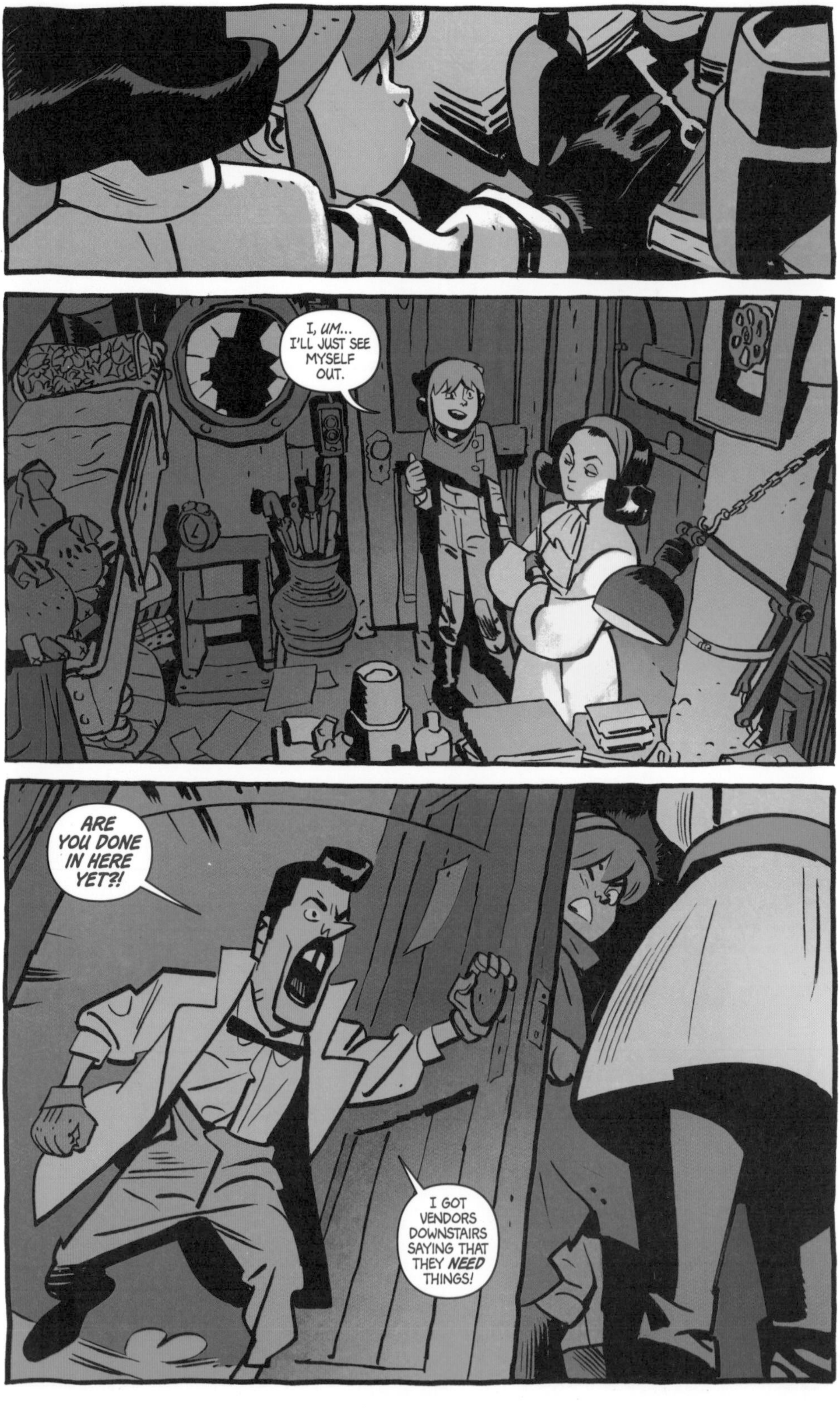
I, *UM*... I'LL JUST SEE MYSELF OUT.
ARE YOU DONE IN HERE YET?!
I GOT VENDORS DOWNSTAIRS SAYING THAT THEY *NEED* THINGS!

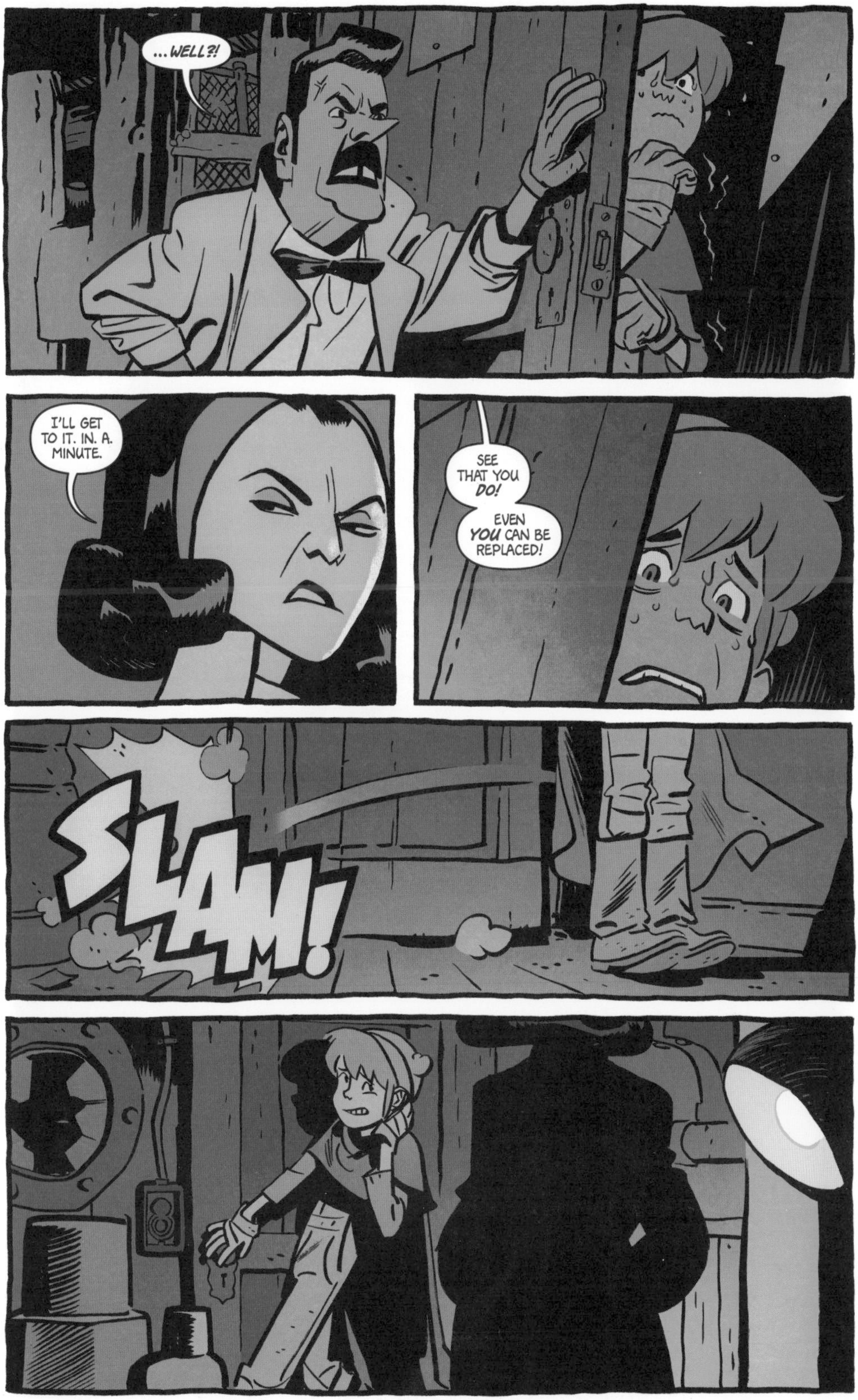
...WELL?!
I'LL GET TO IT. IN A MINUTE.
SEE THAT YOU DO!
EVEN YOU CAN BE REPLACED!
SLAM!

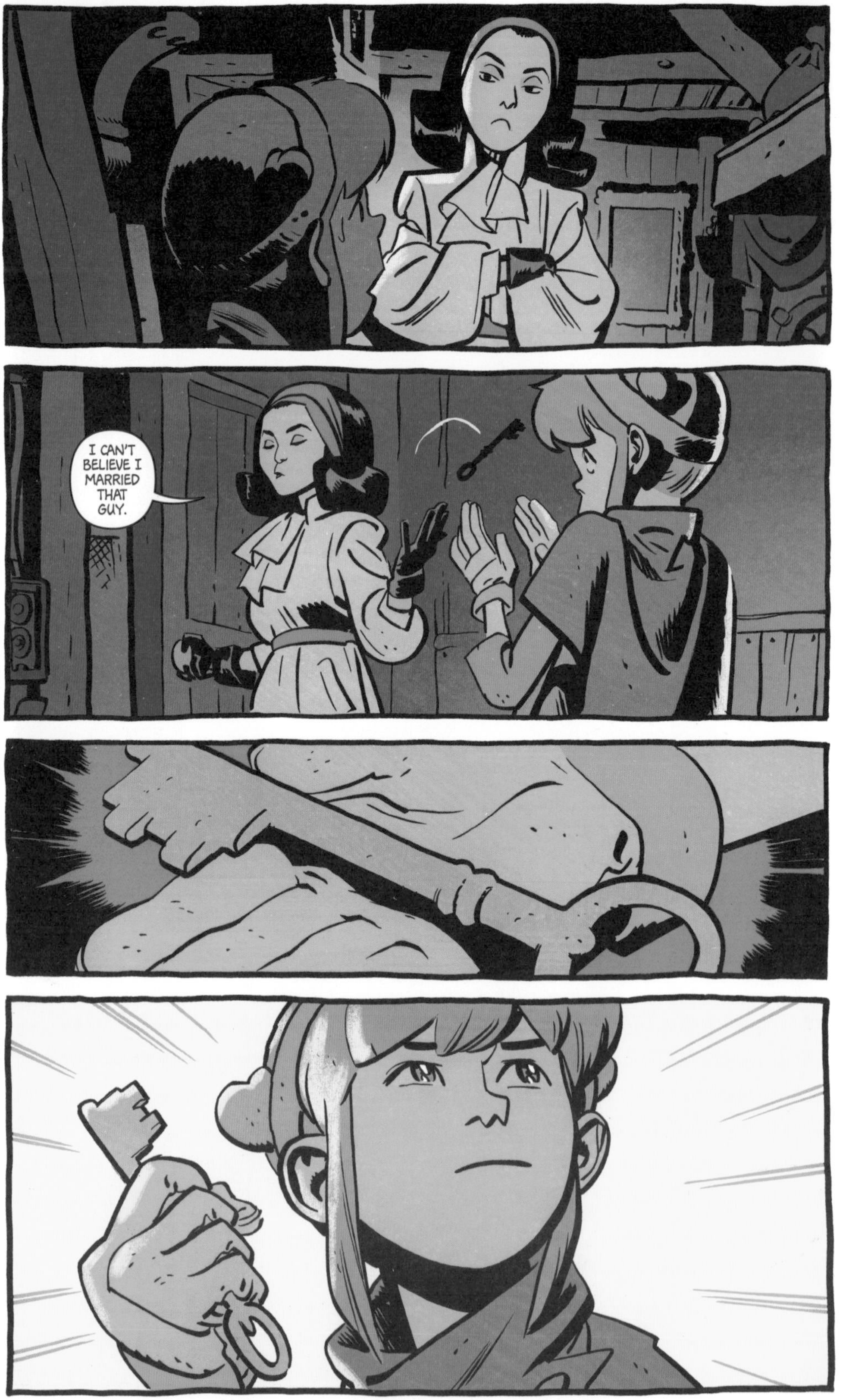
I CAN'T BELIEVE I MARRIED THAT GUY.

CHAPTER 7

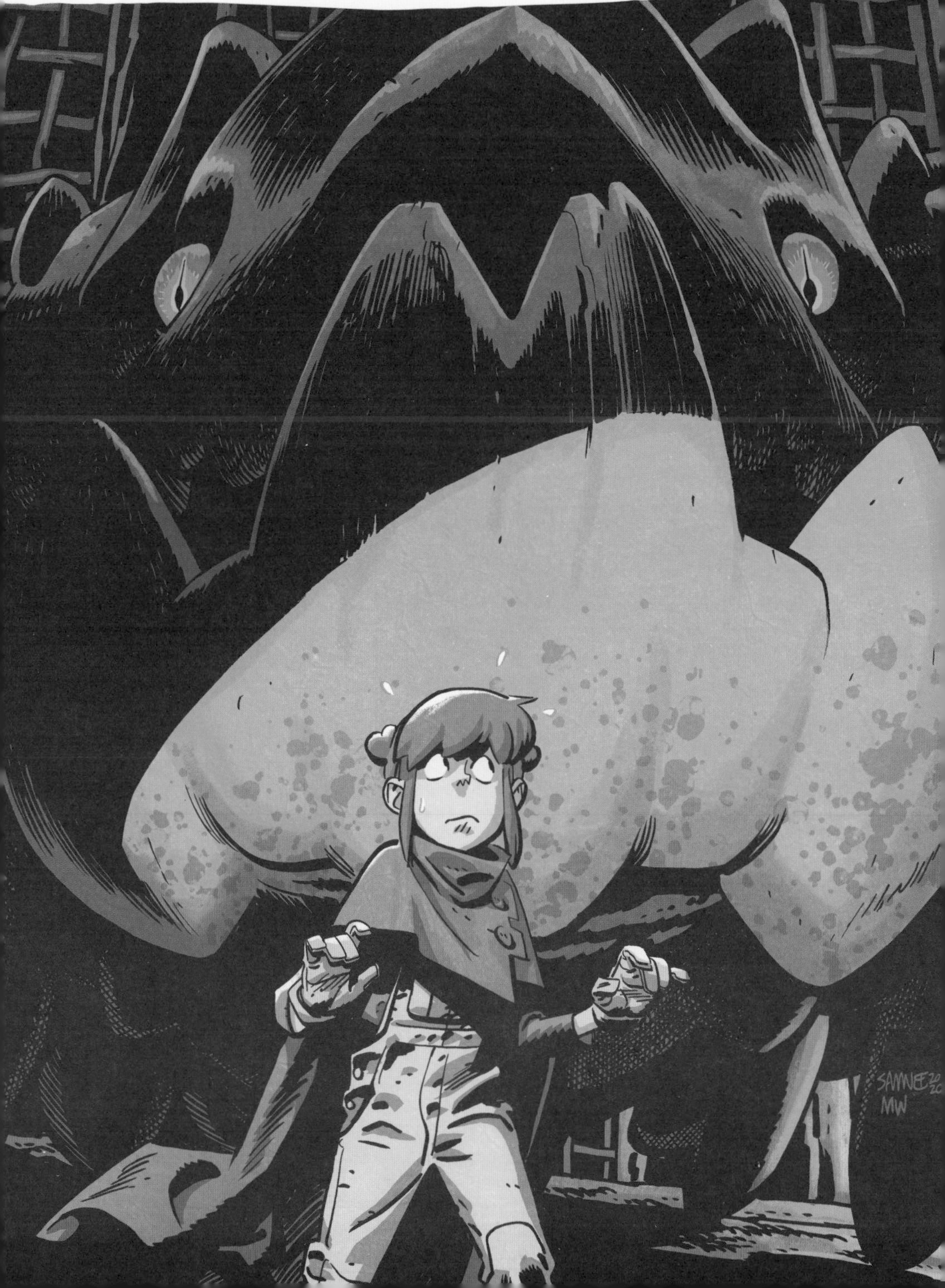

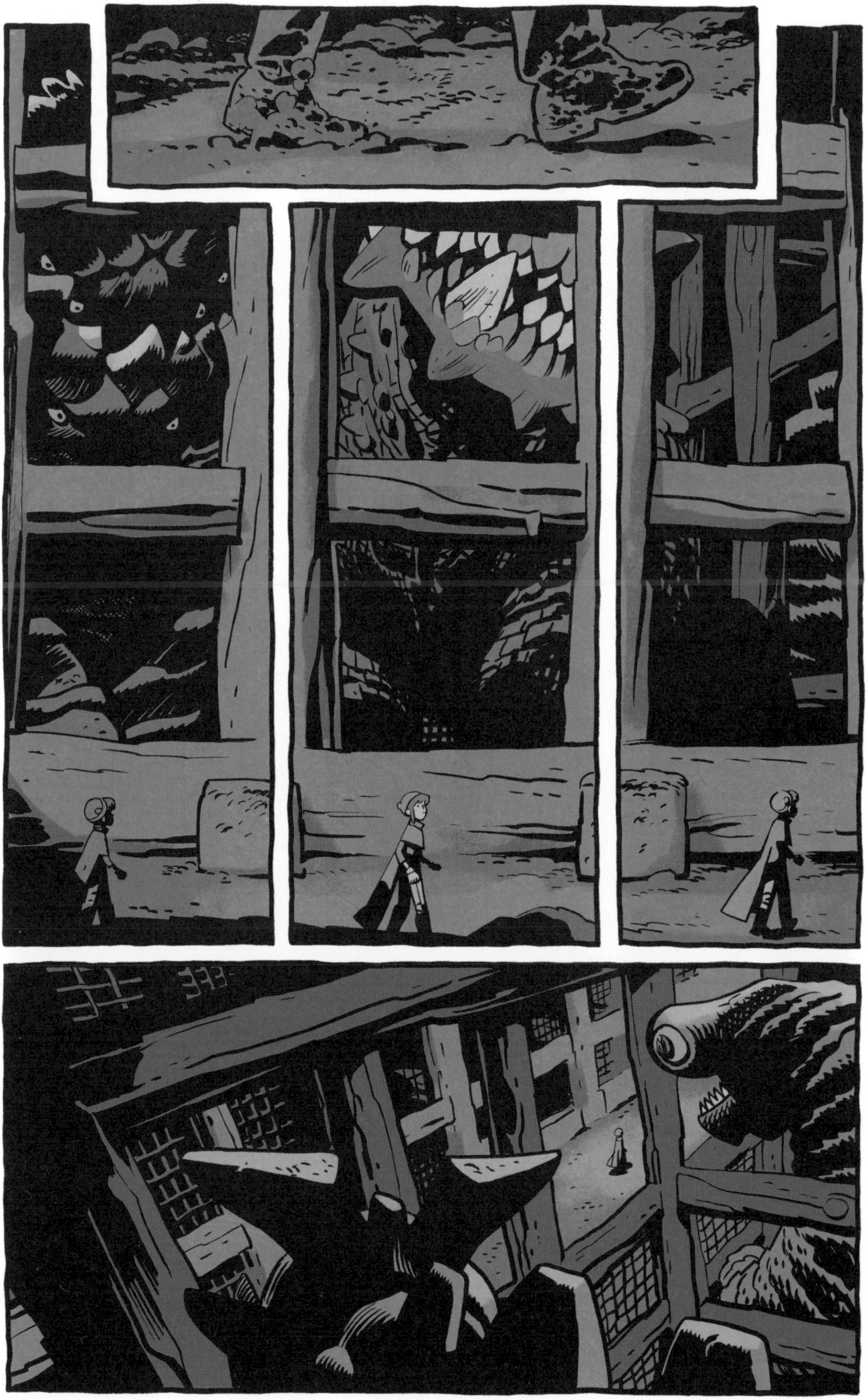

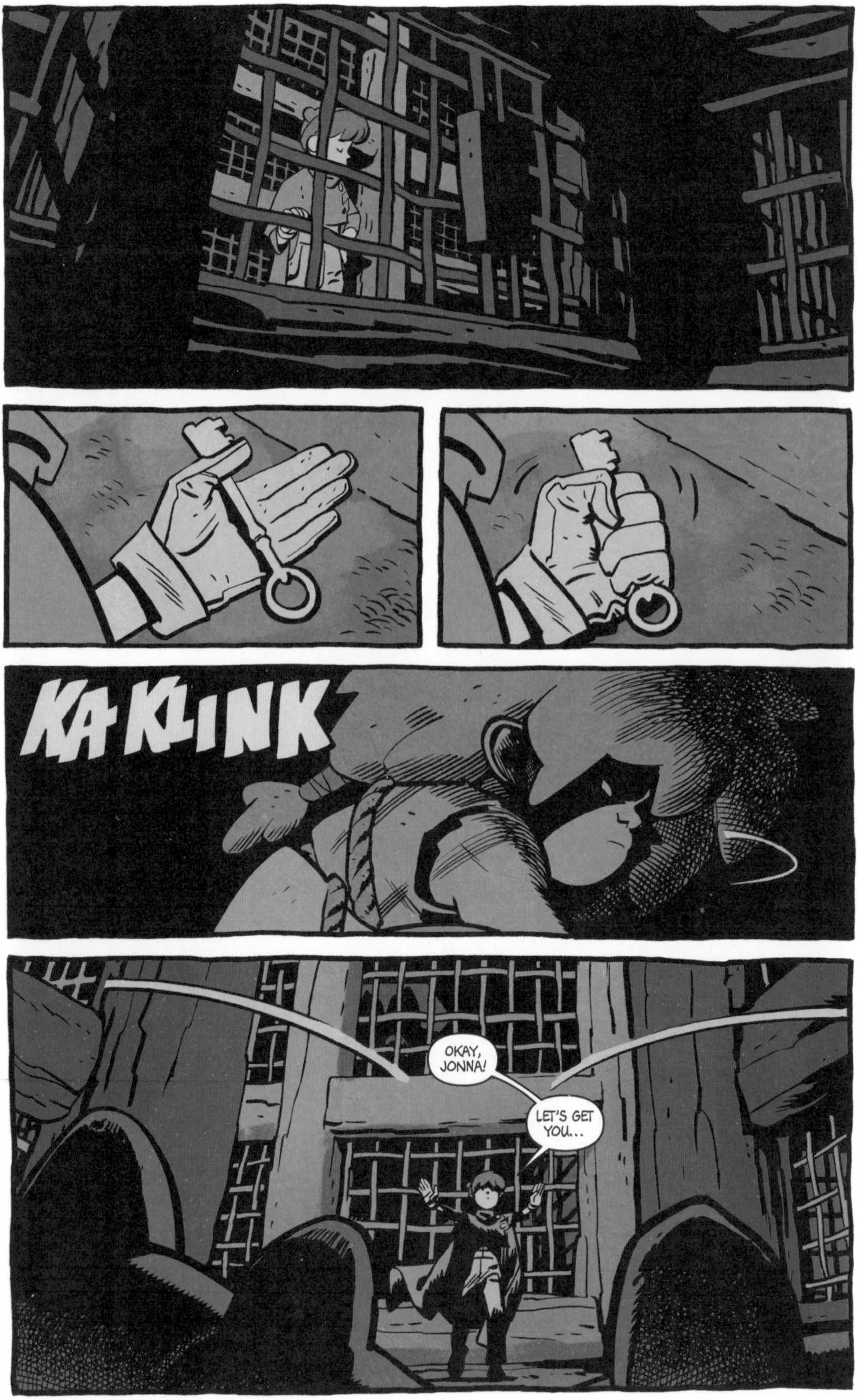
KA KLINK
OKAY, JONNA!
LET'S GET YOU...

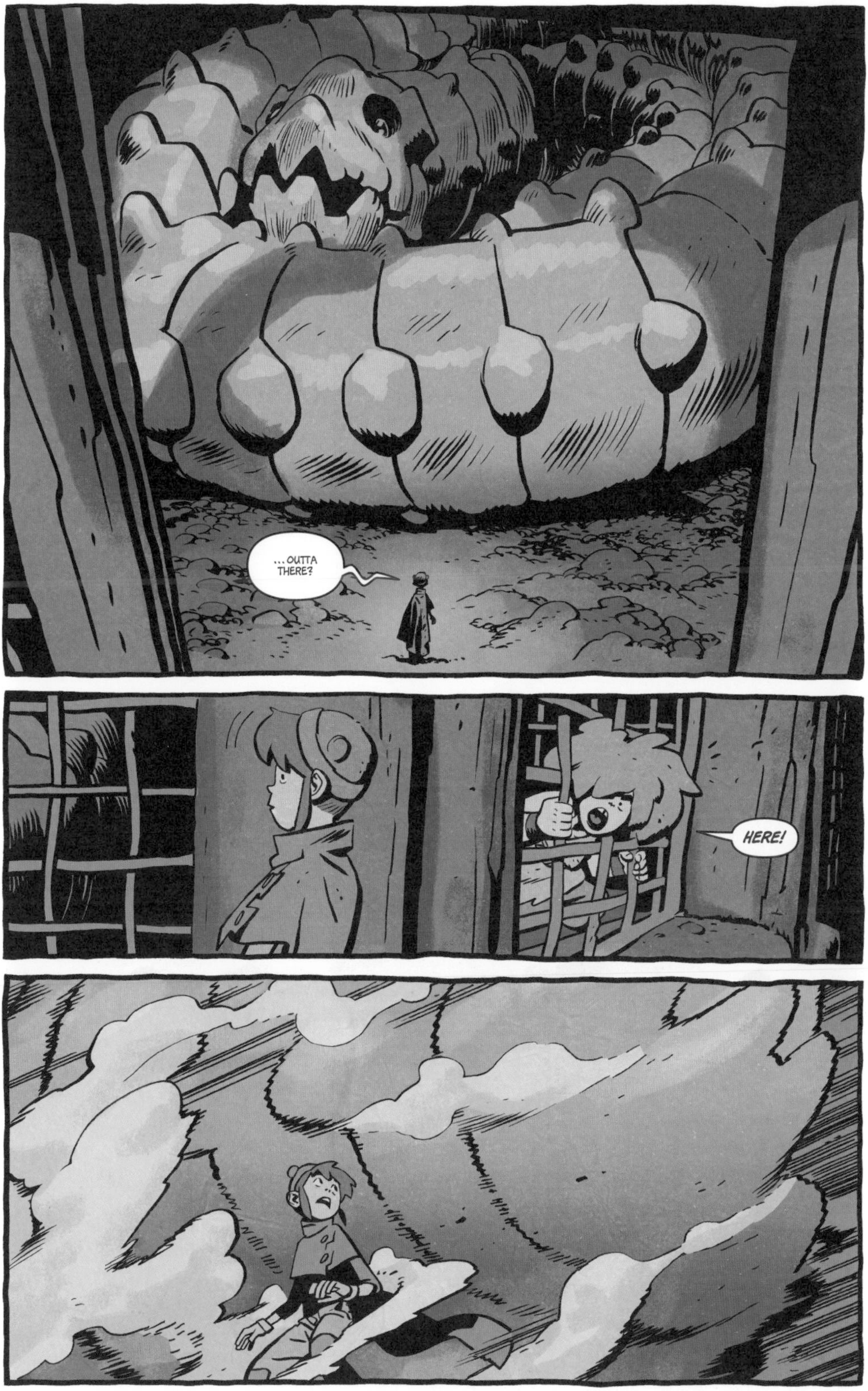
...OUTTA
THERE?
HERE!

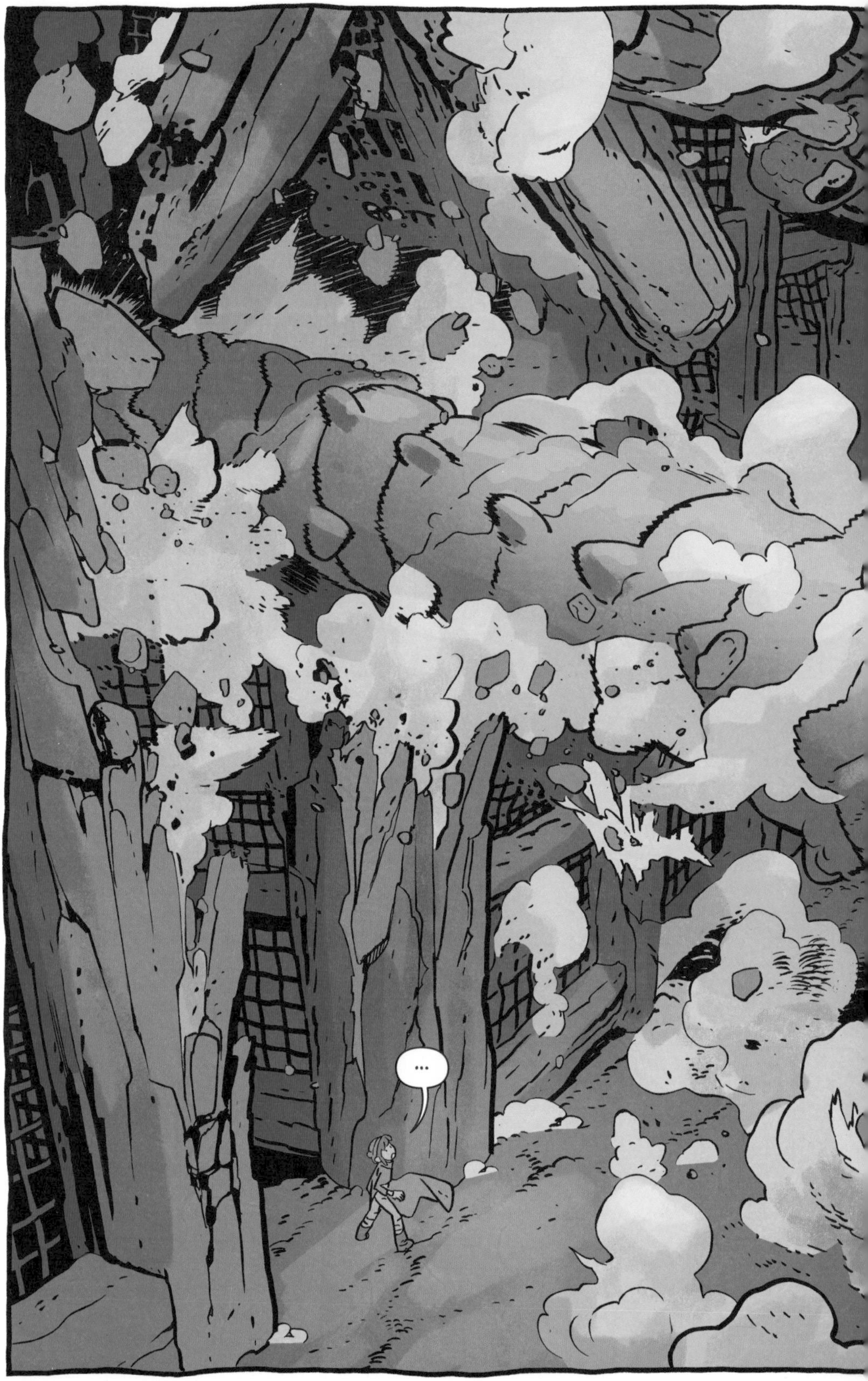
...

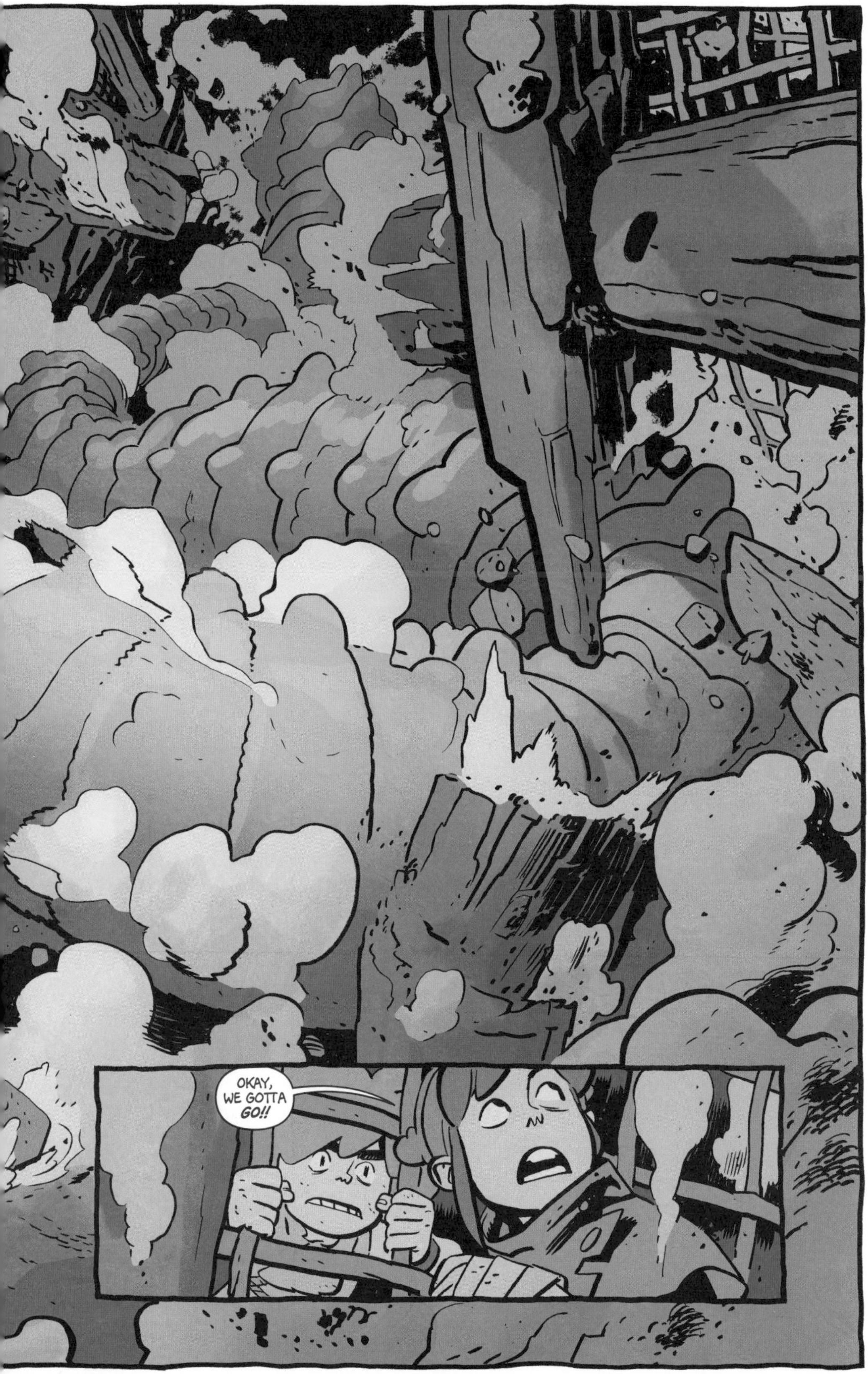
OKAY, WE GOTTA GO!!

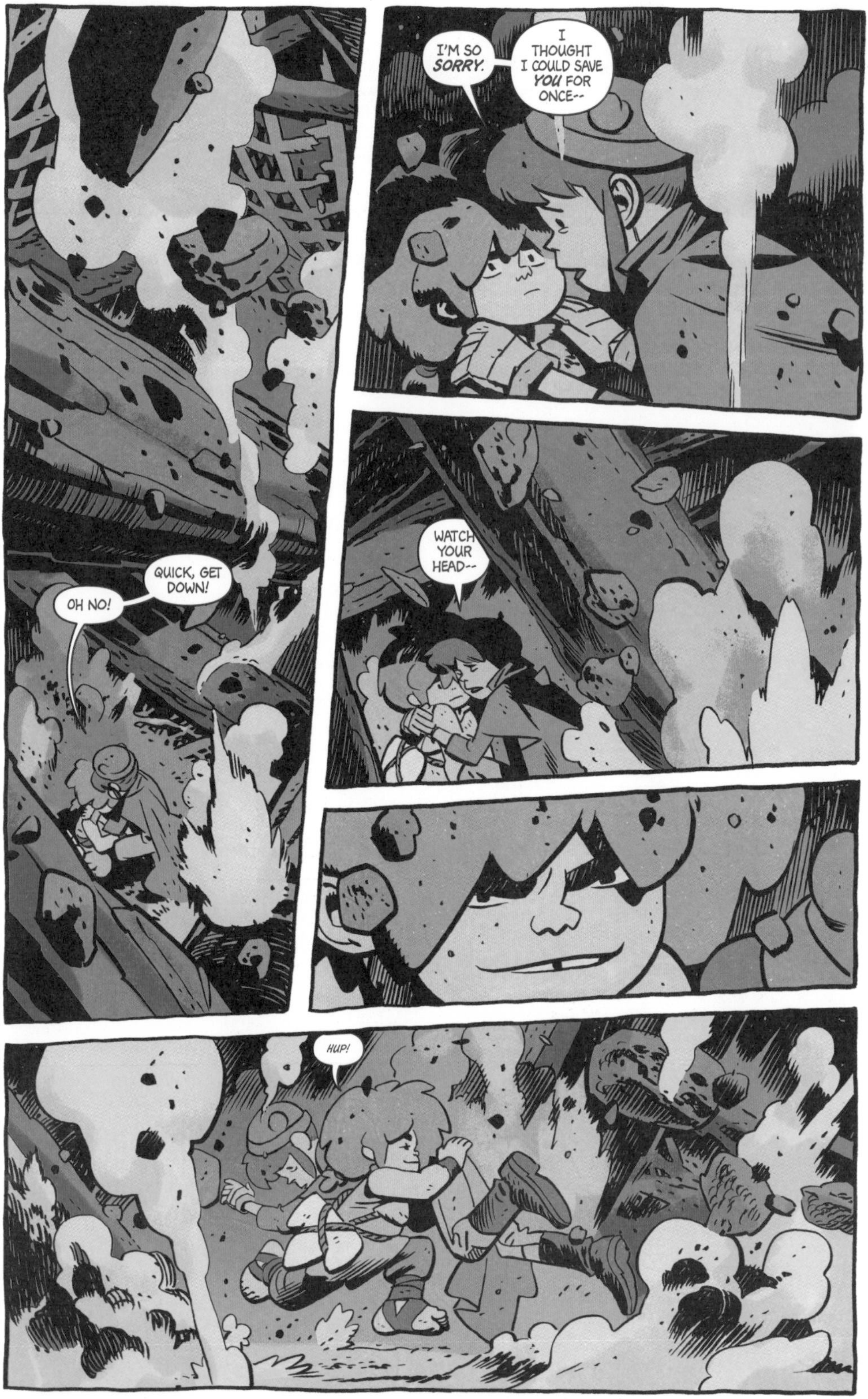
I'M SO SORRY.
I THOUGHT I COULD SAVE YOU FOR ONCE--
QUICK, GET DOWN!
OH NO!
WATCH YOUR HEAD--
HUP!

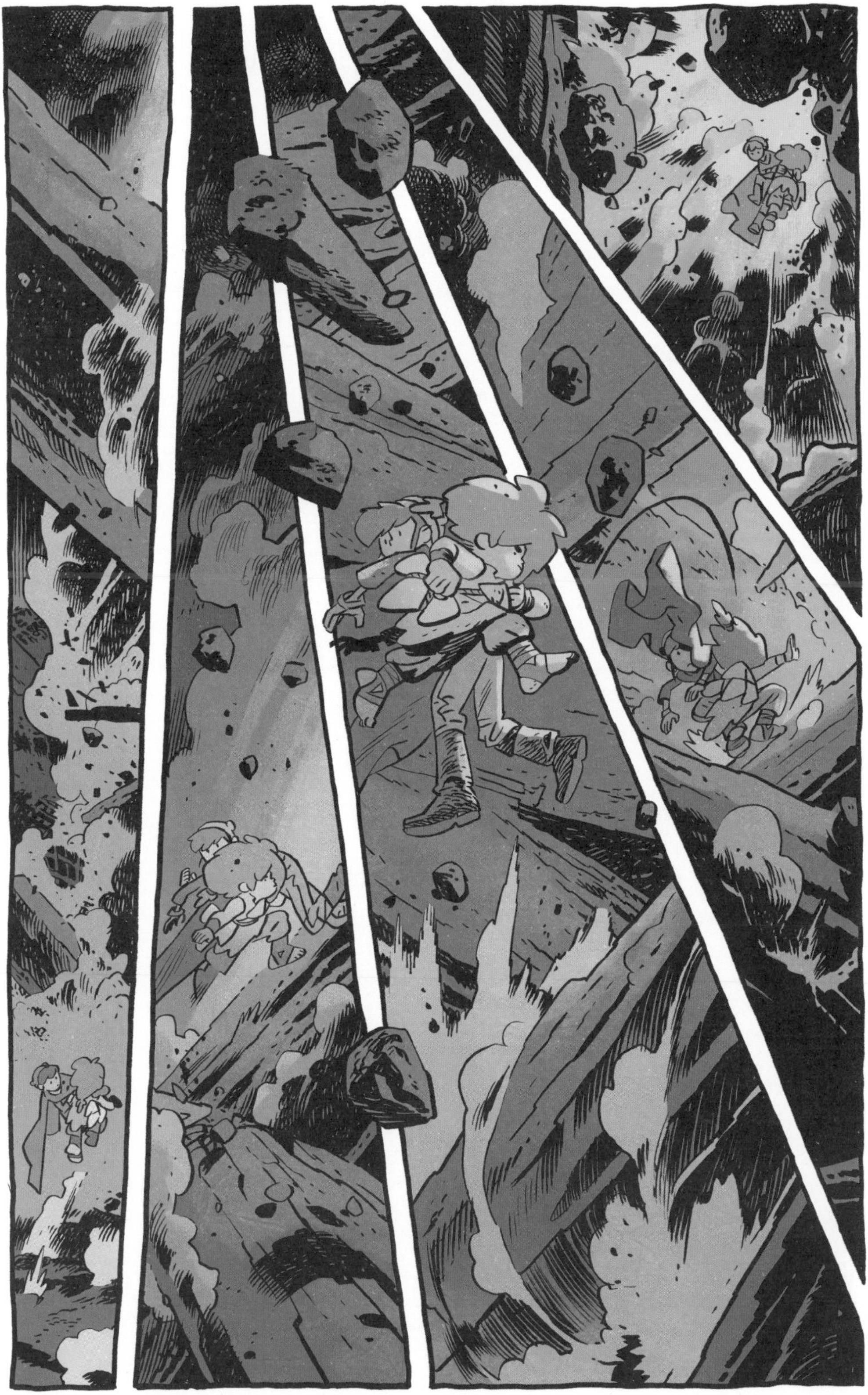

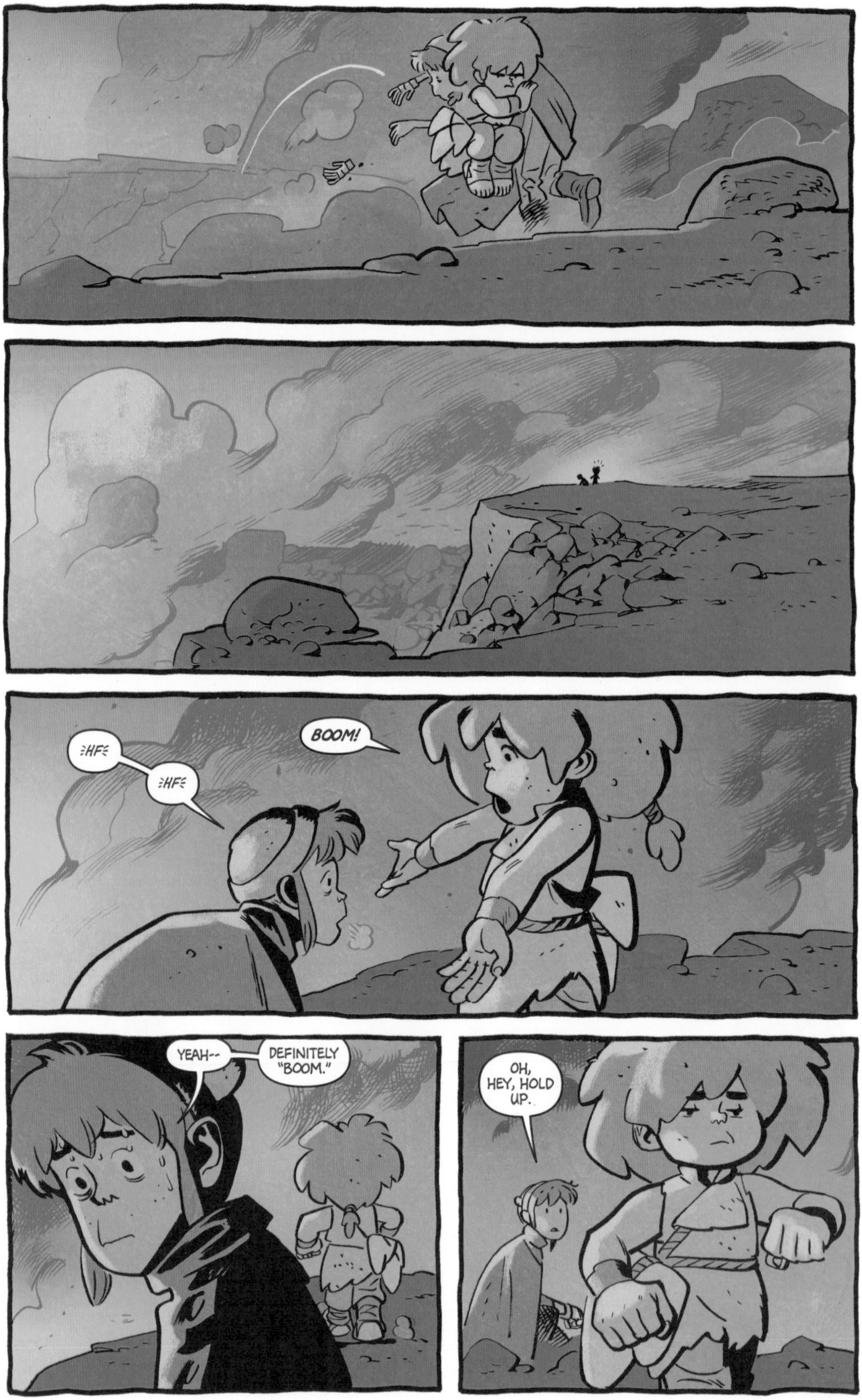

HF
HF
BOOM!
YEAH--
DEFINITELY "BOOM."
OH, HEY, HOLD UP.

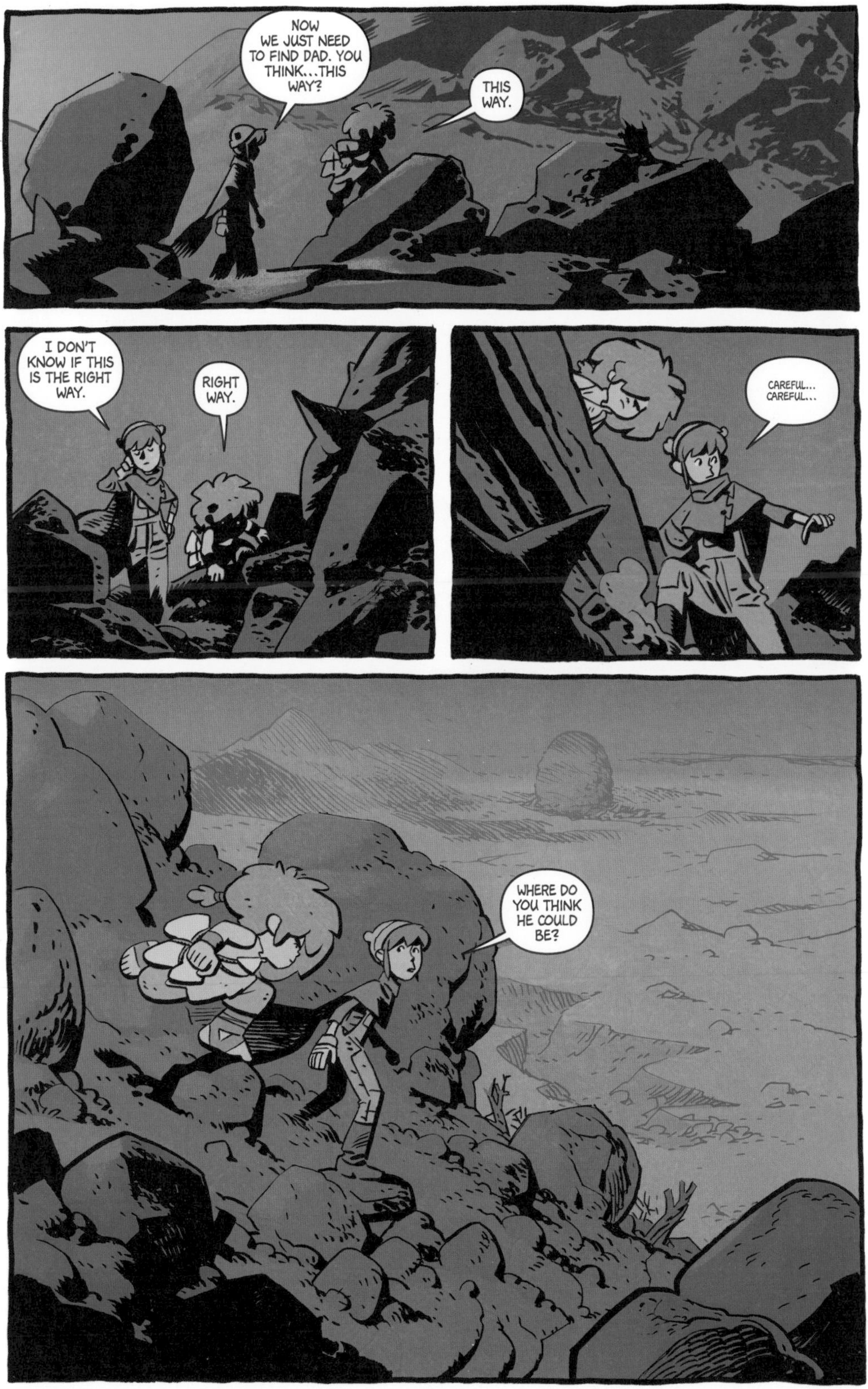
NOW WE JUST NEED TO FIND DAD. YOU THINK...THIS WAY?
THIS WAY.
I DON'T KNOW IF THIS IS THE RIGHT WAY.
RIGHT WAY.
CAREFUL... CAREFUL...
WHERE DO YOU THINK HE COULD BE?

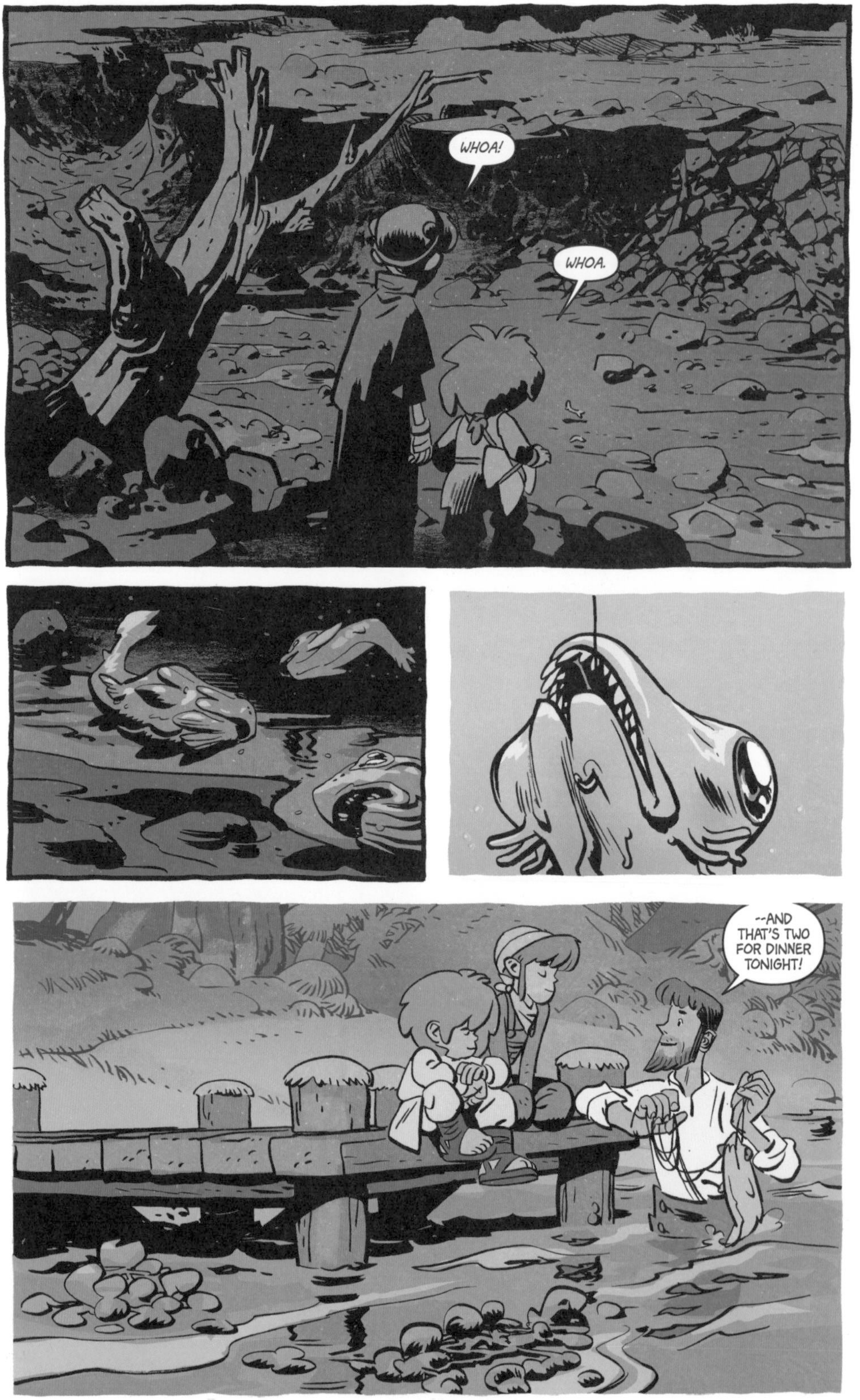
WHOA!
WHOA.
--AND THAT'S TWO FOR DINNER TONIGHT!

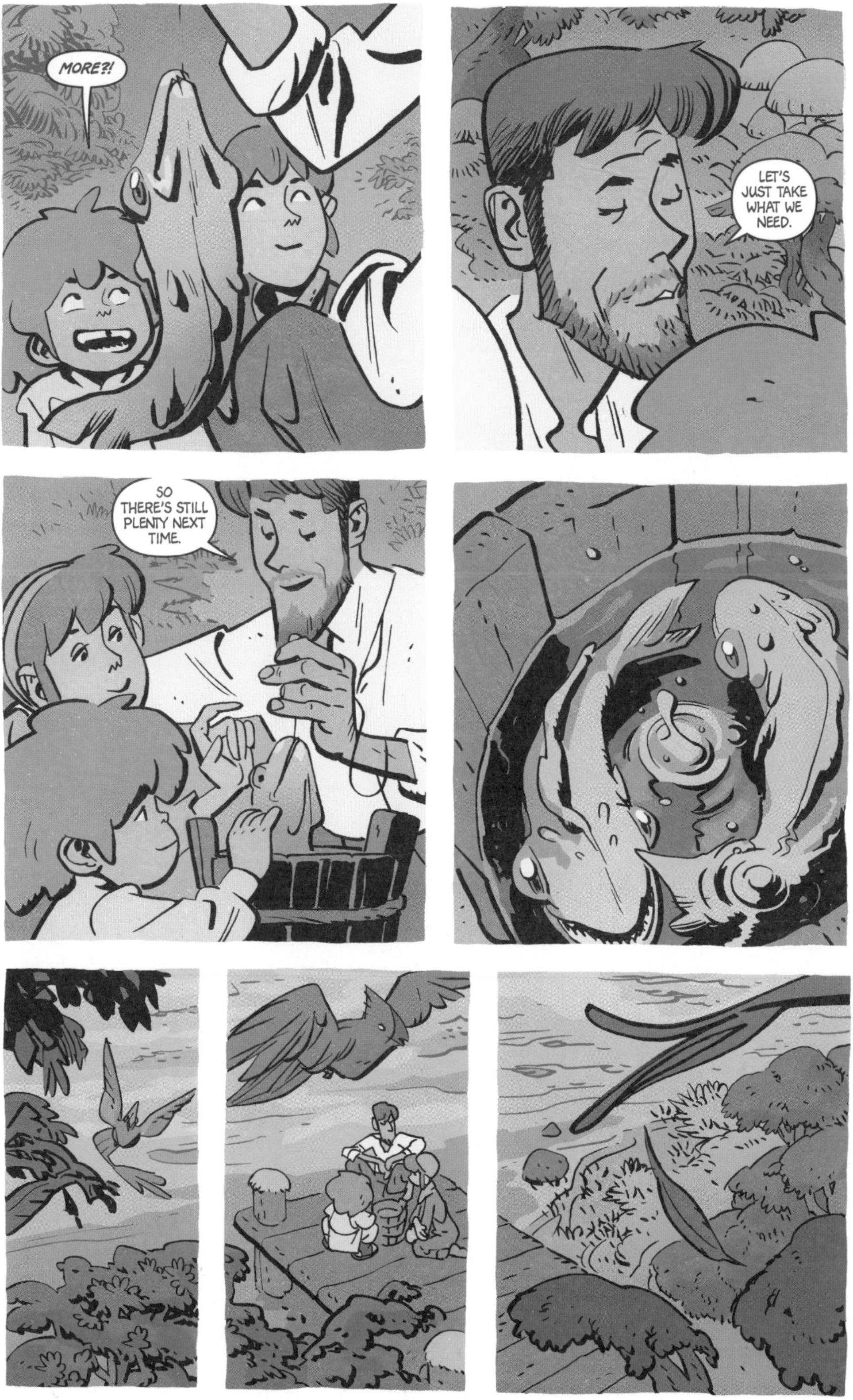
MORE?!
LET'S JUST TAKE WHAT WE NEED.
SO THERE'S STILL PLENTY NEXT TIME.

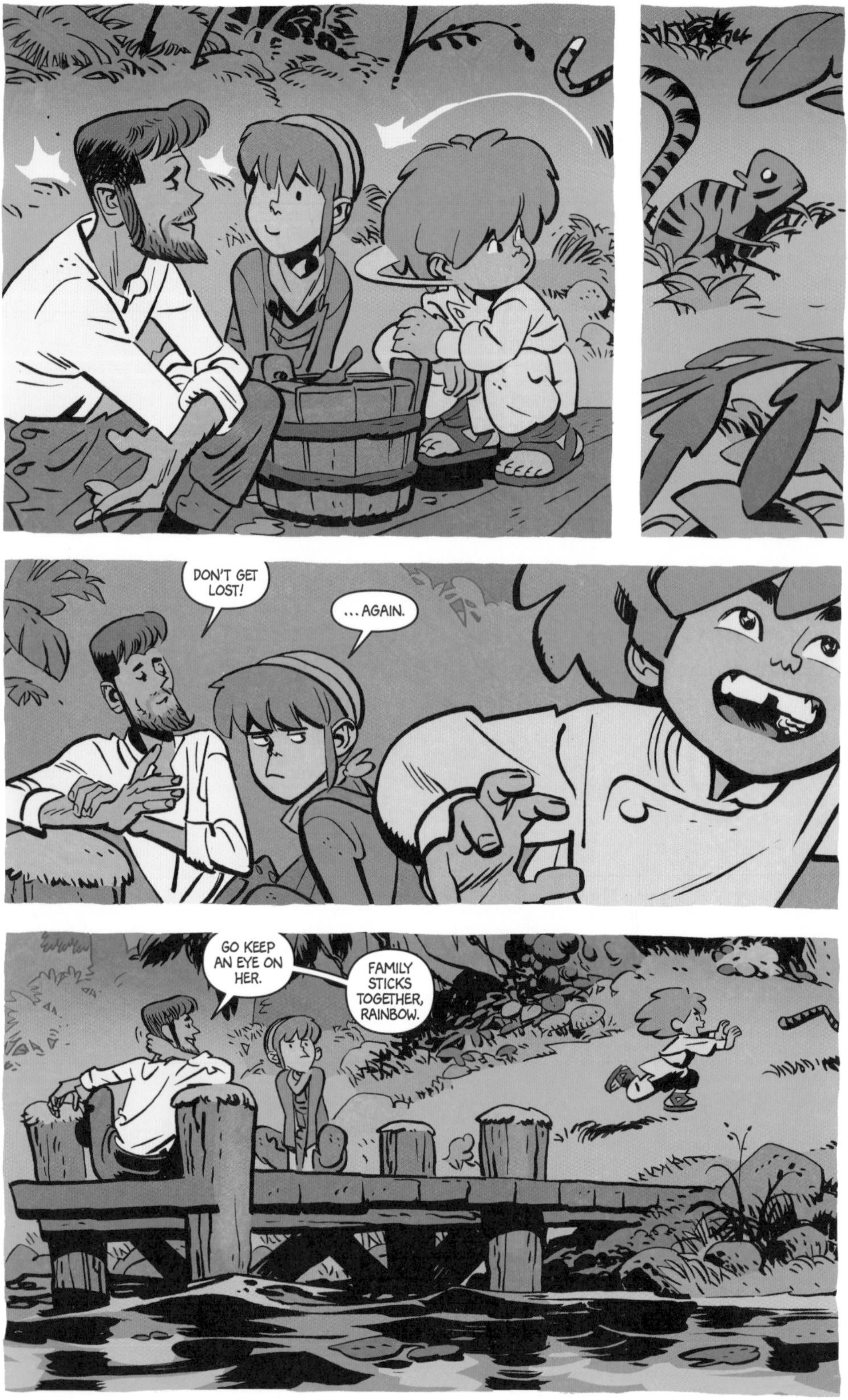
DON'T GET LOST!
...AGAIN.
GO KEEP AN EYE ON HER.
FAMILY STICKS TOGETHER, RAINBOW.

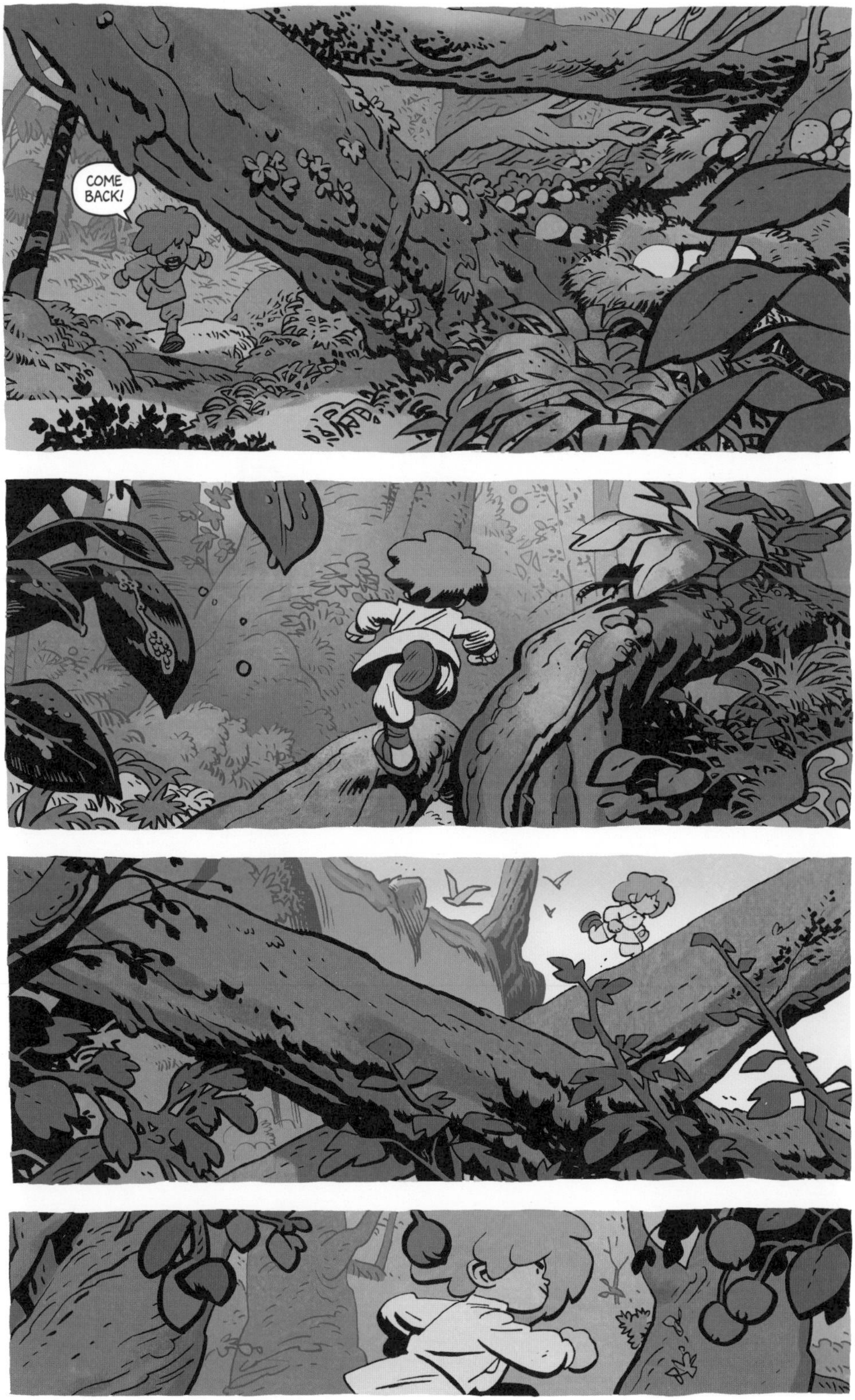
COME BACK!

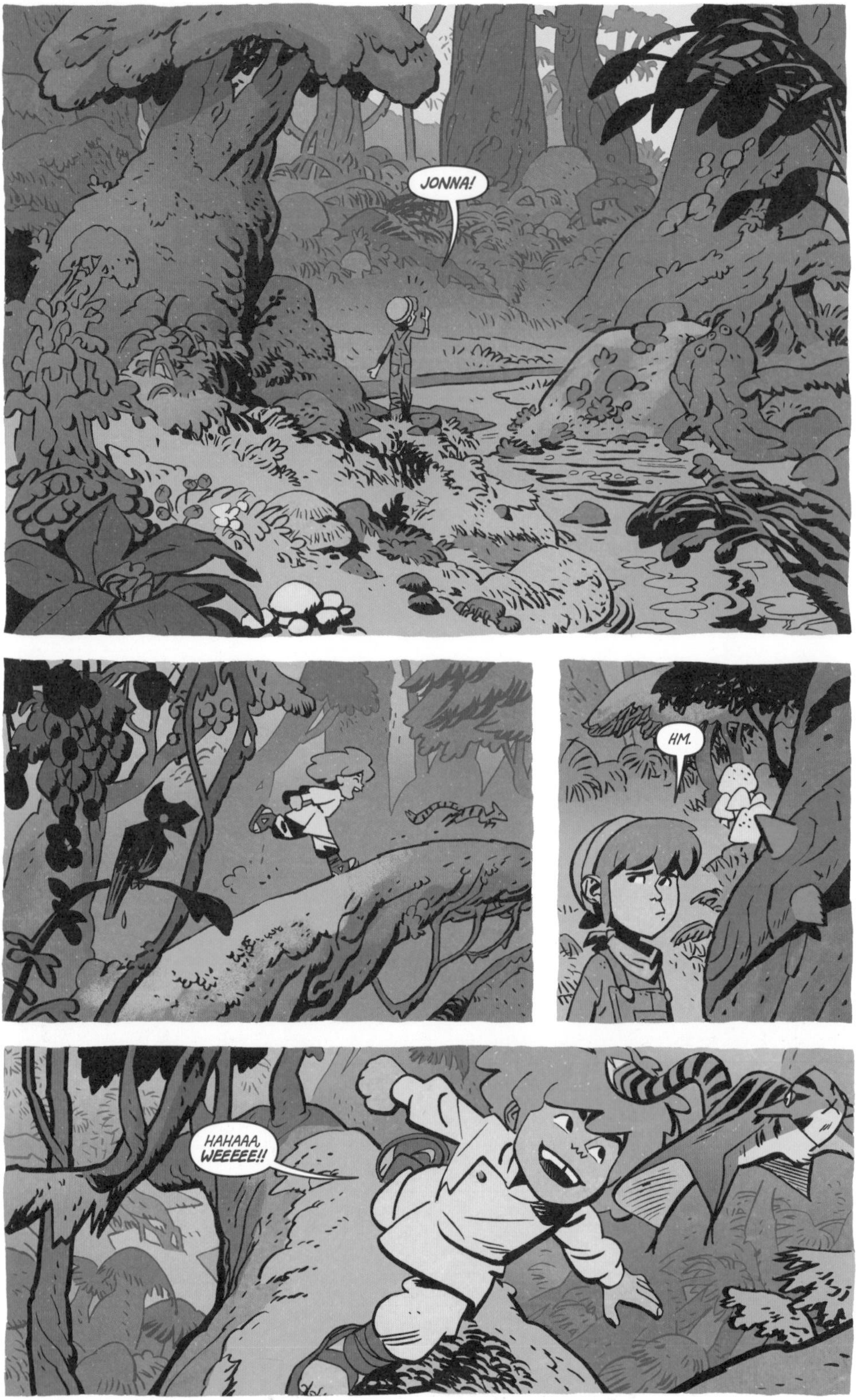
JONNA!
HM.
HAHAAA, WEEEEE!!

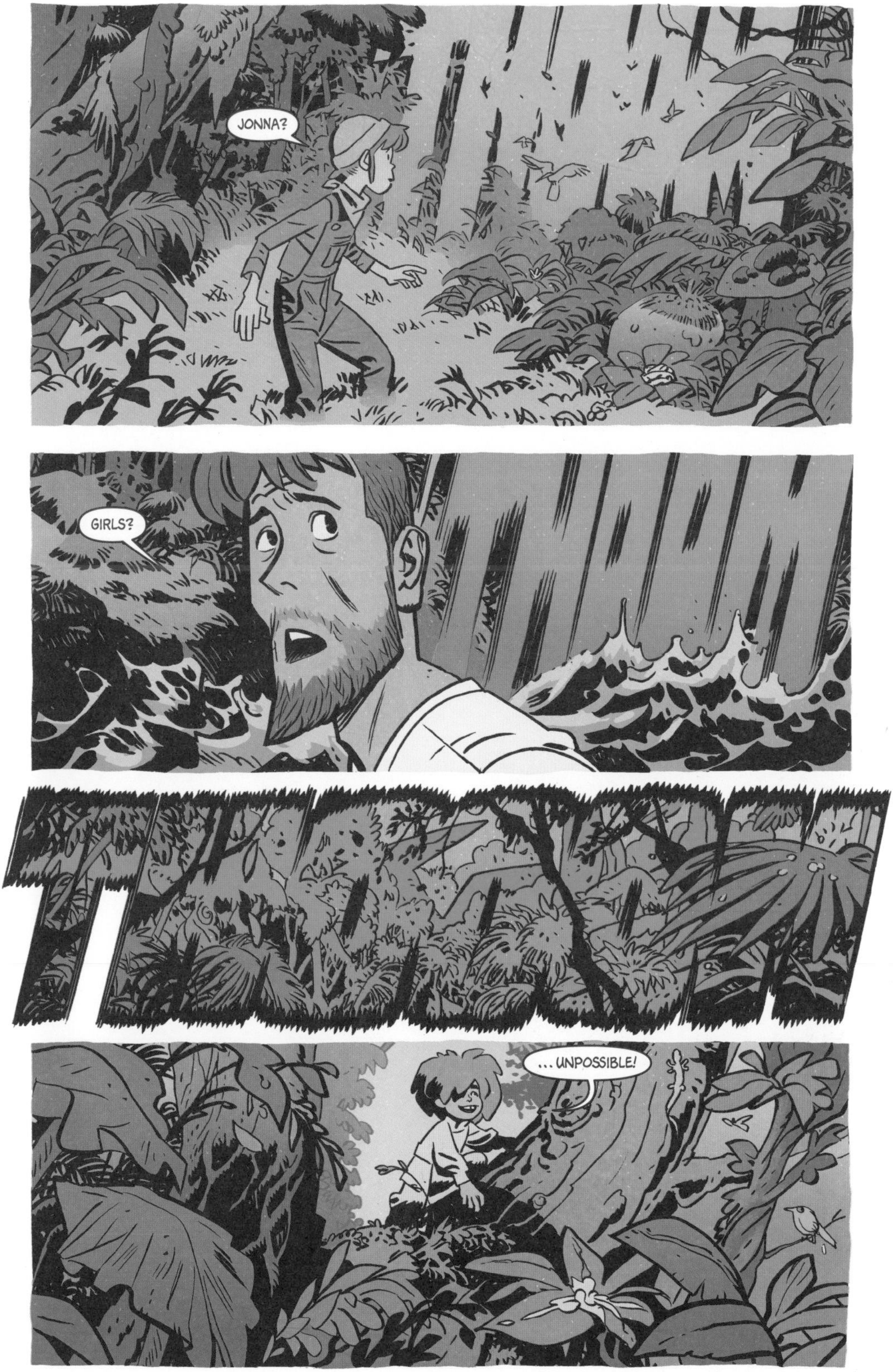
JONNA?
GIRLS?
...UNPOSSIBLE!

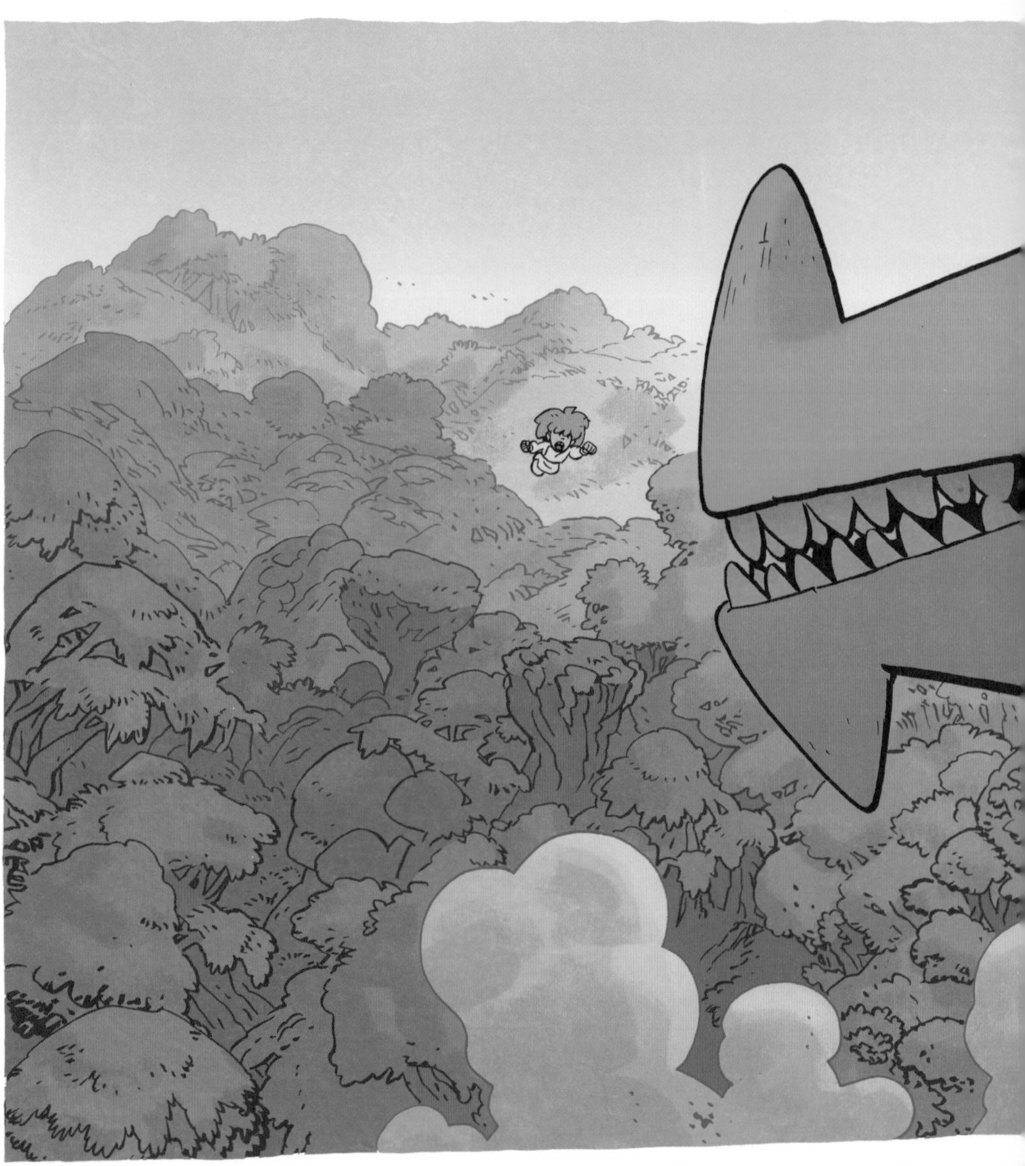
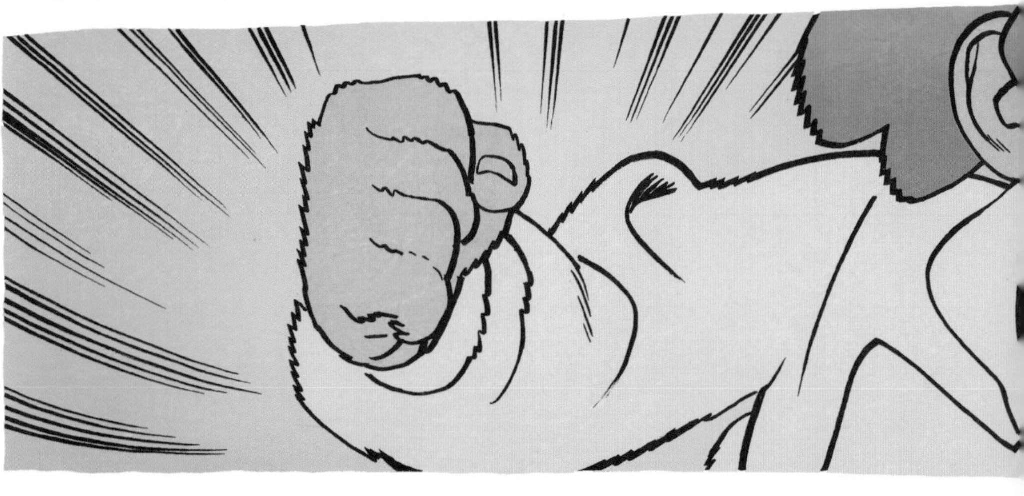

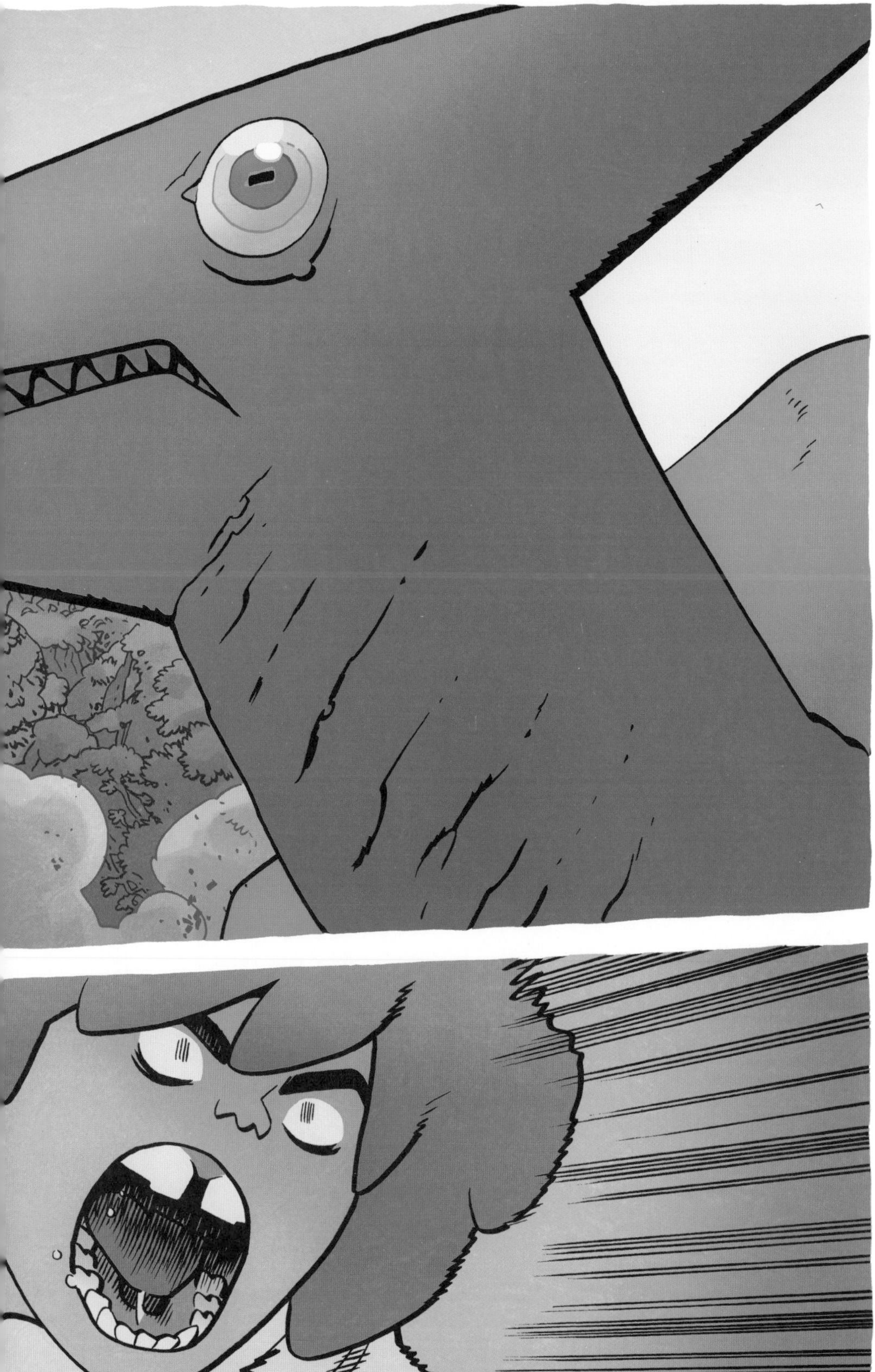

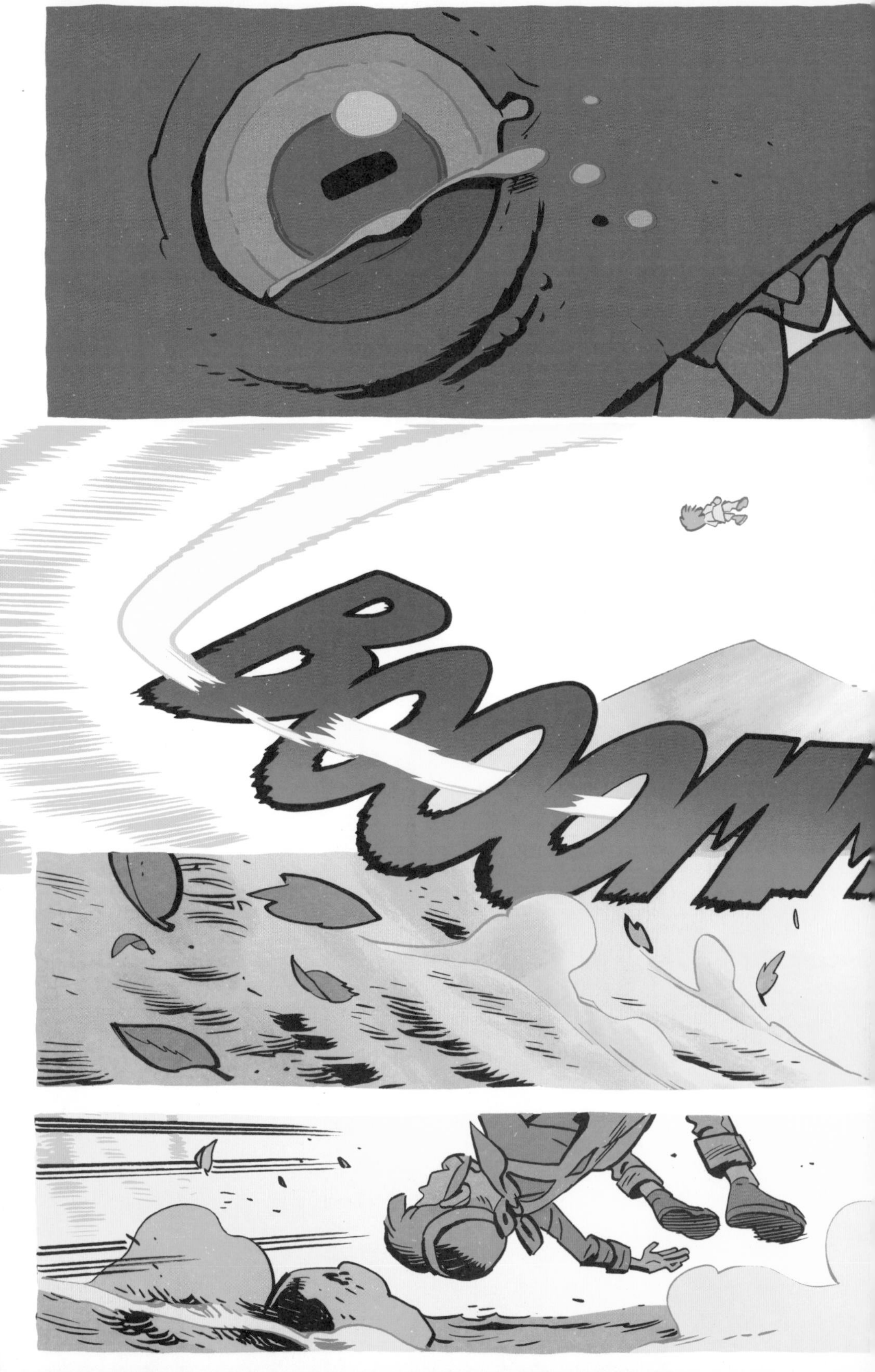
BOOOM

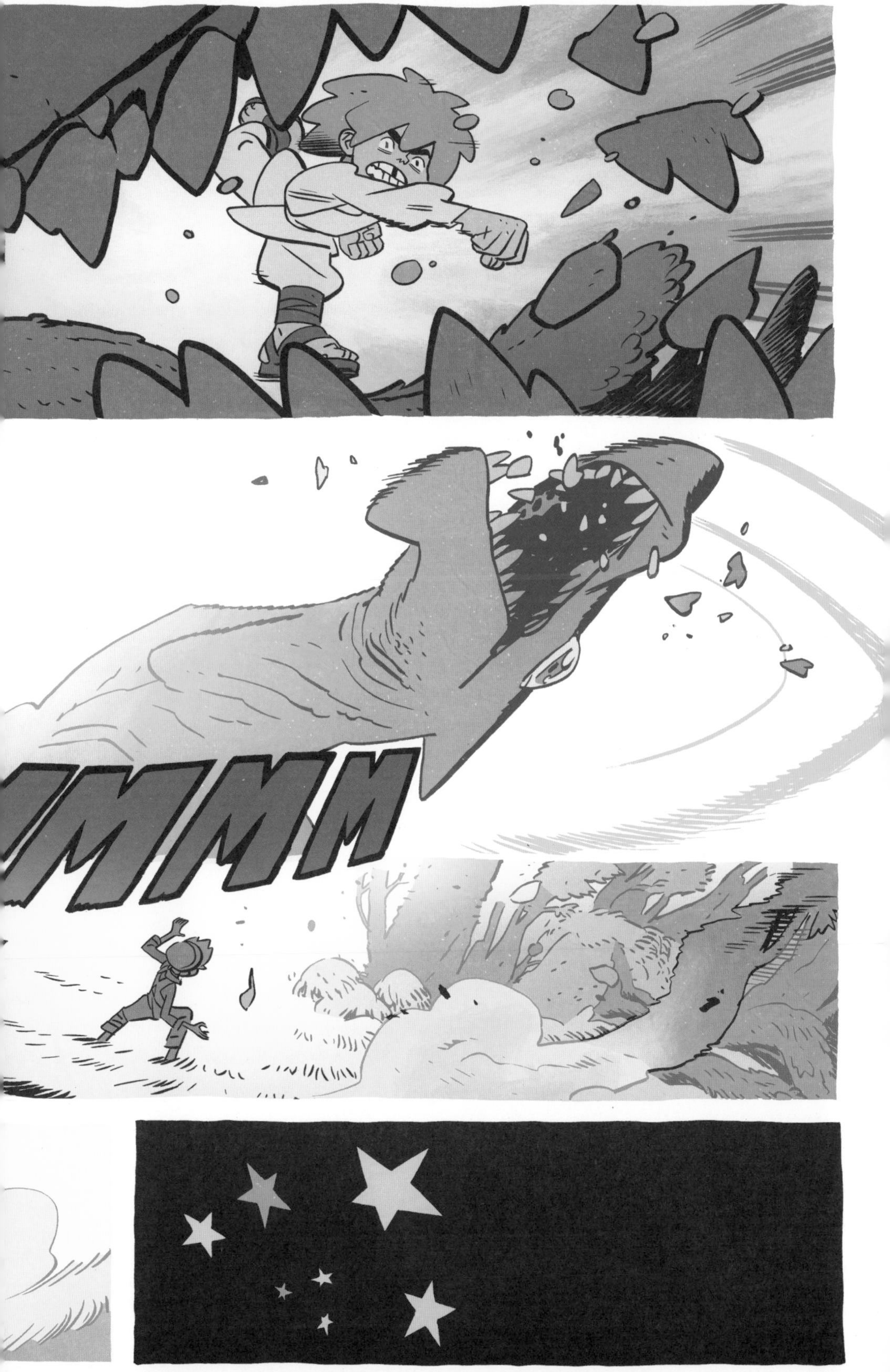
MMM

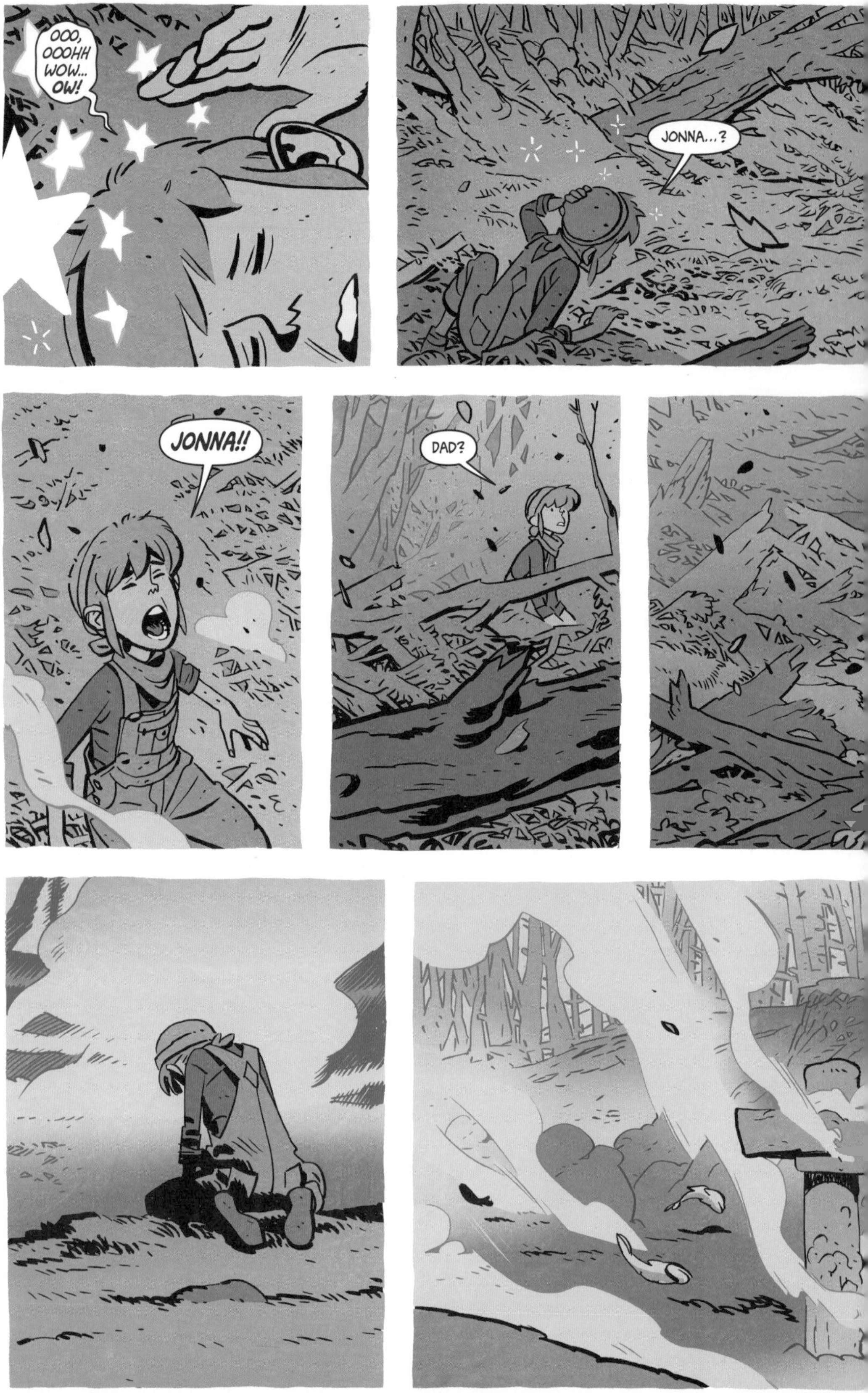
OOO, OOOHH WOW... OW!
JONNA...?
JONNA!!
DAD?

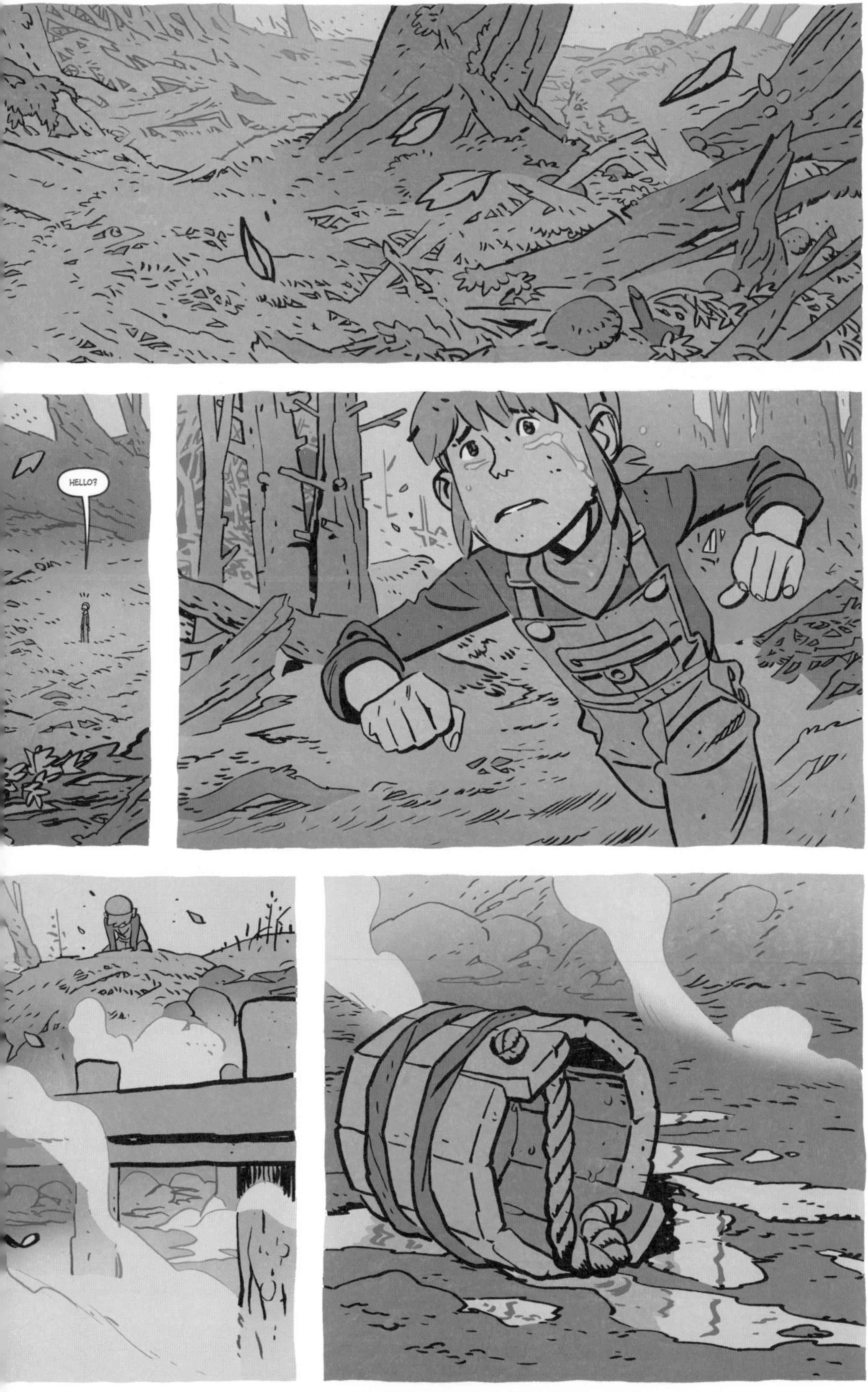
HELLO?

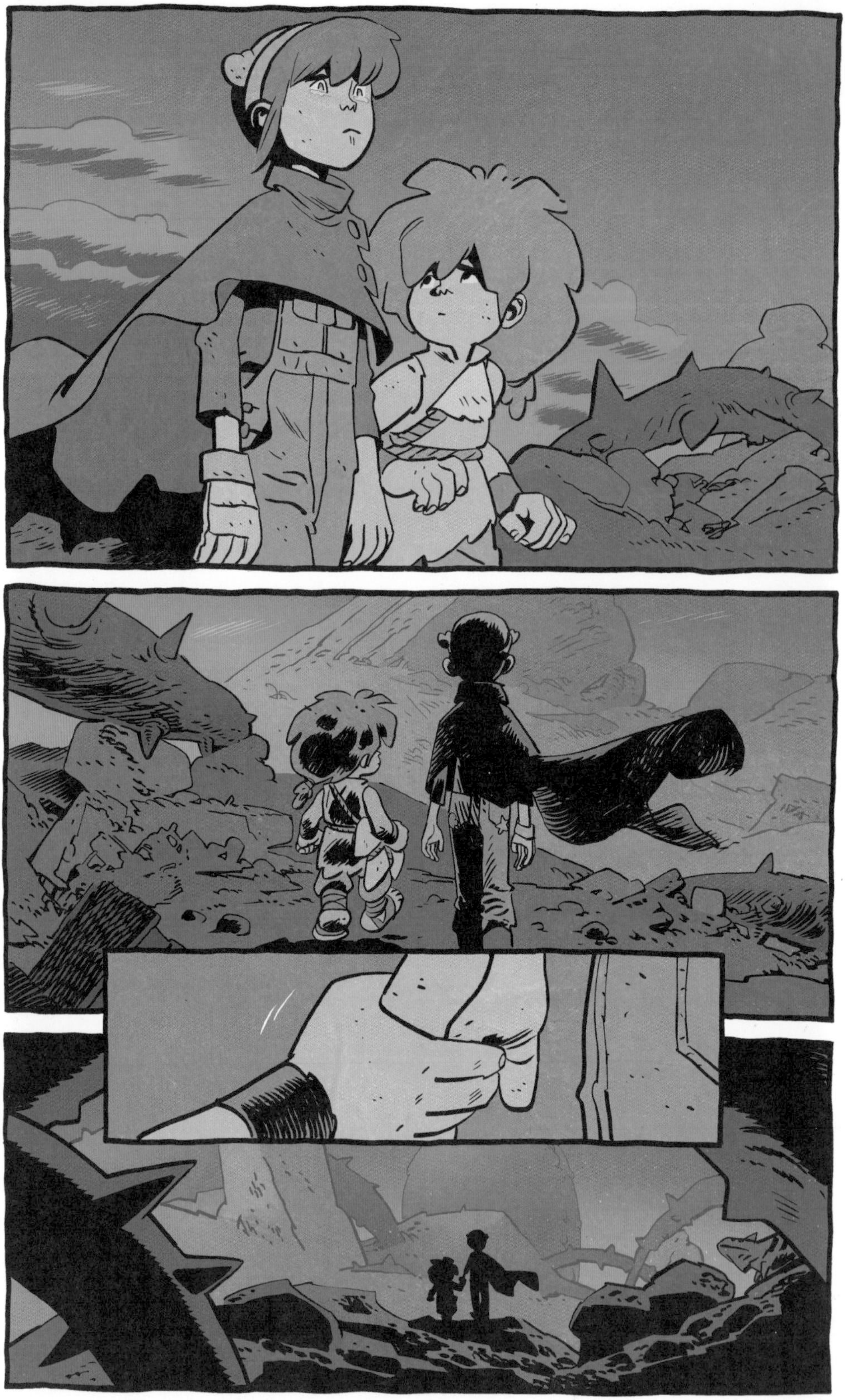

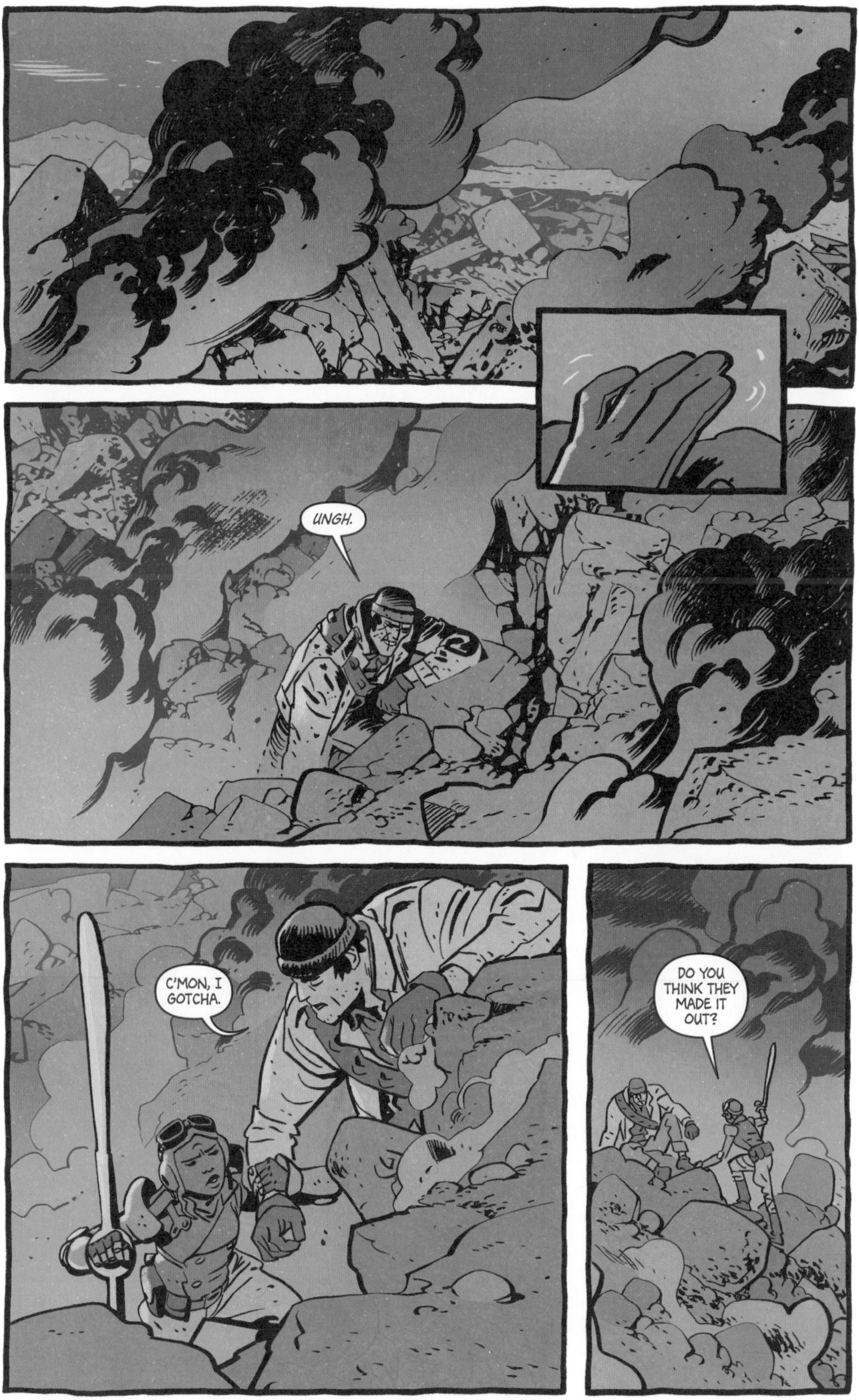
UNGH.
C'MON, I GOTCHA.
DO YOU THINK THEY MADE IT OUT?

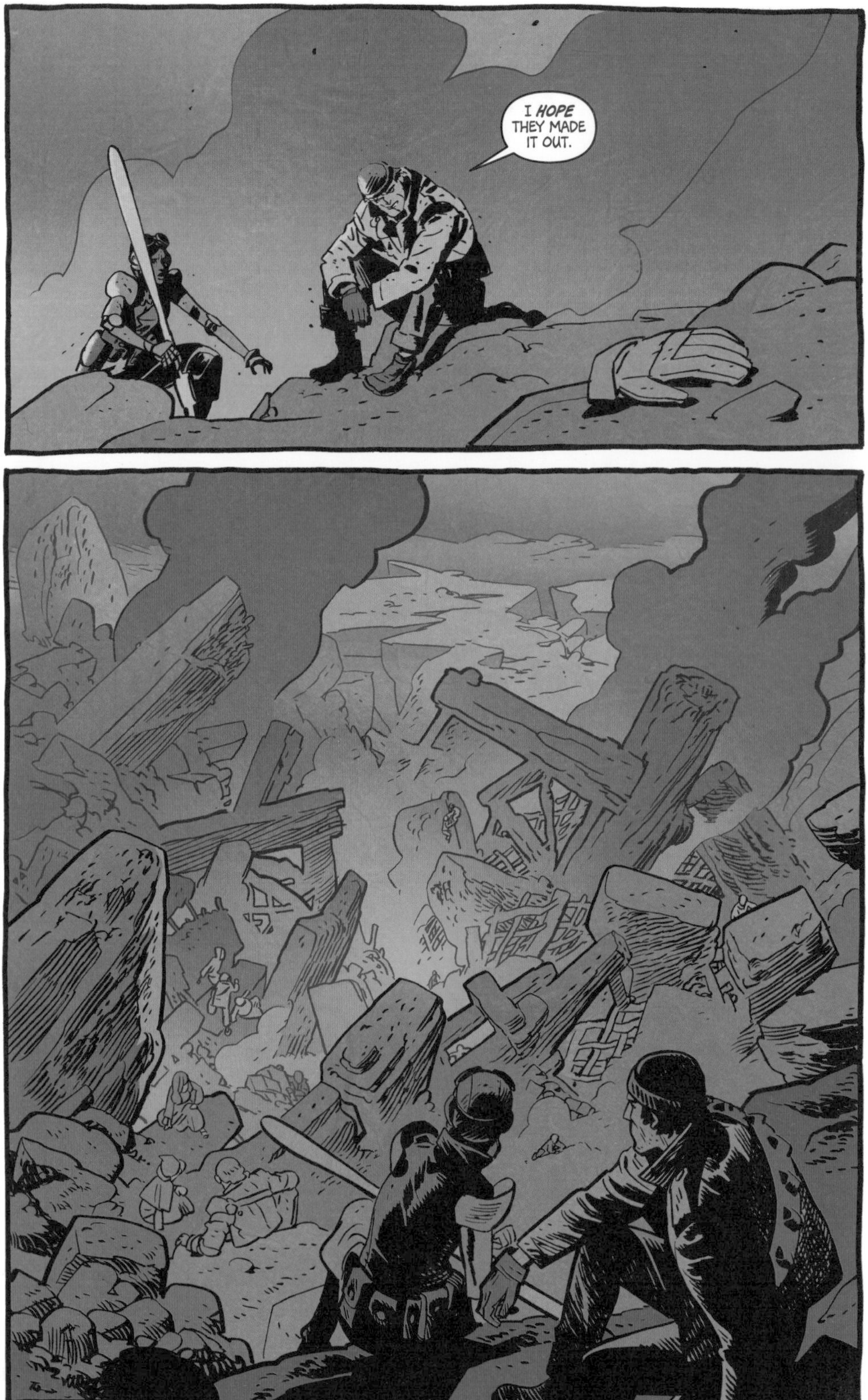
I HOPE THEY MADE IT OUT.

CHAPTER 8

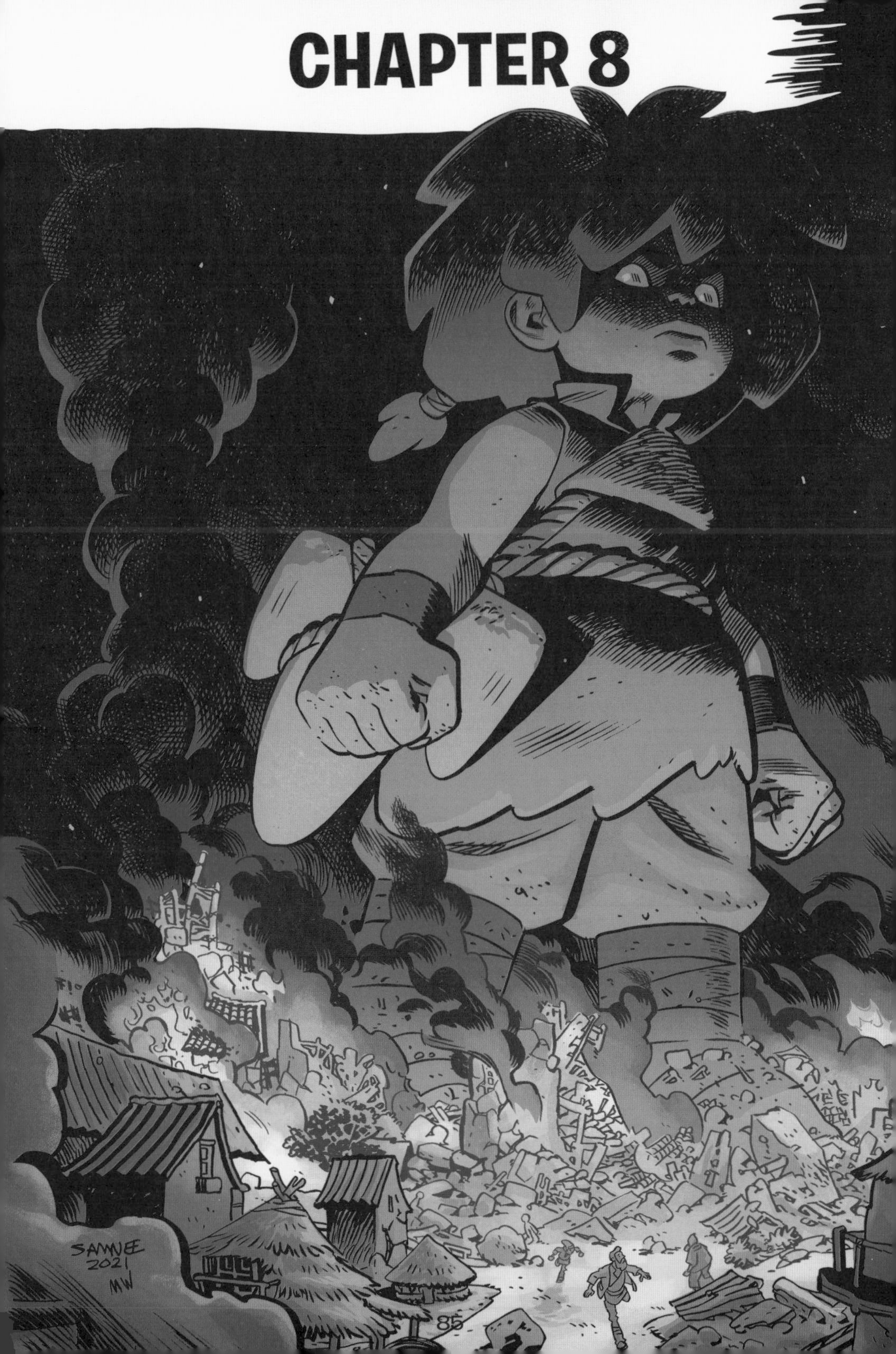
SAMNEE
2021
MW

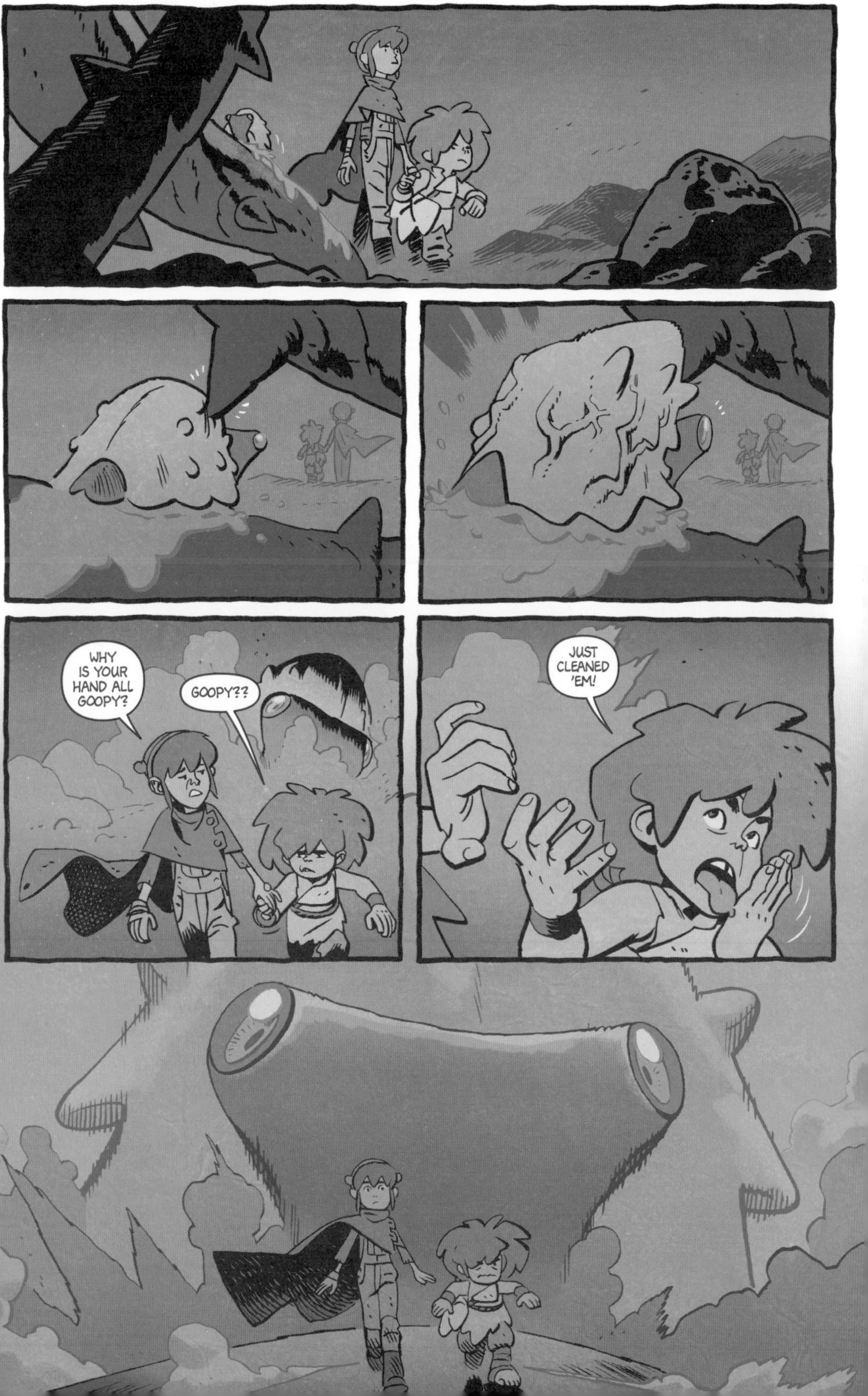
WHY IS YOUR HAND ALL GOOPY?
GOOPY??
JUST CLEANED 'EM!

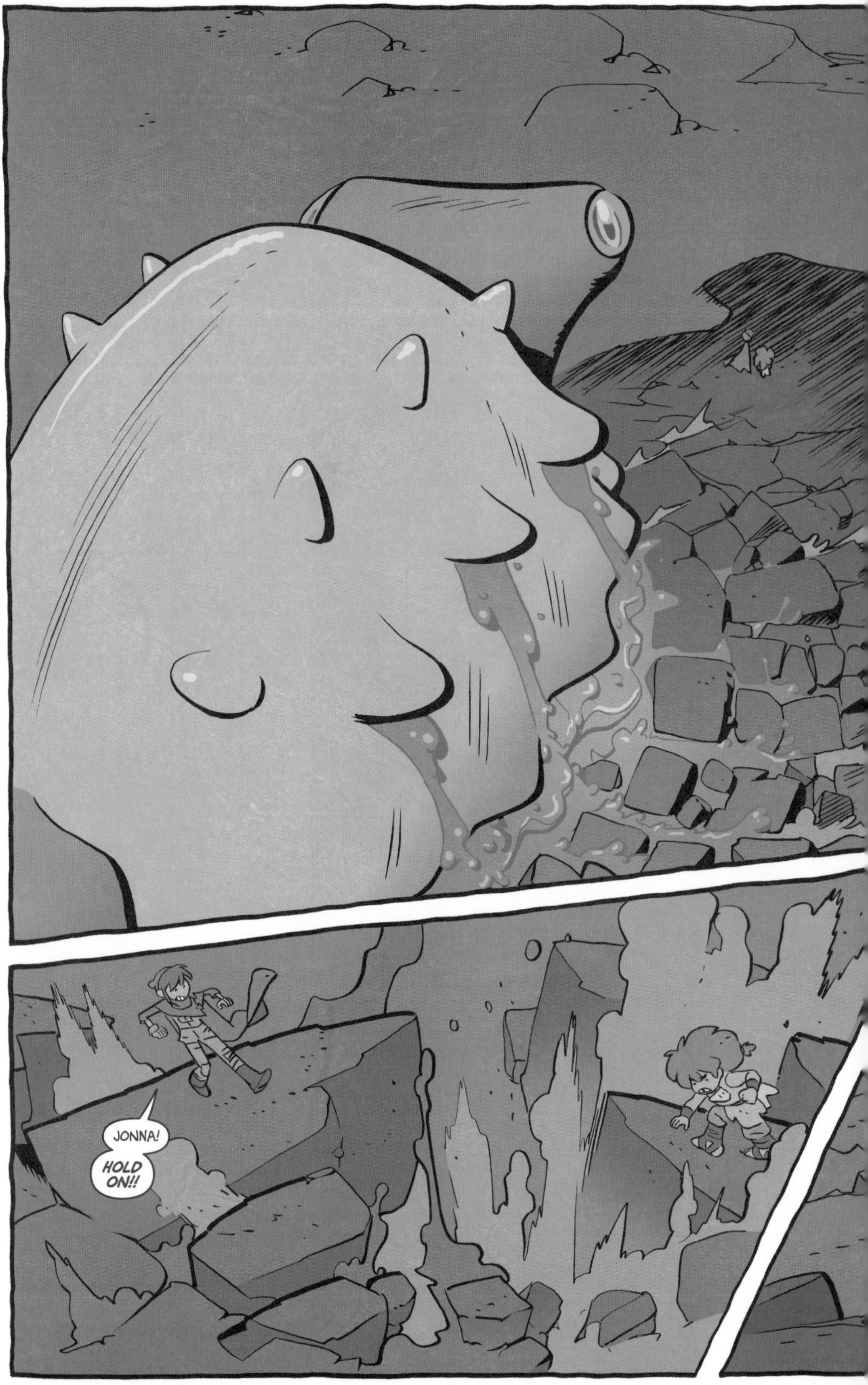

JONNA!
HOLD ON!!

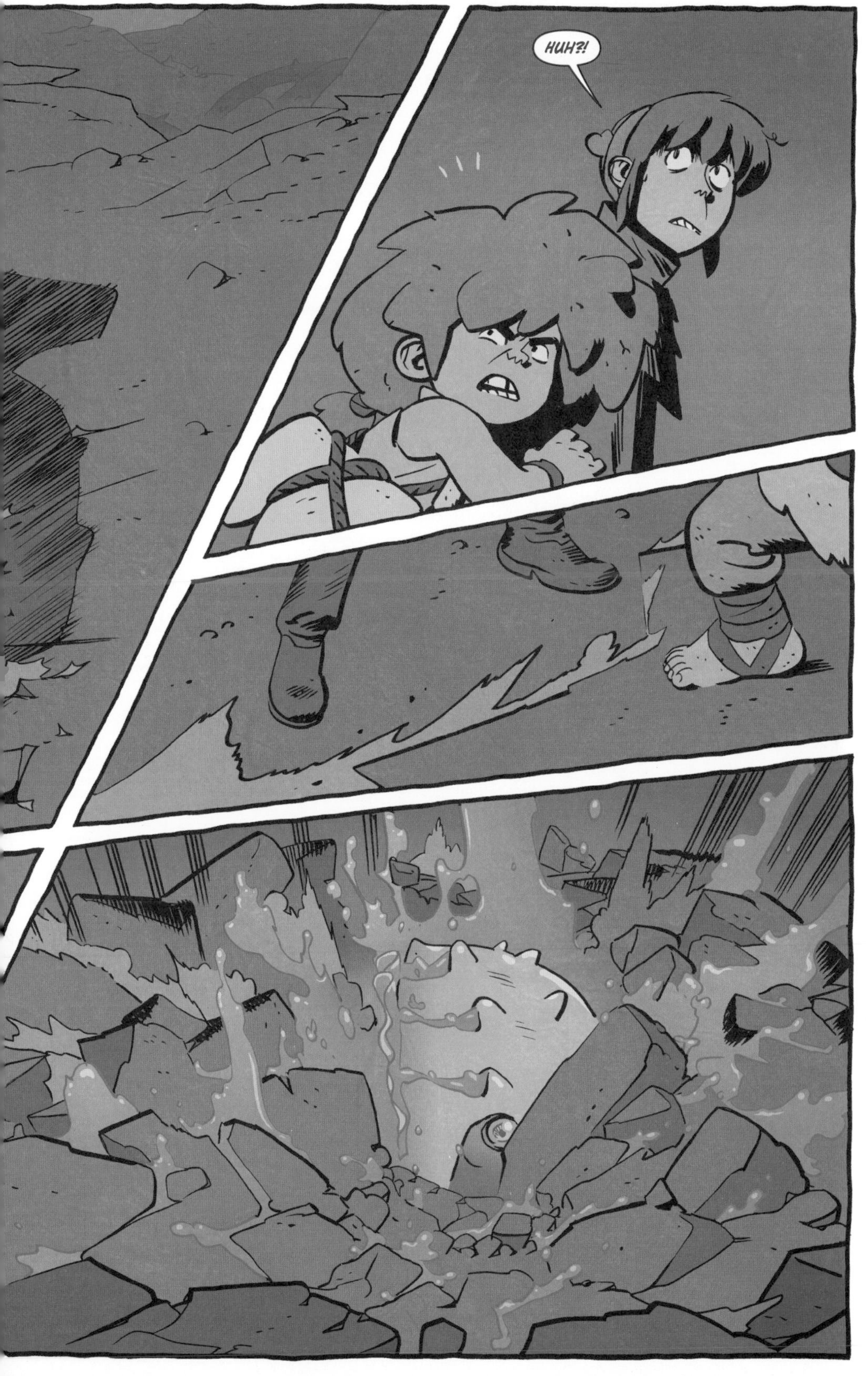
HUH?!

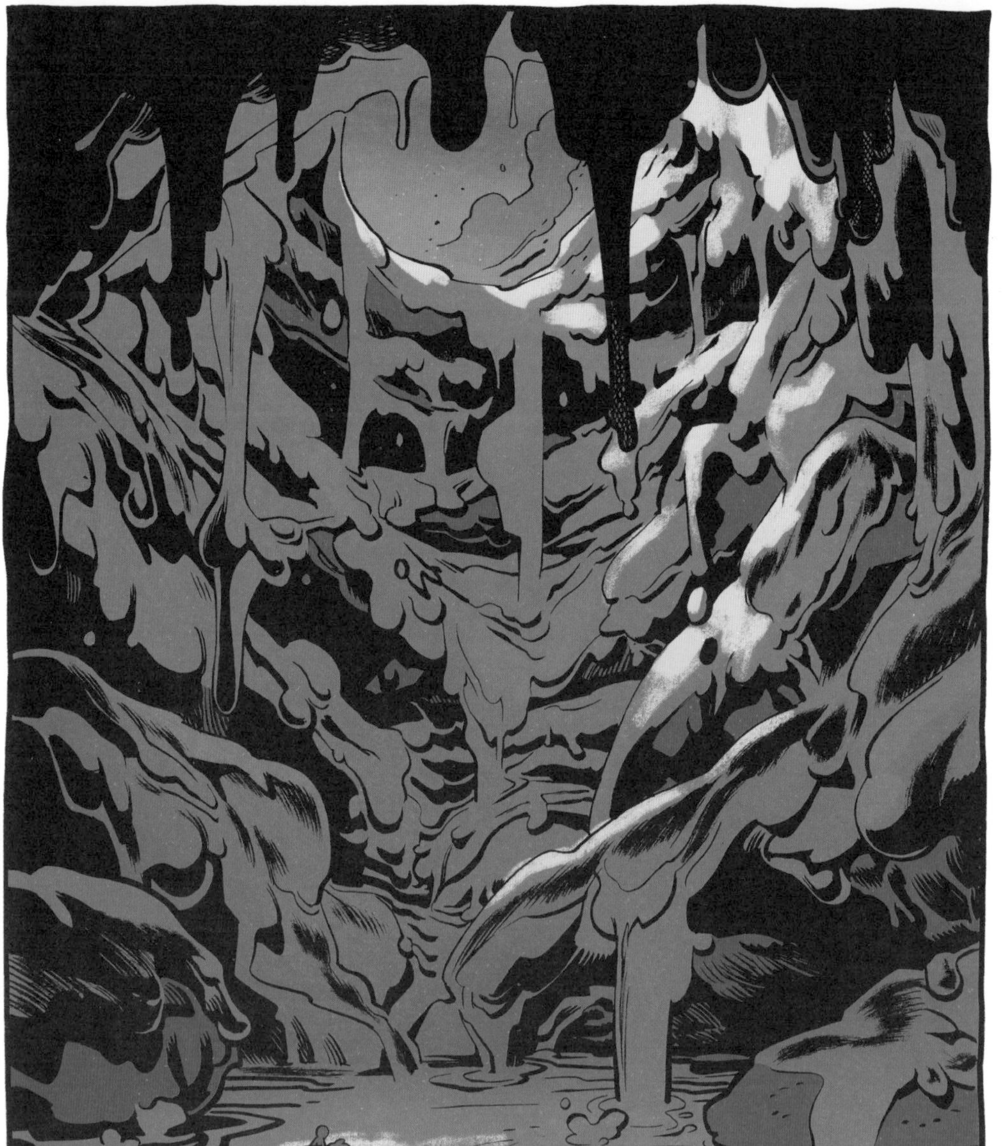

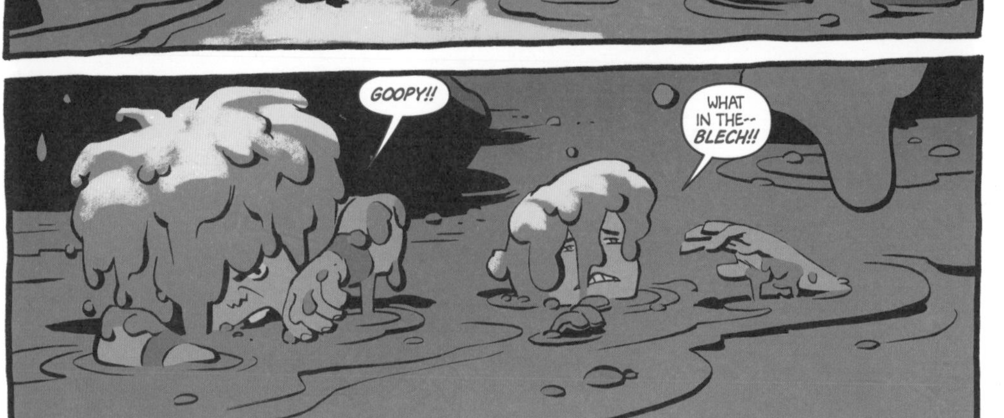
GOOPY!!
WHAT IN THE-- BLECH!!

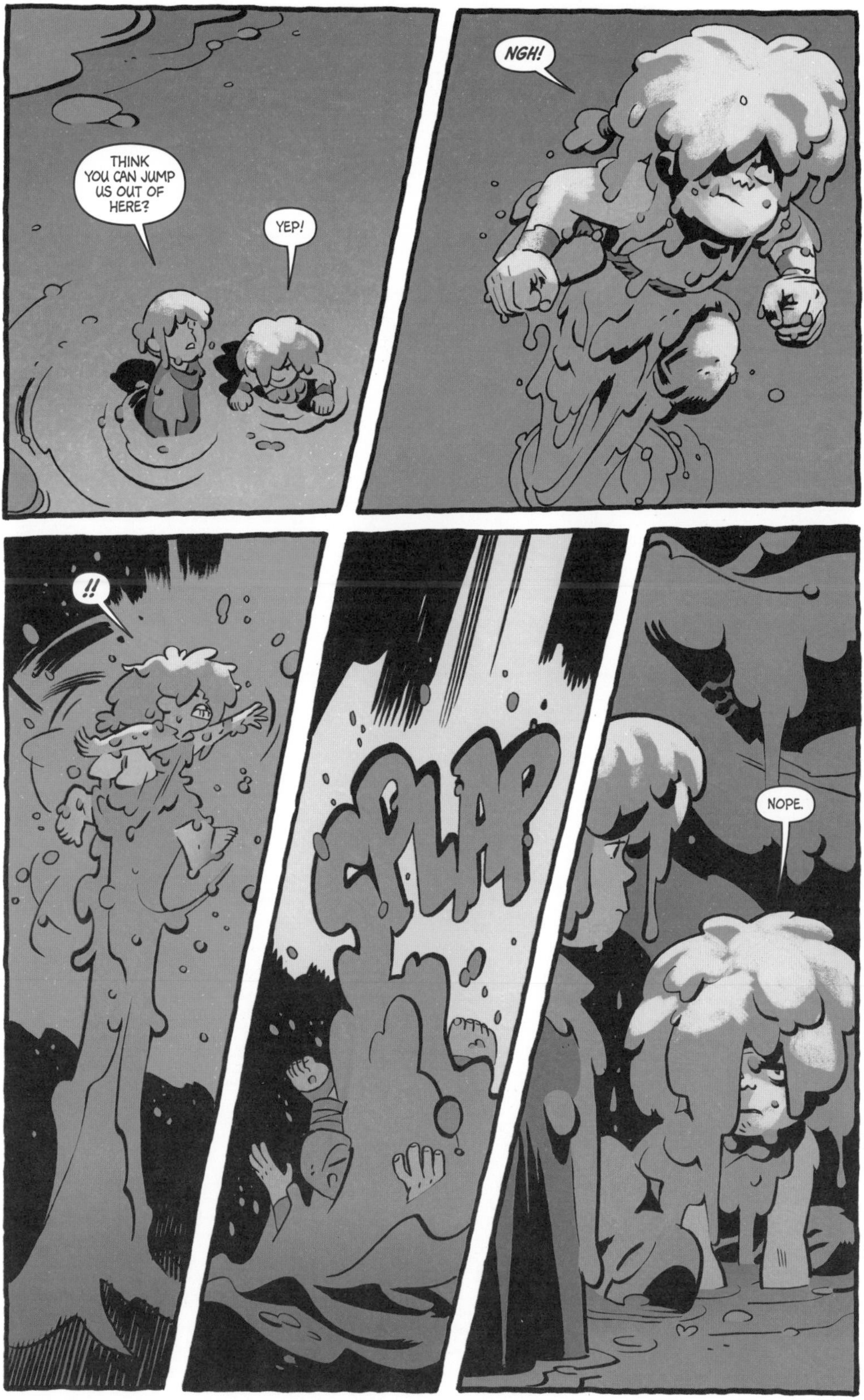
THINK YOU CAN JUMP US OUT OF HERE?
YEP!
NGH!
!!
SPLAP
NOPE.

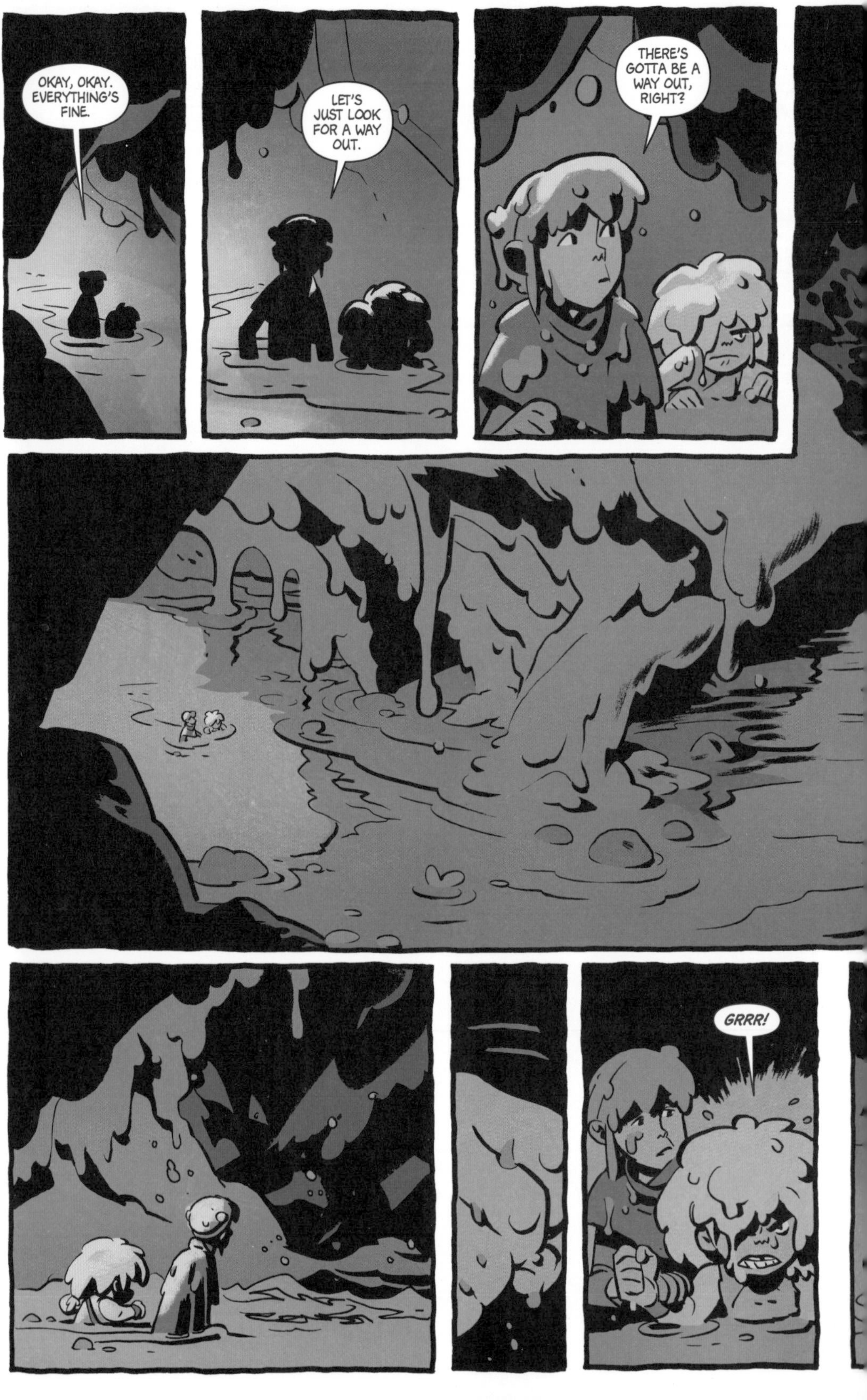
OKAY, OKAY. EVERYTHING'S FINE.
LET'S JUST LOOK FOR A WAY OUT.
THERE'S GOTTA BE A WAY OUT, RIGHT?
GRRR!

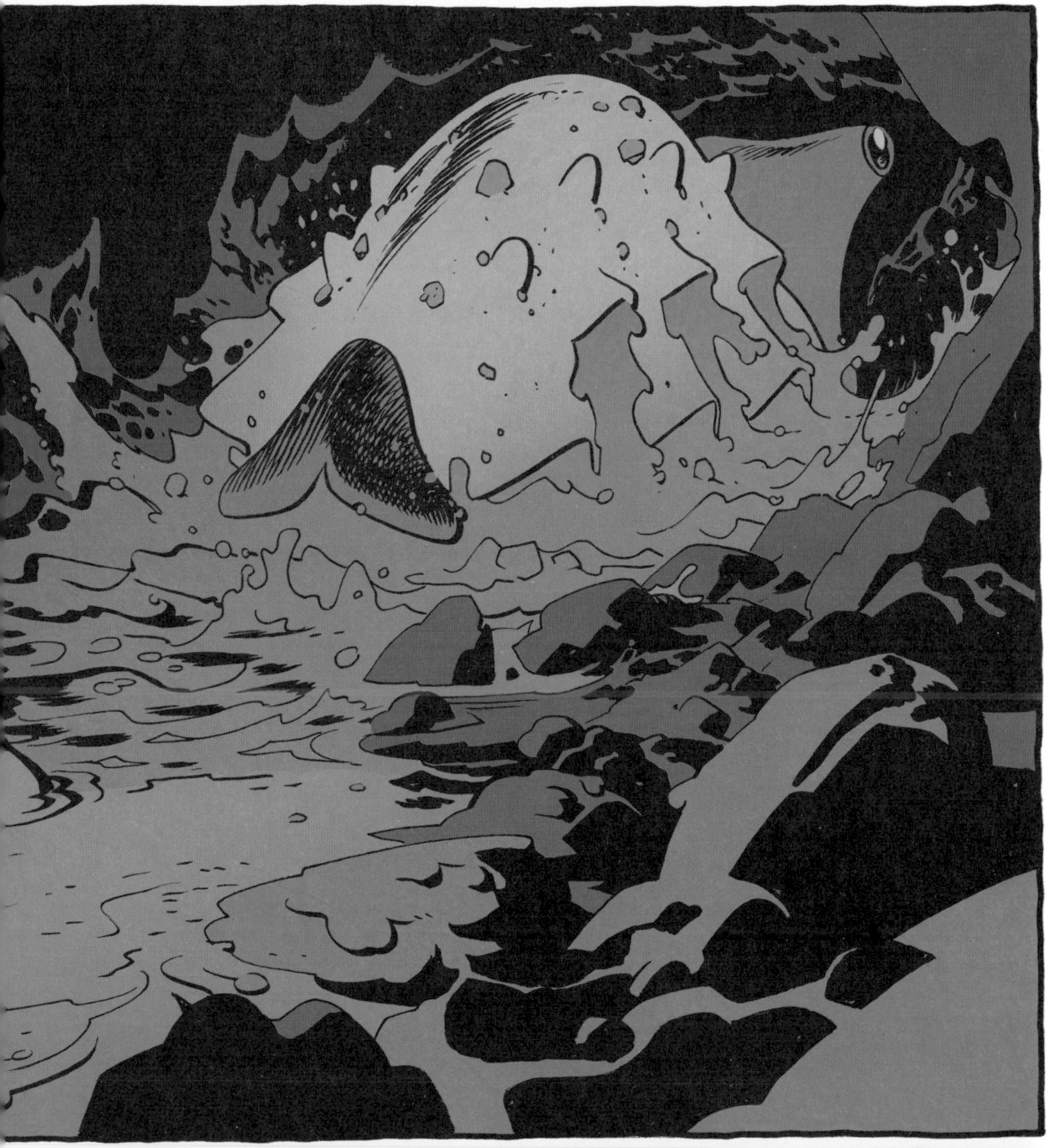

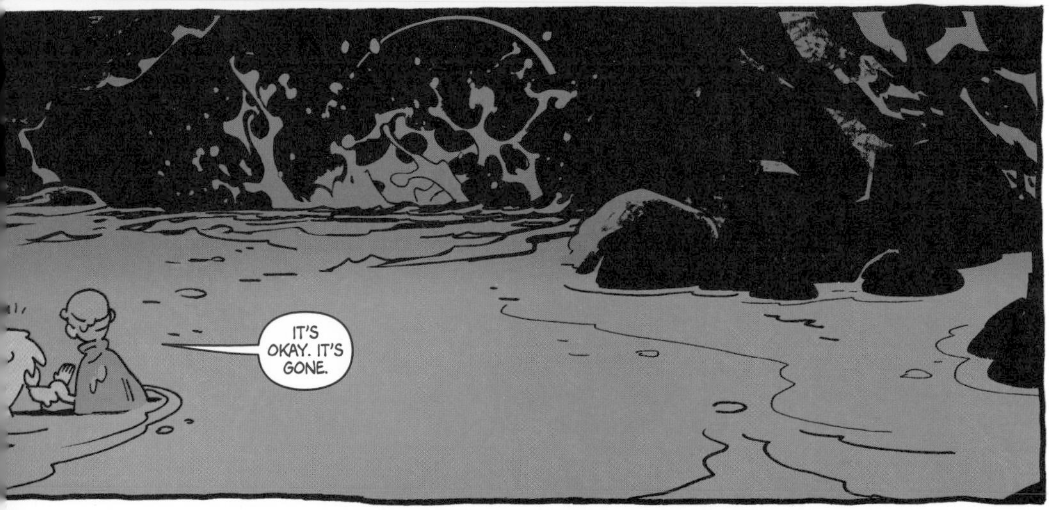
IT'S OKAY. IT'S GONE.

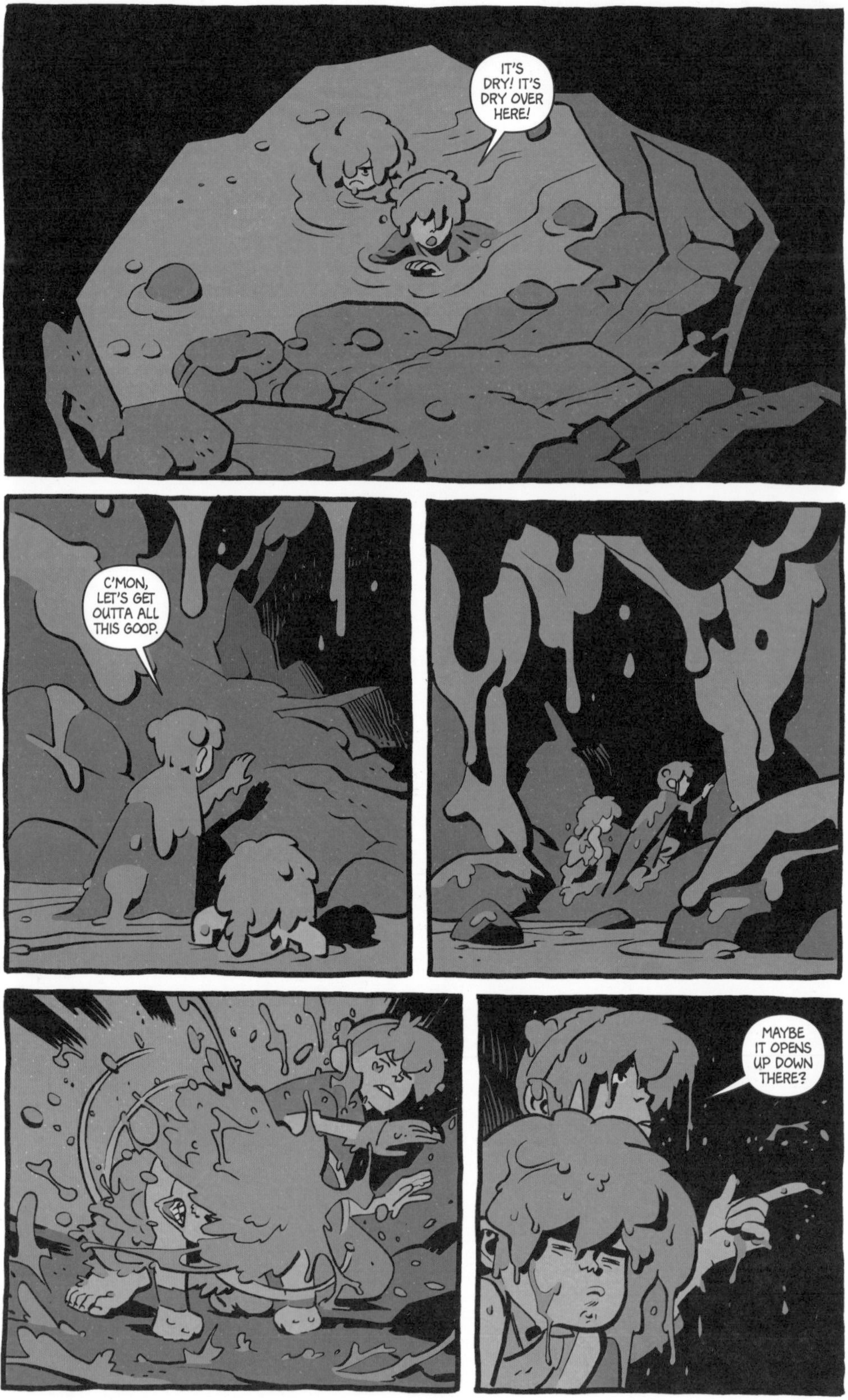
IT'S DRY! IT'S DRY OVER HERE!
C'MON, LET'S GET OUTTA ALL THIS GOOP.
MAYBE IT OPENS UP DOWN THERE?

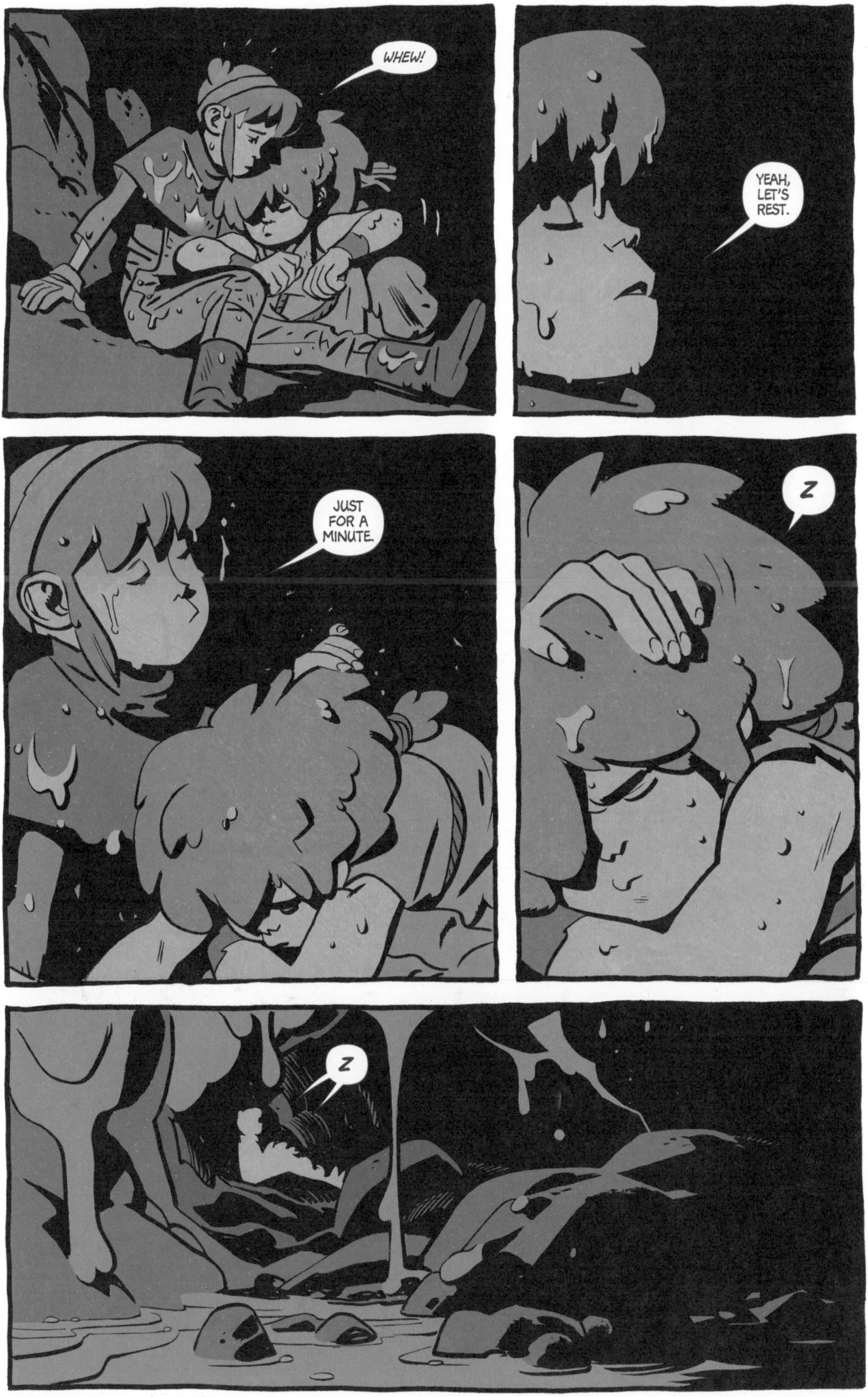
WHEW!
YEAH, LET'S REST.
JUST FOR A MINUTE.
Z
Z

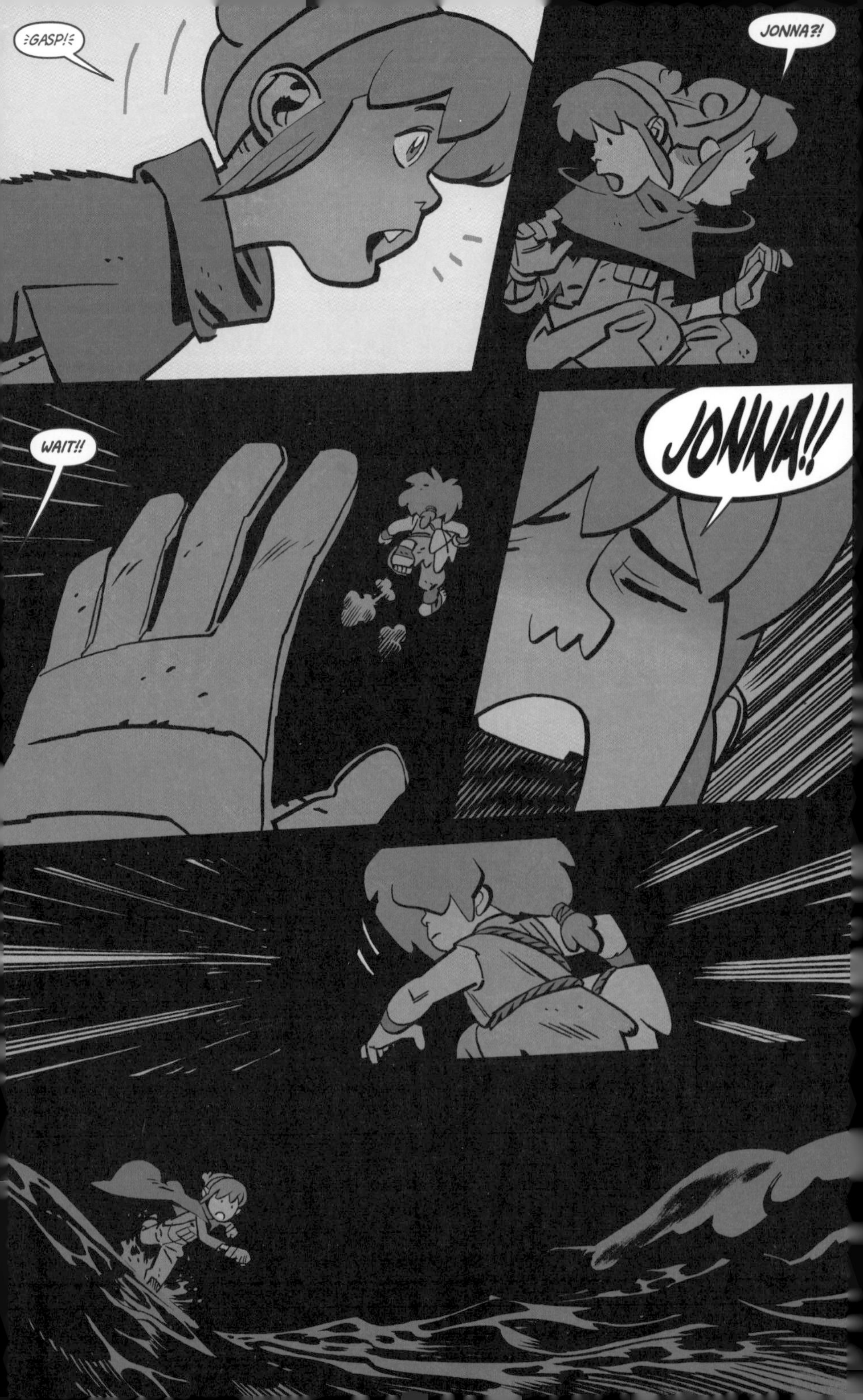
GASP!
JONNA?!
WAIT!!
JONNA!!

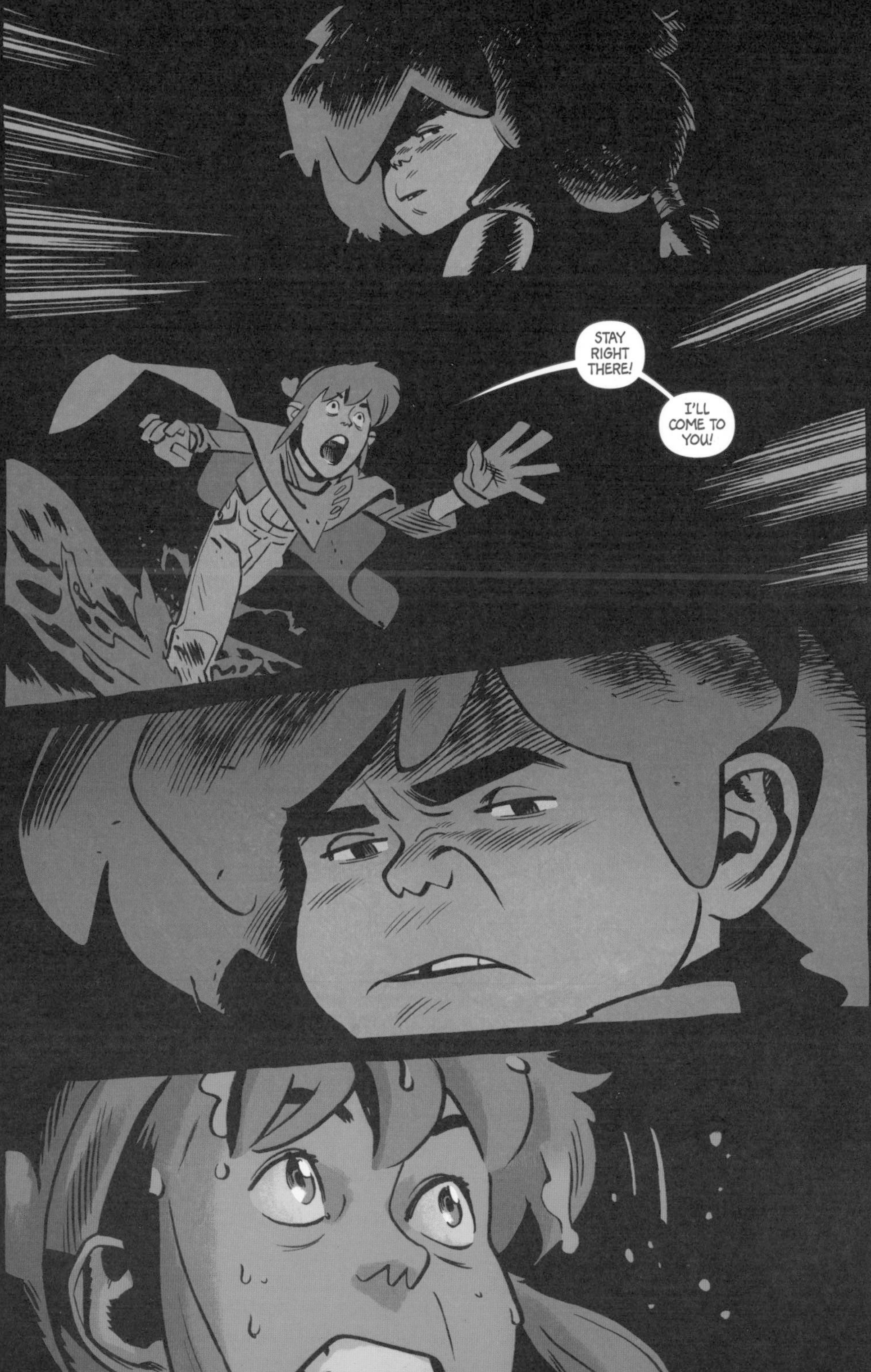
STAY RIGHT THERE!
I'LL COME TO YOU!

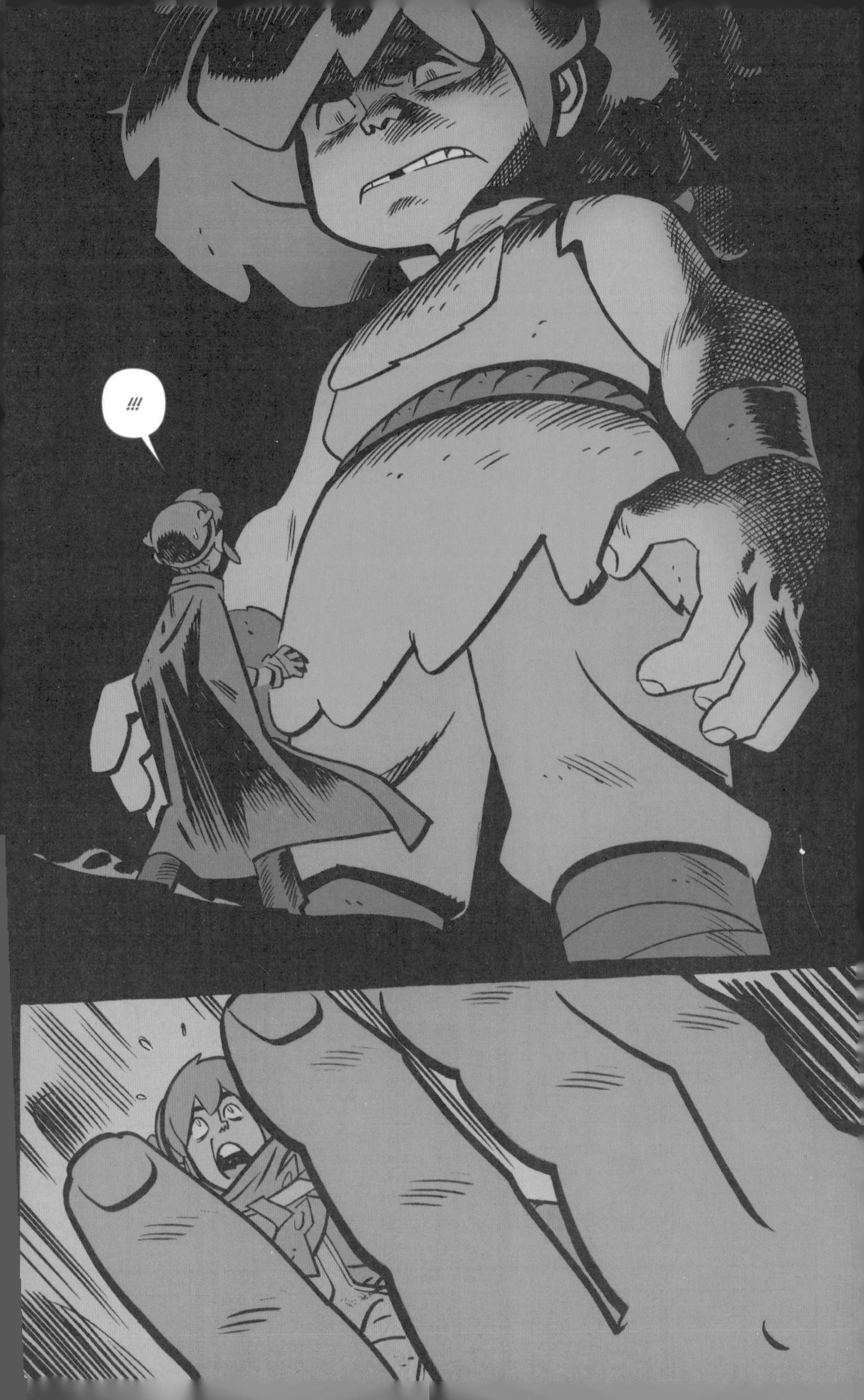
!!!

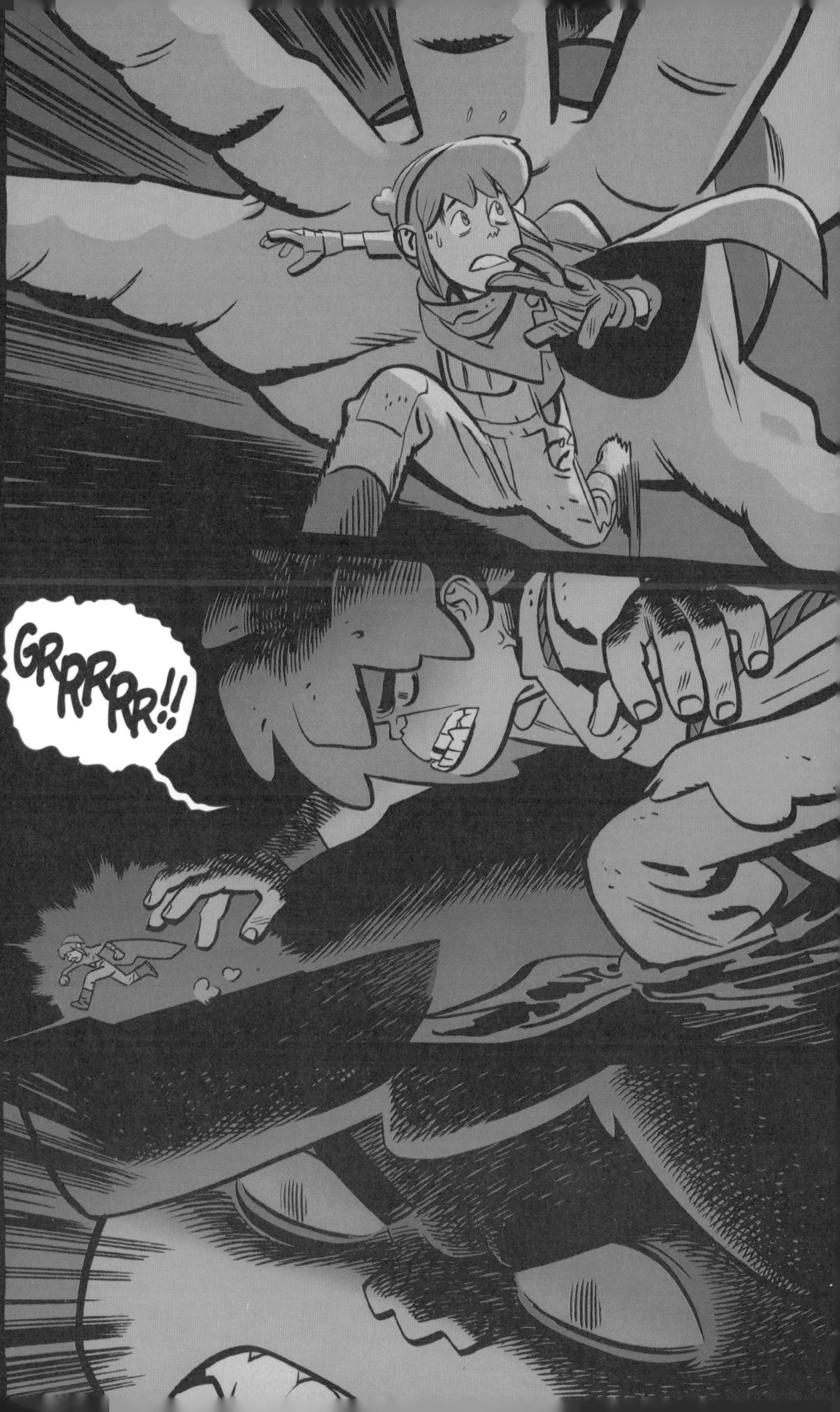
GRRRRR!!

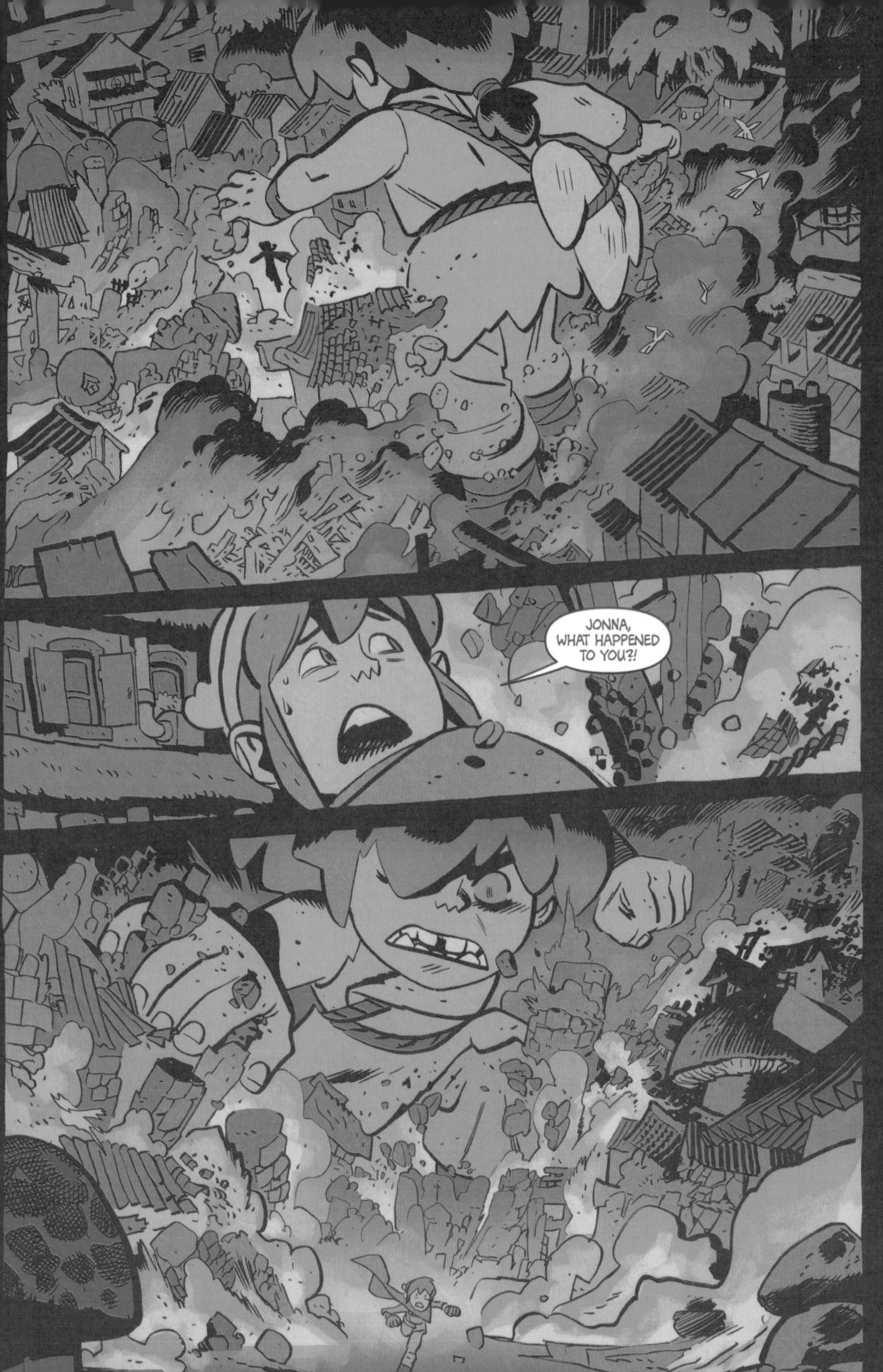
JONNA, WHAT HAPPENED TO YOU?!

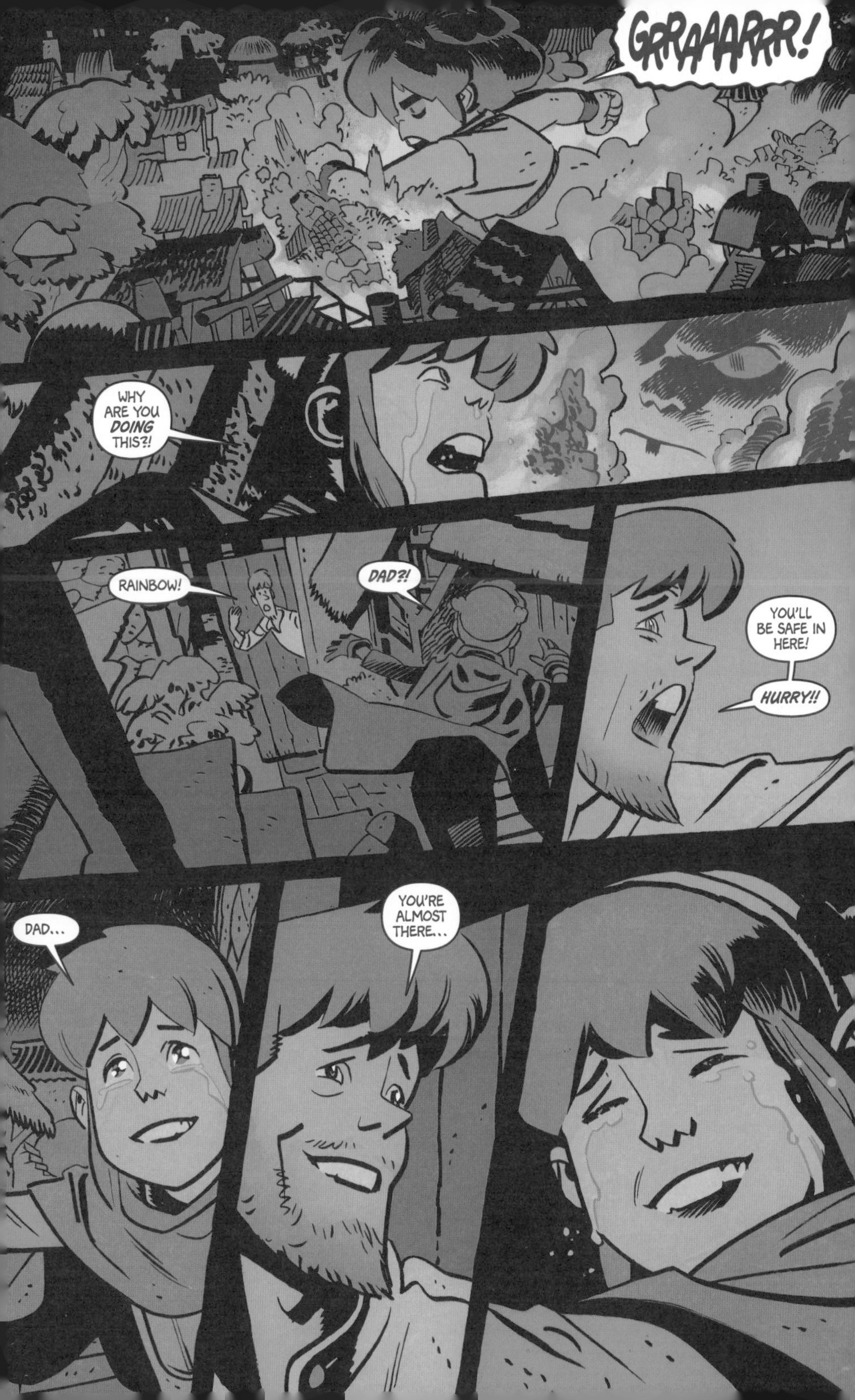
GRRAAARRR!
WHY ARE YOU *DOING* THIS?!
RAINBOW!
DAD?!
YOU'LL BE SAFE IN HERE!
HURRY!!
DAD...
YOU'RE ALMOST THERE...

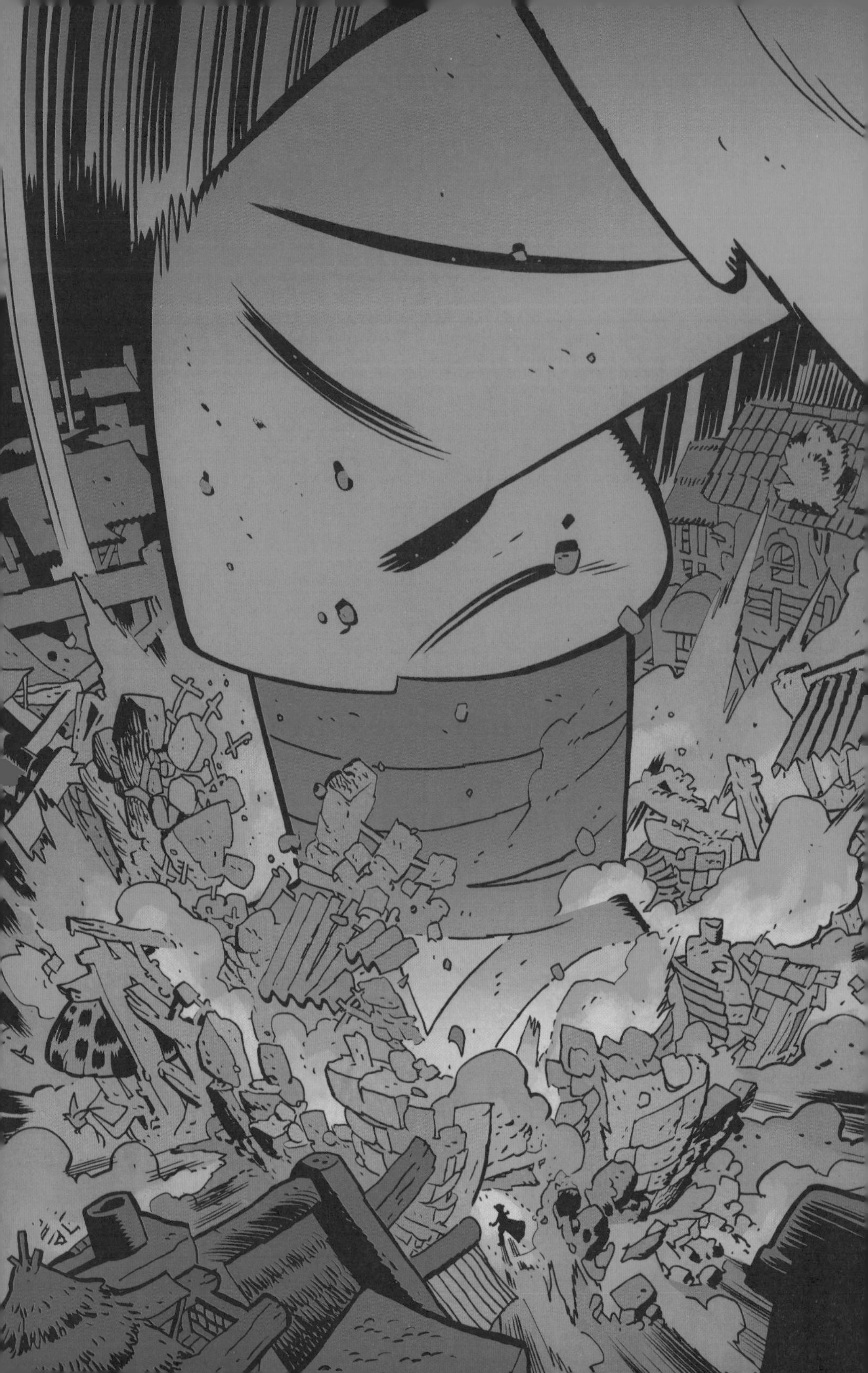

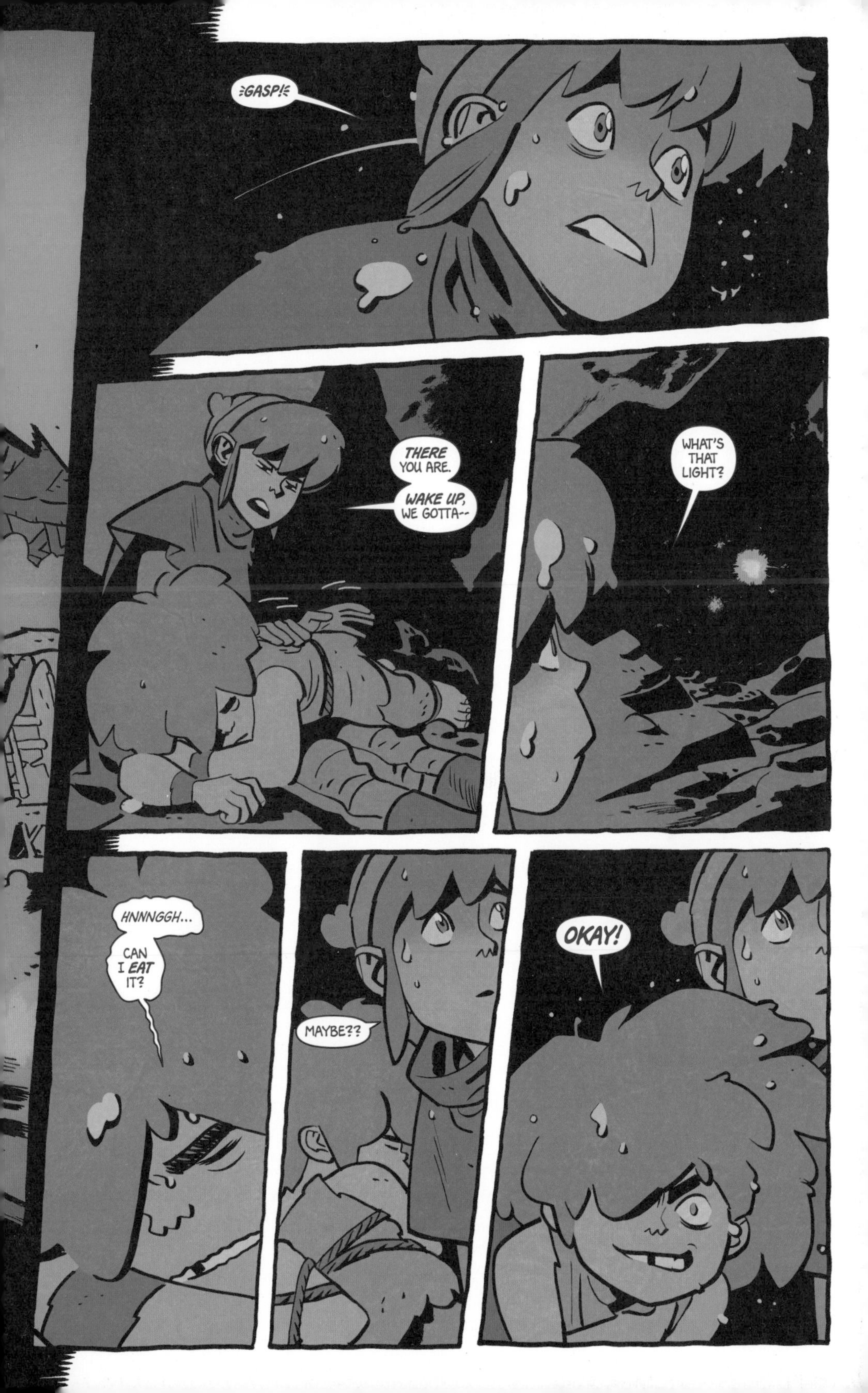
GASP!
THERE YOU ARE.
WAKE UP, WE GOTTA--
WHAT'S THAT LIGHT?
HNNNGGH...
CAN I EAT IT?
MAYBE??
OKAY!

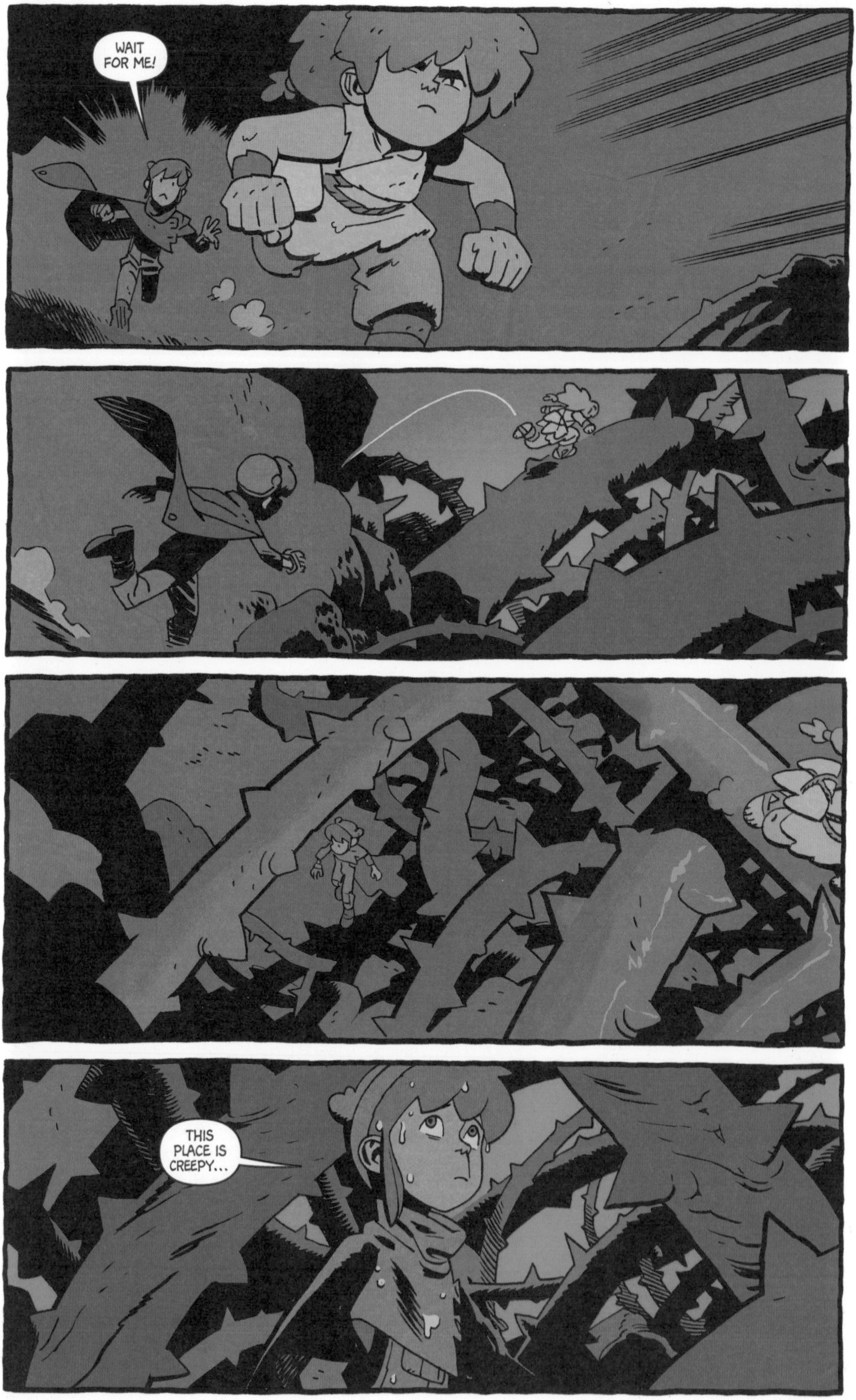
WAIT FOR ME!
THIS PLACE IS CREEPY...

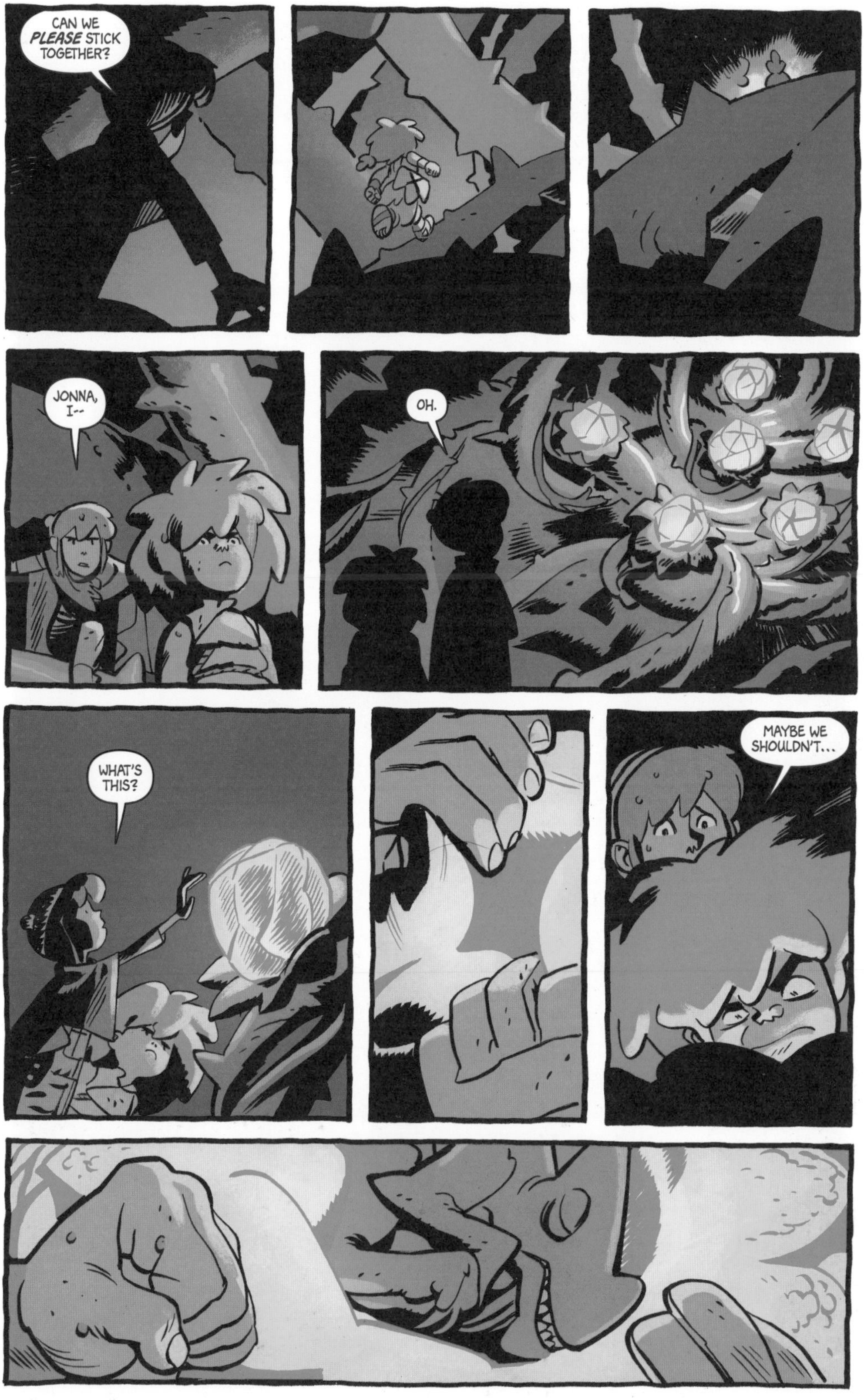
CAN WE *PLEASE* STICK TOGETHER?
JONNA, I--
OH.
WHAT'S THIS?
MAYBE WE SHOULDN'T...

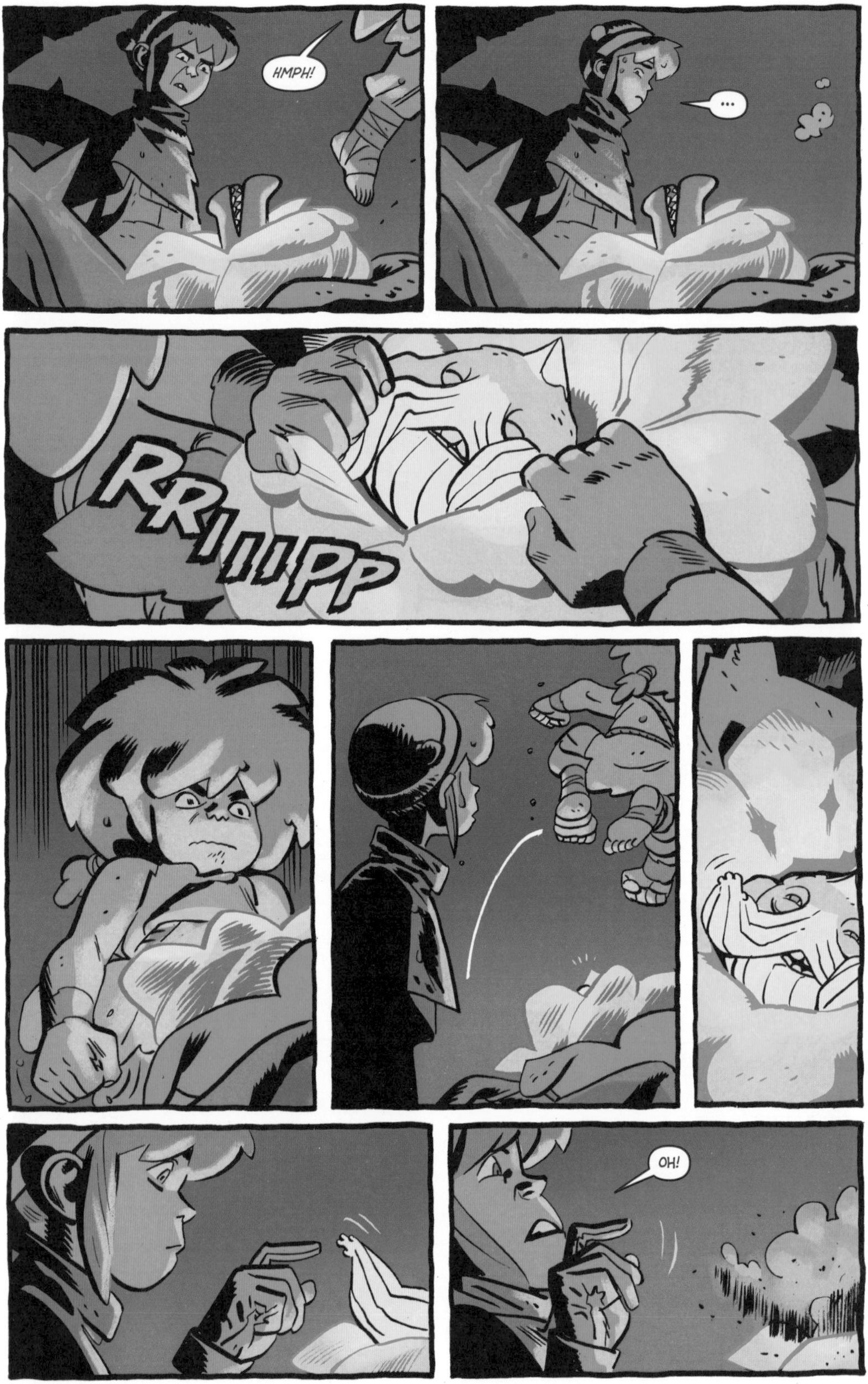
HMPH!
...
RRIIIPP
OH!

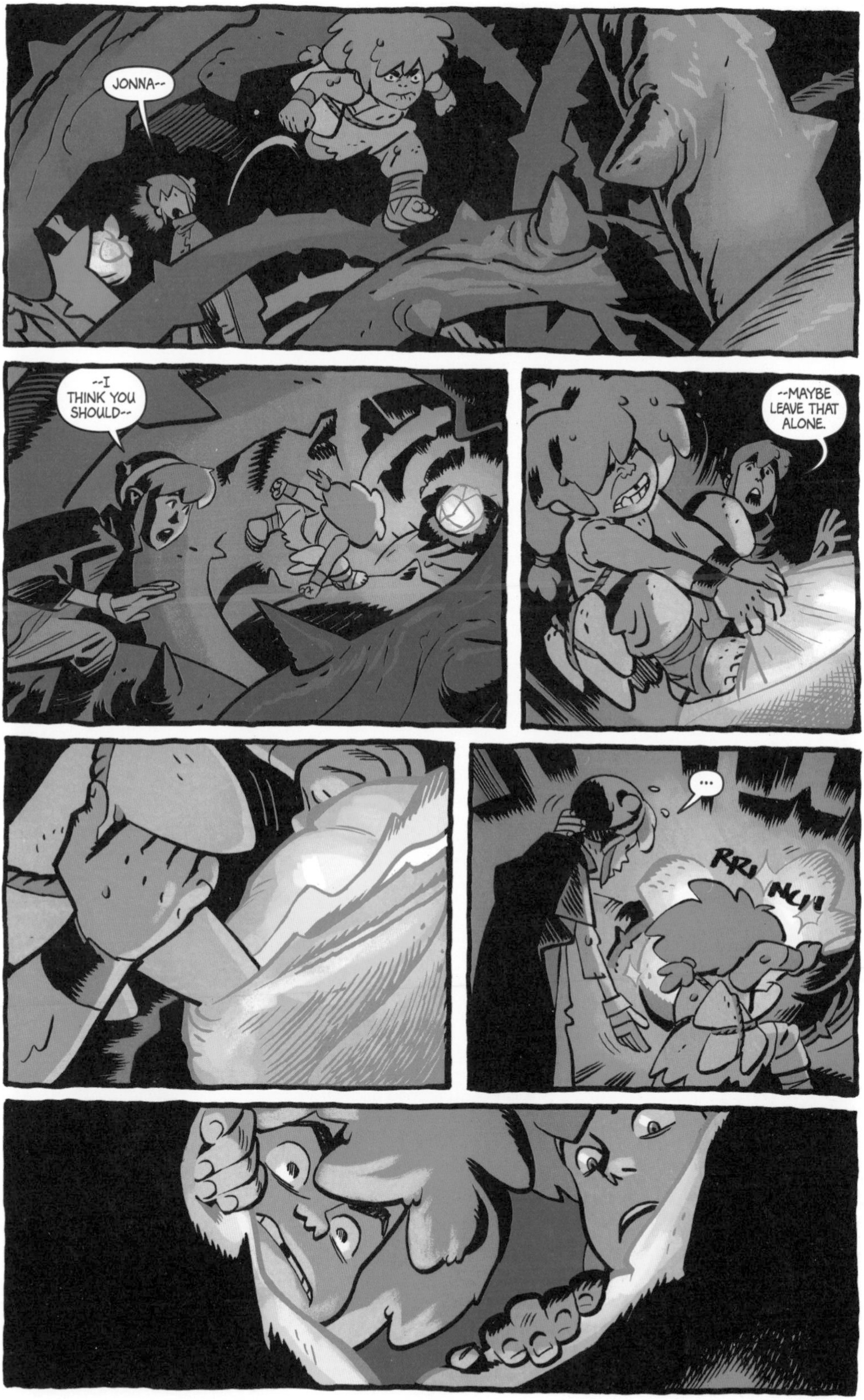
JONNA--
--I THINK YOU SHOULD--
--MAYBE LEAVE THAT ALONE.
...
RRUNCH

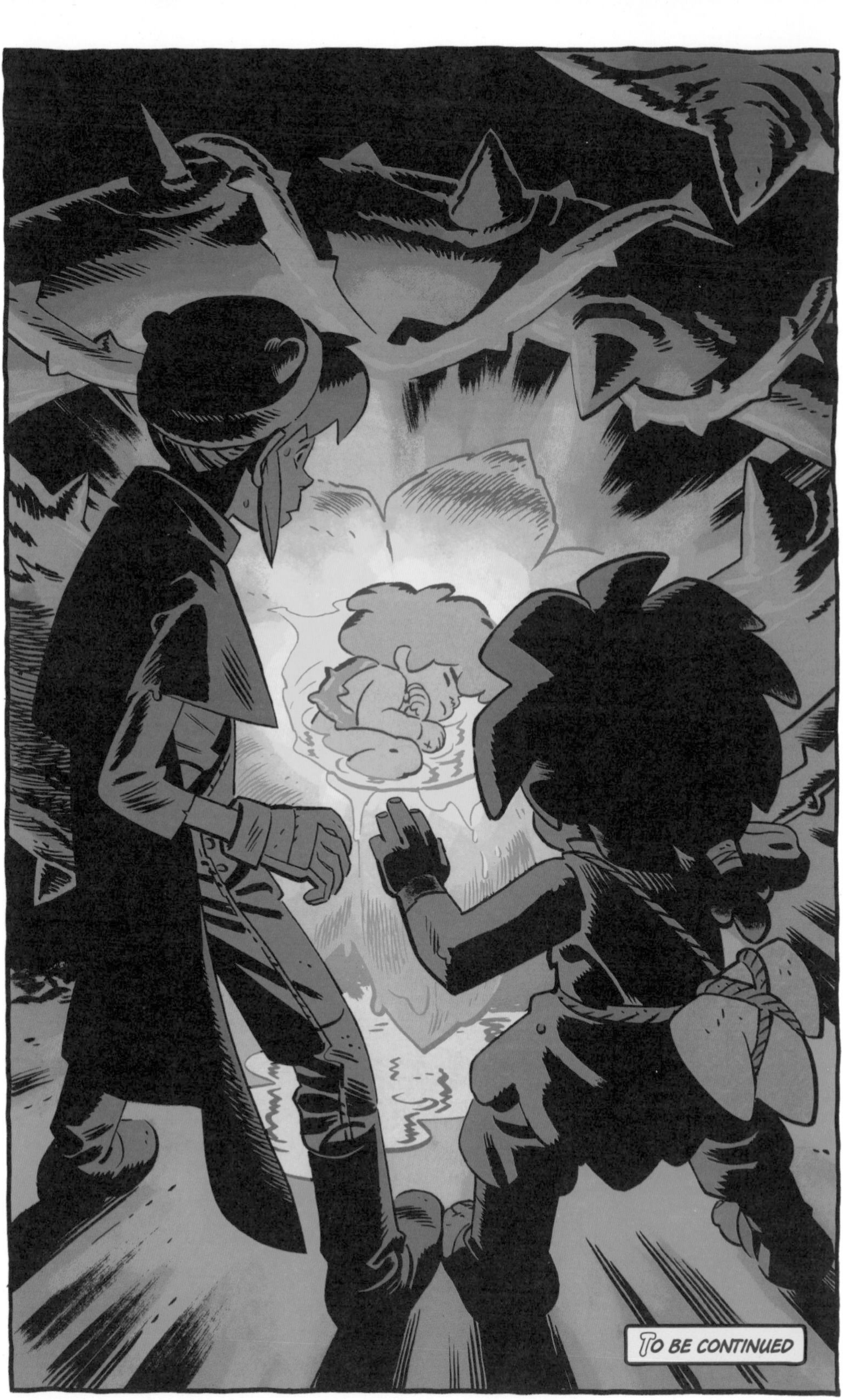
TO BE CONTINUED

TO BE CONTINUED IN

JONNA

AND THE UNPOSSIBLE MONSTERS

VOLUME THREE

BIOGRAPHIES

CHRIS SAMNEE
is an Eisner and Harvey Award-winning cartoonist.
He's best known for his work on *Daredevil, Black Widow,* and *Thor: The Mighty Avenger.* He lives in St. Louis, Missouri, with his wife, Laura, and their three daughters.

LAURA SAMNEE
lives in St. Louis, Missouri, with her husband, Chris, and their three daughters.

MATTHEW WILSON
has been coloring comics since 2003. He's a two-time Eisner Award winner for Best Coloring and has collaborated with Chris Samnee on more projects than he can recall. When he's not coloring comics, he's out on a hike with his wife and two dogs.

CHRISTOPHER CRANK (CRANK!)
has lettered a bunch of books put out by Image, Dark Horse, Oni Press, Dynamite, and elsewhere. He also has a podcast with comic artist Mike Norton and members of Four Star Studios in Chicago (crankcast.com) and makes music (sonomorti.bandcamp.com).

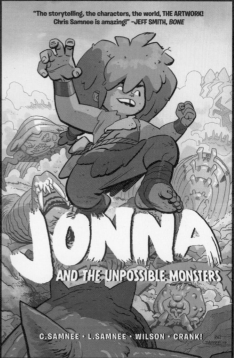
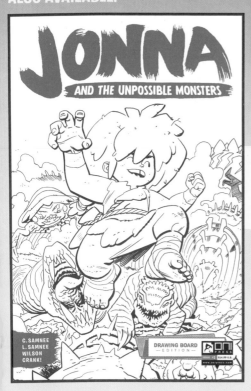

Liked JONNA?

Check out these other great Oni-Lion Forge titles!

PAX SAMSON
THE COOKOUT
RASHAD DOUCET • JASON REEVES

PAX SAMSON VOL. 1: THE COOKOUT
by Rashad Doucet & Jason Reeves

ISBN: 978-1-62010-851-2

SECRETS OF CAMP WHATEVER
by Chris Grine

ISBN: 978-1-62010-862-8

SECRETS OF
CAMP WHATEVER
CHRIS GRINE

JAROD PRATT JEY ODIN
LEMONADE CODE

LEMONADE CODE
by Jey Odin & Jarod Pratt

ISBN: 978-1-62010-868-0

DRAGON RACER
by Joey Weiser

ISBN: 978-1-62010-932-8

DRAGON RACER
BY JOEY WEISER

MAI K. NGUYEN
PILU of the WOODS

PILU OF THE WOODS
by Mai K. Nguyen

ISBN: 978-1-62010-563-4

STAR BEASTS
by Allyson Lassiter & Stephanie Young

ISBN: 978-1-62010-937-3

STAR BEASTS
LASSITER • YOUNG